Praise for *A Fool and His Monet*

"Readers looking for a humorous mystery with a dash of romance may find it here."

—*Library Journal*

"This intriguing look into the world of art theft from the perspective of an FBI agent will keep readers guessing the twists and turns as to the identity and motive of the thief."

—*RT Book Reviews*

"With spunk, humor, and plenty of heart-stopping moments, Sandra Orchard gives readers an exciting string of cases to crack and a character they'll love to watch solve them."

—*Prose 'n Cons Magazine*

"Completely delightful! *A Fool and His Monet* is laugh-out-loud funny! Readers who love Stephanie Plum will delight in Serena Jones and her adventures, her quirky family, and the handsome heroes in her life. An engaging and charming read—I can't wait for more!"

—**Susan May Warren**, RITA Award–winning and bestselling author of the Christiansen Family series

Praise for *Another Day, Another Dali*

"This book was very amusing, as the writer brings together mystery, comedy, love, and family issues to make the perfect story."

—*Suspense Magazine*

"With plenty of edge-of-your-seat moments, *Another Day, Another Dali* gives the plucky Serena Jones—and readers—a new high-stakes case to crack."

—*Relz Reviews*

OVER
MAYA
DEAD
BODY

Books by Sandra Orchard

PORT ASTER SECRETS SERIES

Deadly Devotion

Blind Trust

Desperate Measures

SERENA JONES MYSTERIES SERIES

A Fool and His Monet

Another Day, Another Dali

Over Maya Dead Body

OVER MAYA DEAD BODY

SANDRA ORCHARD

Revell

a division of Baker Publishing Group
Grand Rapids, Michigan

© 2017 by Sandra J. van den Bogerd

Published by Revell
a division of Baker Publishing Group
P.O. Box 6287, Grand Rapids, MI 49516-6287
www.revellbooks.com

Printed in the United States of America

Library of Congress Cataloging-in-Publication Data
Names: Orchard, Sandra, author.
Title: Over Maya dead body / Sandra Orchard.
Description: Grand Rapids, MI : Revell, a division of Baker Publishing Group,
    [2017] | Series: Serena Jones mysteries ; 3
Identifiers: LCCN 2017004560 | ISBN 9780800726706 (softcover) |
    ISBN 9780800728892
Subjects: LCSH: Government investigators—Fiction. | Murder—Investigation—
    Fiction. | Women detectives—Fiction. | GSAFD: Christian fiction. | Mystery
    fiction.
Classification: LCC PR9199.4.O73 O94 2017 | DDC 813/.6—dc23
LC record available at https://lccn.loc.gov/2017004560

This book is a work of fiction. Names, characters, places, and incidents are the product of the author's imagination or are used fictitiously.

17 18 19 20 21 22 23   7 6 5 4 3 2 1

For Lisa Belcastro
Martha's Vineyard tour guide extraordinaire
and self-proclaimed president
of the #TeamNate fan club

I snatched my bag off the luggage carousel at Boston's Logan International Airport and plunked it next to my parents as a sticky-fingered urchin tried to liberate the brightly colored ribbons I'd tied to the handles.

"Look at that little angel," Mom said indulgently to Dad and Aunt Martha.

The pigtailed blonde rewarded them with an impish grin, then skipped toward a grandparently looking couple.

Mom exhaled a wistful sigh. "That should be us."

The *little angel* bypassed the couple and pounced upon another passenger's brightly colored bag, squealing "Doll!"

The sour-faced owner yanked his luggage out of the child's reach.

"Don't stare. It's rude," Mom scolded.

But like a car-wreck rubbernecker, I couldn't rip my gaze away when a gaudy red statue tumbled out of the bag and panic streaked across the man's face. Besides . . . "I'm paid to stare at people."

The little girl scrambled after the souvenir, but a K-9 officer beat her to it.

The souvenir—probably meant to be a miniature replica of a Maya god—reminded me of a case where a crooked European art dealer dipped artifacts in resin to smuggle them out of Egypt. Not that I thought this guy, who'd landed on one of the precleared Caribbean flights, was an antiquities smuggler. Only . . .

Was that sweat popping out on his forehead?

The officer who'd rescued the seemingly cheap souvenir studied it a moment, then crouched low where the dog could sniff it. Sourpuss's fingers danced a number on the sides of his legs before he reached out a shaky hand and asked for it back.

Interesting. I stepped closer for a better look at that *souvenir* and surreptitiously snapped a photo with my smartphone.

"Serena," Mom said, pleadingly this time.

Right. I was on vacation—four glorious days on Martha's Vineyard to relax and celebrate Uncle Jack's engagement. A tingly feeling shivered down the back of my neck as if Mom wasn't the only person eyeballing me. A quick glance about the luggage-claim area pinpointed a military type in civilian clothes, and I had the sudden urge to echo Mom's don't-stare order.

Of course, somehow in the split second, or three, I'd looked away, Gaudy Souvenir Guy had vamoosed.

I returned to my parents. "Hey, where's Aunt Martha?"

Mom did a frantic half jig. "I don't know! She promised me she wouldn't pull any of her crazy antics this time. Ward, did you see where she went?"

Laser-focused on the exit, Dad sloughed off the question

10

with a "Check the restroom" and grabbed the handle of Aunt Martha's bag to lug along with his own.

Aunt Martha had moved in with my parents a year and a half ago, following her hip surgery, and begun accompanying them on holidays. Living under the same roof hadn't curbed her independence one iota.

"Oh dear," Mom fussed.

Aunt Martha scurried toward us from the direction of the exit, not the restroom. Her eyes beamed with that gleeful sparkle they got when she fancied herself on to a good mystery.

I smothered a grin. At least I wasn't the only one making mysteries out of molehills.

"Oh, good, there you are," Mom said and steered us all toward the bus stop. The two-hour bus ride would take us to Woods Hole, where we'd catch the ferry to Martha's Vineyard—another forty-five-minute ride, give or take.

Aunt Martha nabbed a seat next to me on the bus. "He took a cab."

"What? Who took a cab?"

"That guy with the statue you were staring at back there. I tried to catch a glimpse of his name on his luggage tag but couldn't get close enough."

I inwardly groaned. Aunt Martha was in her midseventies and had become an incurable armchair sleuth since retiring from a job as a globe-trotting personal assistant to some corporate bigwig. Trouble was, she didn't know that *armchair* sleuth meant you were supposed to stay in your seat, not chase suspects through airports.

"Aunt Martha, I really have no interest in the man."

"Nonsense. I saw the way he was squirming. He was guilty

11

of something. You couldn't have missed that. Do you think he was smuggling drugs inside that little statue?"

"No, honestly, the thought hadn't even crossed my mind. I'm on vacation, remember?"

"Pffft, tell me you're not going to visit the Artisan's Spring Festival and all the art galleries on the island this weekend."

I shrugged. Aunt Martha knew me too well for me to outright lie. Sure, I rambled through secondhand shops and galleries in every town I visited, but it really wasn't because of my job as a member of the FBI's Art Crime Team. I liked art.

"Besides," Aunt Martha went on, "a little mystery makes everything more fun. Like this mystery bride-to-be your Uncle Jack has swept off her feet."

Uncle was actually an honorary title. Jack was an old college friend of Dad's who'd invited us to vacation on the island every summer. Of course, I hadn't been able to join Mom and Dad since finishing high school.

"Have you ever heard Jack mention her?" Aunt Martha asked.

"No, I haven't talked to him since Christmas." And it was now early May. A lot could happen in the romance realm in four months, especially when you got to be Uncle Jack's age and were still single.

Not that I knew such things from personal experience, being only twenty-nine. The only guys who'd come close to sweeping me off my feet were criminals trying to pull a fancy judo move before they ran.

Although . . . Tanner had nearly dunked me into an algae-filled pond during an ill-fated surveillance op involving paddleboats and mobsters, but that was a whole other story.

And it certainly didn't qualify as romance.

12

My phone beeped, and I glanced down at the text alert. Huh. Speak of the devil.

I opened the text.

Work is oddly peaceful . . . It's almost like I'M on vacation.

A smile curved my lips, but I searched through my emoticons for the happy face that was rolling its eyeballs and hit SEND. Then I added:

Ha, ha. You know you miss me.

"Serena!" Mom was frowning at me. "Is that Tanner? You know we love him, but honey, *you're on vacation*."

How'd she know it was Tanner?

Before I could work that out, my text alert beeped again.

What I miss is your mom's bangers and mash.

A photo of a pathetic-looking take-out burger popped up on my screen.

I laughed out loud. In my rookie days, when Tanner was my field-training agent, Mom had gotten it into her head that if she fed him, he'd make sure I stayed safe.

Boo hoo, I texted back, then conspicuously returned my phone to my purse under Mom's watchful eye.

Mom leaned across the aisle. "You looking forward to seeing Ashley?"

"Sure, it'll be great to see her again." Maybe.

I stomped down on the faint, ridiculous twinge of hurt

that'd never quite gone away. Ashley was Jack's *real* niece, and we'd been bosom buddies as far back as I could remember . . . if I didn't count my last visit to the island. Ashley had gotten mad at me, and I never did figure out why. Not that I'd tried very hard, I guess, after she didn't reply to the last letter I sent her. She seemed to think I should know, and hoping she'd have forgotten about whatever miffed her by my next visit seemed easier than figuring it out. Only with college and all, I stopped spending my summers on the island.

Two and a half hours later, Aunt Martha and I settled in at a table on the restaurant deck of the one fifteen ferry to Vineyard Haven. And . . . whom should I see nursing a drink at one of the tables while perusing what looked like an *art journal*, of all things?

Gaudy Souvenir Guy.

"You're staring again," Mom said, dropping into the seat opposite me while Dad fetched us something to eat.

Aunt Martha glanced over her shoulder and her face lit.

I sent her a cautioning look. Let's just say, Mom didn't share Aunt Martha's penchant for mystery solving. The only mystery she was keen to solve was why I hadn't gotten married yet. And given her grandchildren. Most definitely in that order.

I unscrewed my water bottle cap and downed a swig.

As if Aunt Martha had read my thoughts, or more likely Mom's, she teased, "If I'd known you'd want to man-watch, I would've invited Nate along for you to look at."

I spluttered a mouthful of water across the table. Nate was my apartment superintendent—an apartment I'd taken over from Aunt Martha, complete with a cat, when she moved in with my parents. Dad's allergies meant Harold—the cat—couldn't go.

Then again, maybe it'd all been a conspiracy she cooked up to get Nate to notice me. Come to think of it . . . the airport's metal detector didn't go off when that *supposed* metal hip of hers shimmied past.

I stifled a smile as I mopped up my water with a paper napkin. Nate was a great guy. He had Bradley Cooper good looks and shared my love of both art and old movies. And he annoyed Tanner to no end, which was a fun bonus.

"If Nate was here, then who would watch Harold?" I asked.

"Exactly," Mom said and dismissed Nate with a resolute hand flick. "There will be plenty of eligible young men for her to meet on the island."

Translation—if Nate had been interested in making a move, he would've done it by now.

"Do you really want her falling in love with a man who lives over a thousand miles away?" Aunt Martha countered. "You'd never see your grandkids."

Mom looked startled, then horrified, as if she'd never considered the ramifications. Apparently, the invitation to an engagement celebration on Martha's Vineyard—the perfect setting to entice her single daughter, me, to entertain romantic thoughts of my own—had blinded her to the logistics of who might catch my eye.

Aunt Martha gave me a sly wink, and I grinned. *Thanks for the assist.*

Dad arrived at the table with a large basket of french fries and four burgers, which, thankfully, looked much more appetizing than Tanner's sad little lunch had.

Grinning to myself, I pulled out my phone and snapped a shot of our yummy-looking burgers as Aunt Martha excused herself to wash her hands. I was just typing *Where's the beef? Oh, look, it's on Martha's Vineyard!* when Aunt Martha stopped next to Gaudy Souvenir Guy, and my fingers stilled.

She stooped down, pretending to adjust her shoe, although I'm sure she was eyeballing the tags on his luggage.

Uh oh. Now she was actually speaking to the guy. I hit SEND, then pressed my fingertips to my forehead and watched the pair from behind my hand so Mom wouldn't catch me staring again. The look the guy shot Aunt Martha reminded me of Harold's expression whenever I threatened to give him a bath.

Dad chuckled. "Looks like your matchmaking mission has given Martha ideas for herself," he said to Mom.

Mom spun around to see what he was talking about and gasped. "That man has got to be forty years younger than her."

"Mom, please! Dad was kidding."

Right? I looked to Dad for confirmation, but all he did was smile innocently. "Women can talk to men without it meaning any kind of romantic interest," I added firmly.

As if to illustrate my point, my phone beeped, undoubtedly Tanner's comeback to my smug burger pic.

Mom rolled her eyes. "That kind of thinking is why you're still single."

Okay, that made no sense. I elbowed my dad to nudge him into stepping up to the plate for me. "Would you think a woman was hitting on you just because she talked to you?" *Or texted?*

He pulled his umbrella from his carry-on bag and wielded it like a bobby stick. "Why do you think I always carry this around campus?" He was an economics professor at Washington University. "To beat them off."

Seeing he was going to be no help, I did the only thing I could do. I bit into my hamburger and used the opportunity to check Tanner's response.

I spent the best years of my life training you into
the top-notch agent you've become, and this is
the thanks I get? Cruel, Jones. Cruel.

Chuckling to myself, I keyed in:

Too bad you're so old and washed up. Maybe
you should think about eating better.

I forwarded him the photo I'd snapped of Gaudy Souvenir Guy and added:

Since work is so slow, why don't you get some
intel on this guy that Aunt Martha is surveilling?

Aunt Martha returned to the table looking ready to burst with whatever she'd found out. Thankfully, she had the good sense to not blurt it in front of Mom.

As it turned out, Aunt Martha didn't get a chance to share her discovery with me before we disembarked in Vineyard Haven. I scanned the sea of faces waiting to greet friends and family. "Do you see Uncle Jack anywhere?" I asked.

"No." Dad tapped his cell-phone screen and pressed the device to his ear.

Aunt Martha leaned over to me and whispered conspiratorially, "Charles Anderson."

"I'm on vacation," I reminded her.

She flashed her you-can't-fool-me grin. "He claimed he bought the souvenir for his mother."

I shrugged. "Maybe she likes those sorts of things." Or pretends to, like Dad used to when I gave him all those goofy ties every Father's Day.

"There's no answer at the house," Dad said, pocketing his phone and heading for the street. "He's probably on his way."

We waited on the sidewalk and scanned the parked cars for any sign of him.

After fifteen minutes, Aunt Martha plopped down on her upright suitcase. "Doesn't that old coot carry a cell phone yet?"

Old coot? I was pretty sure Uncle Jack was Dad's age.

"We'll give him another fifteen minutes," Dad said. "That's how long it would've taken him to drive here if he left just before I called."

"But he's never late," Mom said. "Maybe you should call Ashley." Ashley lived in a cottage next to Jack's distant-ocean-view mansion. She, along with her globe-trekking brother Ben, were Jack's only living relatives.

"I don't have Ashley's number on my phone," Dad said. They both looked expectantly at me.

"Sorry. I don't have it either."

Aunt Martha pushed herself up and stomped her foot. I thought she was going to demand we just take a taxi, but she kept on stomping and I realized she probably had pins and needles in her leg.

"Let's take a taxi," I suggested. A few vans were still waiting to offer shuttle services to arriving passengers.

"Good idea," Aunt Martha chimed in, giving her foot one

last stomp. "For all we know, the old coot is out gallivanting with his bride-to-be and totally forgot about us."

Dad and Mom exchanged a what-do-you-think look and peered down the road. "I guess we could watch for his car as we're driving and ask the driver to honk if we see him," Dad finally said.

Five minutes later we were on the road. Jack lived in a gorgeous rural area west of Tisbury Great Pond, about a half hour's drive away in light traffic. This early in May, the tourists that would clog the roads by Memorial Day weekend were still few and far between. Of course, en route we had to drop off a few other passengers, but we still made good time.

Soon after we turned onto Uncle Jack's dirt road, Mom gasped.

Relegated to the back of the van, I bobbed from one side to the other, trying to catch a view past everyone's heads. When I finally did, my stomach dropped.

A police cruiser, its lights flashing, sat outside Jack's house.

2

A police officer burst out of Ashley's cottage, on the other side of Jack's driveway, as we hurriedly unloaded our luggage from the taxi van. "Excuse me, folks. Who are you here to visit?"

"Jack Hill. What's going on? Where is he?" Dad demanded.

The officer pulled a notepad and pen from his pocket. "What's your name and relationship to him, please?" His expression was an unreadable mask that sent chills down my spine.

This was not good. I winged a prayer skyward for Jack's protection, but I had an oppressive sense it was too little too late.

"I'm Ward Jones," Dad snapped. "This is my wife June."

The officer's eyes widened ever so slightly. A common reaction, thanks to the comeback of old *Leave it to Beaver* reruns, since my parents sported the same names as the Beaver's iconic parents.

"We've been friends with Jack since college," Dad went on, oblivious to the officer's reaction. "Now what's happened?"

The officer looked to Aunt Martha and me, clearly expecting us to identify ourselves too.

"I'm their daughter, Serena Jones." To speed things along, I flashed my ID. "FBI Special Agent. And this is my great-aunt, Martha Chandler."

His eyes narrowed on my badge, and I second-guessed the impulse to flash it. "What is the reason for your visit?"

"Jack's engagement party," Dad said, in the tone he usually reserved for recalcitrant students and my brother. "Tell us what's going on."

Ashley stumbled out of her cottage with red-rimmed eyes.

We all lurched toward her and spoke at once. "Ashley, are you okay?"

Ashley tumbled down the porch steps into Dad's embrace. "He's dead. Uncle Jack's dead!" She broke into uncontrollable sobs.

Dad patted her back, a tear trickling down his cheek. His gaze sought Mom's, telepathing anguish, as she and Aunt Martha looked on in stunned silence.

Going into law-enforcement mode, I steeled myself against the emotions clawing at my chest and confronted the officer. "How did it happen, Officer . . . ?"

"Phelps," he said, then seemingly recognizing that I was asking as one law-enforcement professional to another, he drew me aside and lowered his voice. "He fell onto the rocks at Menemsha Hills, fractured his skull."

I swallowed a surge of bile. "So it was an accident?"

"Appears so." He squinted at Jack's house, his jaw muscle twitching.

My pulse quickened. "But you don't think so?" I whispered. Menemsha Hills, with its picturesque lookout, had been one of Jack's favorite hiking trails to shoot photos of sunsets over the water. And this time of year, it would be secluded.

"It's not my call," he said.

That was equivocation if I'd ever heard it.

"I'm with the local Chilmark police detachment," he explained. "The state police have to investigate all unattended deaths. Reinforcements from the mainland are helping the two troopers stationed on the island. But I volunteered to break the news to Ashley since I knew her from school."

A woman I didn't recognize, her skin as pale as her cable-knit sweater, stepped out of Ashley's cottage and hugged the porch pillar, a shell-shocked expression on her face.

"Who's that?" I asked.

"Marianne Delmar."

The fiancée. She was average height and build, with enough gray in her stylishly cut hair to suggest she was comfortable in her own skin. At least, until she'd heard the news about Jack. Her eyes were puffy from crying.

"She's the one that found Jack," Officer Phelps added.

My heart jumped. *Found* him? Or *pushed* him?

I hated myself for the thought. This was the woman Jack loved, had planned to spend the rest of his life with.

Mom and Dad urged Ashley back inside the cottage, expressing their condolences as they reached Marianne.

Aunt Martha broke away from the procession and joined Officer Phelps and me. "Was Marianne hiking with Jack?" she asked.

He hesitated.

"Oh, c'mon, young man," Aunt Martha pressed. "You know as well as I do that it'll be on tonight's news. Or I

22

could just march on inside and ask the poor grieving women myself. Is that what you want me to have to do?"

He glanced toward the now empty porch and seemed to come to a decision. "Ms. Delmar said she and Jack had a brunch date planned. When he didn't show, she and her daughter drove around looking for him and spotted his vehicle parked at Menemsha Hills."

"Did the coroner specify a time of death?" I interjected.

"Between eight and eleven last night."

"And Marianne was *where* at that time?" Aunt Martha and I asked simultaneously. After all, we didn't know her. And maybe Jack really didn't either.

"It'll be up to the state police to establish the alibis of possible suspects . . . if it comes to that. But rest assured the scene is being thoroughly processed. There was no obvious evidence of foul play that I could see."

"You have a murder here . . . what? Once every twenty years? Would the cops know a murder if they saw one?" Aunt Martha griped.

A redhead driving a sporty red Mazda careened into Ashley's driveway, then sprang out of her car and stormed toward us in her designer boots, her gaze fixed on Officer Phelps. "Jack was killed, wasn't he?"

"This is Marianne's daughter, Carly," Phelps informed us, ignoring the young woman's hysteria.

She inhaled, puffing up her small stature an extra half inch, and raked her gaze over me, then Aunt Martha. "Who are you two?"

"Friends of Jack's."

"And of Ashley too, I suppose?" she snapped.

Aunt Martha and I exchanged a glance. What was this woman's problem with Ashley?

She snorted. "I thought as much. Well, I'll tell you something you probably don't know. Jack had an appointment with his lawyer for Monday morning. He was going to add Mom to his will."

I nodded, since the plan seemed perfectly reasonable, given their pending nuptials.

Officer Phelps jotted the information onto his notepad.

"And you can bet your badge," Carly went on, jabbing one perfectly manicured finger at his book, "Ashley and that lazy brother of hers weren't happy about getting squeezed out of the picture."

Aunt Martha stomped her foot for real. "Are you accusing Ashley and Ben of murdering their own uncle?"

"You bet your pink patoozies I am."

Ashley, who must've stepped back onto the porch to see what all the yelling was about, crumpled to the floor.

Another guy plowed up the driveway past us, took the porch steps two at a time, and slid to his knees at Ashley's side. He cradled her head and patted her cheek, urging her around as the rest of us stared at him dumbfounded. His dark chiseled features looked familiar. He scooped her into his arms. "Get out of my way," he said to my parents and Marianne, who'd stopped frozen in the doorway.

As he maneuvered past them, Aunt Martha and I hurried inside too.

He set Ashley down on her sofa. "Will someone please tell me what's going on?"

"Who are you?" Mom blurted.

"Preston?" I said on an exhalation as my mental Rolodex

24

locked on to why he looked so familiar. "Preston Sullivan Frasier?"

His gaze skittered over everyone else before settling on me. He looked puzzled.

And why would I think he'd remember me? We'd only gone out a few times, and that was ten years ago.

"Preston," Ashley whimpered, coming around. She threw her arms around him and sank into another crying jag as Dad broke the news about Jack's death.

"You must be Ashley's fiancé," Mom cut in, apparently catching sight of the rock on Ashley's left ring finger the same moment as me.

"No way!" I blurted before I could censor my surprise. Preston was an academic type who loved art and history and *loathed* sunbathing on a crowded beach, Ashley's favorite pastime.

Ashley pushed her face away from Preston's damp shoulder and swiped at her stray tears. "I was going to surprise you with the news this weekend," she said sheepishly.

Looking at me, Preston tilted his head, recognition finally lighting his eyes. "Serena? Serena Jones. It's good to see you." He pushed to his feet and pulled me into a hug. "I wish it could've been under happier circumstances."

Carly snorted. "*You* should be happy. Your fiancée's inheritance is secure."

"Carly!" her mother exclaimed as the rest of us gaped at the woman's callousness.

Everyone except Aunt Martha, that is. She grabbed Carly by the arm and herded her out the door. "It's time for you to leave."

"With pleasure. C'mon, Mother," Carly called over her shoulder as Aunt Martha shoved her across the threshold.

"I'm sorry," Marianne whispered, hurrying after her. "She easily gets emotionally distraught and tends to overreact."

Officer Phelps followed the pair out, no doubt to get the lowdown on the evil step-child-to-be's fantastical theory in case that lack of "evidence of foul play" just meant the killer was smart.

Aunt Martha closed the door behind them. "Pay her no mind," she said to Ashley. "The grief clearly sent her over the edge."

Except . . . Carly had been right about one thing. Money was pretty much the number one motive for murder. "Where's Ben?" I asked. Ashley's brother spent most of the year back-packing around one country or another, freelancing human-interest stories to any outlet that would buy them. But I'd expected him to be home for the engagement party.

"Oh no!" Ashley shot a worried glance at Preston. "I forgot. Uncle Jack was supposed to pick Ben up from the ferry this morning. We have to go get him."

"His flight must've been delayed," I said.

"She's right," Preston agreed. "Otherwise, he would've found his way here by now."

Ashley grabbed her cell phone and thumbed through some screens. "He hasn't texted me." She tried his number. "He's not picking up."

"He could still be on the plane," Preston soothed.

"Or forgotten to turn his phone off airplane mode," Dad interjected. "Do you know what flight he was coming in on?"

"Uncle Jack would have it on his calendar in the kitchen."

"I'll go look," I volunteered.

Phelps was still talking to Carly and Marianne in the drive-way, so I slipped out the side door and crossed the yard. Like lots of people on the island, Jack never locked his house, and with any luck I'd be in and out before Phelps could hassle me.

The side door opened into his kitchen. I let myself in, and my throat caught at the familiar home smell that hadn't changed in all these years. I wrestled down the swell of emotion and focused on the wall calendar. It had the time of Ben's ferry on it but nothing about his flight. The phone also hung on the wall. I scanned the countertops for a notepad, envelopes, anything that Jack might've jotted the information on. I should've known better. Uncle Jack had always been borderline compulsive about keeping everything in its place.

The phone book drawer! I jerked open the cupboard drawer closest to the phone and found the mother lode. A three-messages-per-page book, complete with yellow carbon copy duplicates. And Jack, bless his compulsive soul, had written the date and time of every call he deemed important enough to keep a record of. His neighbor seemed to call a lot with one complaint or another about the latest "sculpture" Uncle Jack had added to his garden. Some areas of the Vineyard had bylaws restricting lawn ornaments and various other things, but not in this area. I snapped pics of a couple of the pages that recorded the neighbor's rants and then flipped to the last used page. Tiny remnants of perforated paper indicated a page had been removed, complete with its duplicates. I carefully pried up the blank top layer of the next page to see if Jack had pressed hard enough for his message to appear on the carbon copy of the set below.

My heart jumped. FBI-Boston was written neatly at the top with Monday's date and the time of 9:05. Scrawled in the message area was a name I recognized—Isaak Jackson, a member of the Art Crime Team working out of Boston—

along with the word *vacation*. Why was Jack calling the FBI's art crime detective?

I squinted at the memo below the first. A call with Isaak, maybe. The print was too faint to be sure. Same for the last memo, except it might've had Ben's flight information. I could make out the word *terminal*, but not the number or time.

At the creak of a floorboard in the next room, I glanced out the kitchen window. Officer Phelps was still at Carly's car. So, who was in the house?

The hairs on my neck prickled. My back was to the archway between the kitchen and the next room, with table and chairs the only cover between it and me. Reaching for my gun, I spun and ducked in one motion.

"Drop the weapon or I'll drop you," a deep male voice ordered.

3

"FBI, drop your weapon," I ordered, glaring at the massive man looming over me with his Glock, held in latex gloved hands, pointed at the kitchen chair uselessly shielding my chest. Then recognition dawned. "Isaak?"

The agent's eyes narrowed.

I laid my gun on the floor and, straightening, raised my hands in surrender. "Serena Jones. With the FBI Art Crime Team, St. Louis. We met at the conference in New York. Remember?" As the youngest agent on the twelve-member team, I should be pretty memorable.

But a couple more heartbeats passed before he said "right" and holstered his gun. "What are you doing here?"

"Jack Hill is an old family friend." I lowered my hands and returned my gun to its holster too. "What are you doing here?"

"Hill's niece gave me permission to search the place," he said quickly.

Ohh-kay. So, no search warrant. Tension tightened my

chest. Was he trying to save time? Or looking for something without cause? "What are you searching for?"

"Anything that may tell me what Jack knew about an antiquities smuggling ring."

"A smuggling ring? What are you talking about?"

"He called headquarters on Monday. Said that his nephew had information. Asked about making a deal."

No. No. *This couldn't be good.* "Is Ben in jail?"

"Who's Ben?"

"Jack's nephew." I willed my hammering heart to slow. "His ferry was supposed to arrive this morning."

"*Supposed to?*"

"Ben hasn't shown up."

Isaak rammed the butt of his hand into the doorjamb and let out an expletive.

"What did Jack tell you about this smuggling ring? Do you think they killed him?" My throat tightened. "Got to Ben?"

Isaak shook his head. "No clue. I never talked to Jack. He left a message with headquarters, because I'm *supposed* to be on vacation with my family. But when I picked up my messages and found out he lives here, I decided to take a couple of hours to meet with him. Only . . ." Isaak waved his hand about the empty room.

I swallowed hard, a chill skittering down my spine. With the rise in global terrorism and reports purporting that antiquities smuggling had become the second-largest source of income for at least one major terrorist group, the government paid close attention to the slightest whiff of antiquities smuggling these days. And not just the FBI. Homeland Security, Customs, the coast guard, and no doubt the CIA were on high alert.

"Whatever Jack uncovered must've got him killed." *Maybe Ben too*. The pressure in my chest intensified. Antiquities smuggling was an appealing way to make cash. Artifacts didn't set off metal detectors or attract gun- or drug-sniffing dogs. And with the ever-growing thirst of collectors, terrorists had little trouble finding eager buyers. Not that we should be surprised by their initiative. The Nazis and Khmer Rouge had financed their endeavors the same way.

"The police say Hill's death was an accident," Isaak said. "He fell down the stairs to the rocky beach and hit his head."

Swallowing hard, I blocked out the image. "But"—I glanced out the window at Officer Phelps still talking to Carly—"you told them what was going on, didn't you? That maybe he didn't *just fall*."

Isaak blew out a huff of frustration and stalked back to the living room. "Yeah, but the police didn't find evidence of anyone else being there."

I hurried after him. "But someone's been here. A page was torn from his message book. We need to get an evidence team in here."

"State police already has one on the way."

Of course, they would. Probably weren't happy about Isaak getting here first.

A massive drafting table dominated Jack's living room, flanked by a second smaller table covered with photographs. Jack was an architect, the "Hill" in Hill and Dale Architects Ltd., and still very much old school. Not only didn't he use a computer to do his drafting, he still used 35mm film to take photographs. My gaze skittered to a photograph on the wall of Ashley and me digging a moat around our sand castle.

I could still remember the day he took it. I blinked back tears.

Isaak flicked through a stack of photos of the interior of an uber-luxurious home Jack was probably redesigning or perhaps had designed. "He's got dozens of photos of homes whose owners could easily afford to collect antiquities, but I'm not seeing anything suspicious in any of these." He tossed the photos back on the table.

I scanned the photos. "Whoever ripped the page from the message book could've already scoured the house for anything else incriminating." I scanned the bookshelves filled with books and magazines on architecture, art, and archeology. I ran my finger along the spines of the archeology magazines. "Last December's issue is missing."

"A missing magazine doesn't mean anything. He probably lent it to someone."

"Did you check the darkroom?"

"Yeah, just a few photos of another mansion hanging from a clothesline."

I opened the door off the end of the hall and looked for myself. "Did you take down some of these?" I pointed to the couple of empty spaces on the line.

"No, it was like that when I came in."

"Did you see the negatives?"

"Never thought to look."

I pulled down the binder in which Jack had always neatly filed them away in plastic sleeves. The negatives for the photos on the line weren't in it. I checked the enlarger and in and around the table and nearby drawers. Nothing. "Did you ask the police to check Jack's wallet or pockets for photos, notes, anything?"

"They said his wallet and camera were on him. That's

why they ruled out a robbery." Isaak's cell phone twerped and he glanced at the screen.

"I'll check his personal effects when they're returned to Ashley," I said. "In the meantime—"

"There's no meantime." Isaak thumbed something into his phone and stalked to the kitchen. "I'm sorry about your friend, but my family is waiting for me. And you're way out of your jurisdiction."

"But—"

He yanked open the side door. "When Hill's nephew shows up, I'll talk to him. Until then, this is the state police's case." He strode down the driveway, where a car had just pulled up with a female driver and two girls in the backseat.

"Wait. You're leaving?"

"Yes." He got into the car, and all I could do was gape as it pulled away.

The state police showed up a few minutes later while I was going through Jack's desk, still trying to hunt down Ben's flight information. And let's just say finding me there didn't endear me to them. After I finally convinced them I was on their side, they thanked me for my input and then asked me to leave.

By that time, Officer Phelps, Carly, and Marianne were gone, but our luggage was still sitting where we'd dropped it. I trudged over to drag it to the cottage and put a call in to Tanner in St. Louis.

"Let me guess," Tanner teased. "You saw Bruce Willis jogging on the beach and thought of me."

"Ha. You're not *that* old," I shot back.

"Glad to hear you recognize I'm a couple of characteristics up on Willis," Tanner retorted.

"A couple? What's the second?"

"I have hair."

I rolled my eyes and refrained from fibbing that I kind of preferred bald men. Bantering about actors with Tanner after what happened to Uncle Jack today just didn't feel right. "Hey, can you do me a favor," I said instead.

"Another one? Your aunt's Charles Anderson was clean, by the way. Did you get my text?"

"No, I missed that. Uh, could you check with Customs to see if Ben Hill of Martha's Vineyard has returned to the country yet?"

Tanner's voice instantly sobered. "What's going on? You're supposed to be on vacation."

"There's been a suspicious death."

"Someone you know?"

"Yes." My voice cracked. I pressed my lips together and breathed in hard through my nose.

"Serena? You okay?"

"Uncle Jack is dead."

Tanner uttered a sympathetic moan. "What do you need me to do?"

"Find Ben. He's Jack's nephew and was supposed to come in on this morning's ferry."

"Okay, I'll see what I can find out. How . . . how did Jack die?"

"The police say it was a hiking accident." I couldn't help it. I burst into tears.

"Shh," Tanner said gently. "Take a deep breath."

"I'm sorry."

"Nothing to apologize for." He fell silent as I pulled myself together.

"I'm okay now." To help me hold my emotions in check, I piled Aunt Martha's bag on top of mine and wheeled them toward the cottage.

"You sound as if you don't believe it was an accident."

I told Tanner about my encounter with Special Agent Jackson.

"And you think this Ben Hill might be involved?"

"No. *No!* Not in Jack's death." I set the bags next to the porch and confided my fear that Ben was also a victim.

"Okay, I'll see what I can find out."

A smidgen of peace eased the tension gripping my shoulders. I could always count on Tanner.

Dad came out and helped me retrieve the last of the luggage. "You were gone a long time. Did you find the flight information?"

"No, but Tanner's going to track it down for me."

Dad nodded. He had a deep respect for Tanner. Besides sharing meals with my family, Tanner had been one of Dad's favorite economics students back in his university days. "I'm sure Ben will call as soon as he's able. Ashley wants you to stay with her as planned." Dad's voice cracked. He cleared his throat. "Preston said the rest of us could stay at his house up the road until after the funeral."

"That's nice of him."

Dad glanced back at the cottage and lowered his voice. "Did the officer say anything to you about the investigation that might give credence to what Carly said?"

"Of course not." I mentally debated telling Dad about my encounter with Special Agent Jackson. But Dad looked so emotionally wrung out, I decided against burdening him with a believable reason Jack might've been murdered. "Don't pay any attention to that woman. You know Ashley and Ben would never hurt Uncle Jack."

"You're right. I can't believe anyone would. He's the nicest guy you'd ever want to meet."

I pulled Dad into a hug. "I'm so sorry." Dad hadn't missed a summer visit with Jack in all the years I could remember. Jack's passing would leave a man-sized hole in his life.

Preston chose that moment to step out onto the porch. Our gazes touched, and he ducked his head apologetically.

I stepped out of my dad's arms and reached for a bag handle.

"I'm going to walk back to my house and bring the car down for the luggage," Preston said. "It's only half a mile, but I don't think we'll want to lug the bags that far."

"I'll join you," I said. "My legs could use a stretch."

Dad didn't look as if he thought my heading off with Preston was a good idea, but Preston was Jack's longtime neighbor and an art history professor, not to mention Ashley's fiancé. If Jack had confided in anyone about an antiquity ring operating on the island, it would've been Preston.

We fell into step beside each other on the dirt road, the distant sound of crashing waves and the occasional cry of a seagull filling the silence. I inhaled deeply, savoring the scent of sea air, as childhood memories of skipping along to keep up with Uncle Jack's long strides washed over me.

"What are you doing with yourself these days?" Preston asked.

"I'm a special agent with the FBI," I said, surprised he hadn't heard that much from Jack. Seizing the opportunity to segue into asking about the antiquity ring, I added, "I'm also a member of the FBI's Art Crime Team. Have you heard of it?"

"Of course. It was formed after all those antiquities were pillaged from Iraq. I even consulted with an agent on a case one time."

"Really?"

"No, wait. I believe it was with the Homeland Security Agency. They found several looted Iraqi artifacts in someone's luggage at the airport and asked for my assistance with authentication."

"Wow, so you've clearly established a solid reputation in your field. I'm impressed. Do you enjoy being a professor?"

"Love it. Nothing better than being paid to study and teach about your passion."

The fervor in his voice reminded me of how Uncle Jack used to talk about architecture. I choked down the swelling lump in my throat and grasped for a nonchalant tone. "Have you encountered any antiquities on the island? Of questionable provenance, I mean."

He laughed. "Are you asking me out of curiosity or as an FBI agent?"

I stopped and looked up at him. "That sounds like a *yes*."

His eyes twinkled. "You know as well as I do how many super-rich summer residents the island boasts." He resumed walking. "I'm sure several are in possession of stolen antiquities, although I doubt they're aware of it."

"Seriously?" I lengthened my stride to keep up with him. "Even with all the news coverage over the last few years?" The antiquities trade was considered a gray market since it was nearly impossible to distinguish legitimate antiquities from looted and trafficked ones.

"Yeah, I'm always stunned by how little my first-year students know about the problem or the laws forbidding the removal of artifacts from numerous countries. And they're *into* art history."

"Did you and Uncle Jack discuss antiquities?" My heart hammered my ribs. I sucked in a deep breath and willed it to slow. "I mean, archeology was always a fascination of his, right?"

"Was it ever! He wove ancient elements into several of his architectural designs."

"Did he ever mention seeing an antiquity he thought may've been looted?"

Preston tilted his head, snagging my gaze. "Why would you ask that?"

My heart beat louder than the pounding surf as I debated how much to say. Preston's knowledge of both the island's avid collectors and of antiquities in general would prove invaluable to the investigation. But . . . could I trust him?

The image of Ashley clinging to him, her engagement ring glistening on her finger, rose in my mind. If Uncle Jack had given his blessing on their engagement, he couldn't have had any qualms about Preston's scruples. *Right?*

I squinted up at Preston. "Jack contacted the FBI about an antiquity smuggling ring on the island."

"Well, he was speculating it was that organized," Preston said.

"He talked to you about it?"

"Briefly. I got the impression he was hoping I'd refute his concerns."

I winced. I could only think of one reason Jack would hope that—because Ben was involved.

"Are you here to investigate his allegations?" Preston asked.

I decided against telling him that Jack died before he

could communicate them. "Yes, I am." As soon as I figured out what they were exactly. "But I'd appreciate it if you didn't say anything to my family. They have enough to deal with . . ."

"Of course. And if I can help in any way, please ask. You can count on me."

"I appreciate that. Thank you."

As the rambling raised bungalow Preston had taken over from his parents came into sight, Preston slowed his pace. "You may want to talk to Ashley. She works for a caterer who does parties for all the super-rich. You never know what she may've seen. Just the other day she mentioned being creeped out by the African artifacts one host had around."

"That's good to know. Thank you."

▪▪▪

After my parents and Aunt Martha headed over to Preston's for the night, Ashley offered scant insight into antiquities collectors on the island before nodding off on the sofa. I covered her with a blanket and picked up the framed photo that had fallen from her grasp. It was of Uncle Jack with his arms around Ashley and Ben, standing on Jack's business partner's boat with the wind whipping their hair and all of them grinning for the camera.

Tears flooded my eyes. *Oh, Uncle Jack.*

I nearly dropped the box of tissues I'd just picked up when my cell phone rang. With a worried glance at Ashley's still-sleeping form, I stepped outside to take Tanner's call and swiped a hand across my wet cheeks.

"Hey, sorry it took so long to get back to you."

Tanner's voice encircled me like a comforting hug. "No

problem. Your looking into this for me helped more than you know."

"How's everyone holding up?"

"As well as can be expected. Ashley texted Ben but still hasn't heard from him. I hope you have good news for us."

"Well, I'm not sure if you'll think this is good news or bad news. The Customs agent I talked to said Ben left Egypt three weeks ago for Belize, then hit Mexico a week later. He cleared Customs in Boston yesterday afternoon."

"Yesterday?" My thoughts scattered. Sinking to the porch steps, my gaze drifted to Jack's house and the darkening sky beyond.

"Yeah, his plane landed just after two local time."

"I guess he could've spent the night in Boston and missed his bus to the ferry this morning." Except . . . he would've called.

"Not what you wanted to hear?" Tanner said.

"No," I admitted. What if whoever got to Jack got to Ben too?

"Serena?" he said softly.

I gulped back a rising sob. Why'd he have to pick tonight to be so *nice*? I was barely holding it together. I could keep a stiff upper lip when he cajoled me out of fretting with a teasing *Serene-uh*, but this gentle caring . . . "I should go."

"Let me know if you need me to look into anything else for you. Okay?"

"I will. Thanks." I hung up quickly and pressed a tissue to my eyes.

My phone beeped—a text from Tanner. *It's okay to cry, kiddo.*

I lost it.

A flash of light from inside Jack's house caught my eye, and I sprang to my feet. The state police had all cleared out hours ago. Blinking away my tears, I hurried across the yard for a closer look. No car was around. Whoever was snooping in Jack's house had walked or been dropped off.

I squinted up the road. Aunt Martha could've easily walked the half mile from Preston's house. And snooping around for a lead was exactly the kind of thing she'd do. Reaching the house, I peeked into the window. She was pawing through a drawer in the end table on the far side of the couch, her back to me. She suddenly turned.

My heart ricocheted off my rib cage. *That's no she.* I shrank back against the side of the house, praying the guy hadn't spotted me.

He was average build and height, but with a dark ball cap shielding his face, I couldn't make out any other features. Clearly he was looking for some sort of paperwork, something small enough to fit in a drawer, anyway. Evidence that might give him away as Jack's killer?

One thing was for sure. If he'd killed once to cover a crime, he wouldn't hesitate to do it again. I thumbed 9-1-1 into my cell phone and snuck another peek in the window.

The flashlight beam swept past the living room window and disappeared in the direction of the bedrooms.

"Wait a minute." I ended my call before it rang through. There was something way too familiar about the prowler's gait. Crouching low, I ran past the living room window and pushed onto my tiptoes to peek into the first bedroom window. Dark. I peeked into the next one, just as the flashlight beam swirled into view.

I jumped back, muffling my gasp. Scrounging up my

courage, I peeked again. Sure enough, I'd been right about the gait. It was Dad's. I tapped on the glass.

He jumped and flicked off his flashlight.

"Dad, it's me. Serena. I'm coming around," I said loud enough for him to hear me through the closed window. I ran around to the kitchen door and let myself in. "Do you mind telling me what you're doing here? I thought you were Jack's killer!"

He winced, making me regret my description choice. "I'm looking for something."

"What?"

"I'm not sure. That's why I didn't say anything to you earlier."

"Can you give me a hint?"

"About a month, or maybe six weeks ago, Jack called and asked me some financial questions."

"Okay." Since Dad was an economics professor, I didn't see what was so unusual about that.

"His business partner had complained that Jack's refusal to 'get with the times' was hurting their business and made an offer to buy him out."

My thoughts raced. "Was it a good offer?"

"Fair, but Jack isn't, uh wasn't, sixty yet, and with investments as volatile as they are these days, I advised him to hold on to the business for a few more years."

"So now you're thinking maybe his partner didn't take Jack's decision too well?" I asked softly.

Dad let out a pent-up breath. "Something like that, yeah."

"His death isn't your fault, Dad."

"Can you check it out? You know, quietly. Make sure the police haven't overlooked something." Dad's face twisted

42

with pain. "You've met his partner. He's impossible to reason with. I'm afraid if Jack didn't buy into his new plan, Frank Dale may've made it happen for himself."

"Okay, Dad, I'll look into it first thing in the morning. You better head back to Preston's now, or everyone will be wondering what happened to you."

"I told them I needed to be alone awhile. That I wanted to walk along the beach."

"That sounds like a nice idea. Mind if I join you?"

He clasped my hand, and we walked in companionable silence along the trail Jack had blazed through the scrub brush and sea grasses to the water.

"It's a lot longer walk than I remembered," Dad said at about the quarter mark. In the distance, the water was eerily still. And dark. Dad suddenly stopped and blurted, "You don't think Ashley or Ben could've killed him, do you?"

"Not Ashley. She's genuinely heartbroken. And what would be her motive? I'm sure Preston makes more than enough for them to live on. And I doubt Jack intended to cut her and Ben out of the will altogether anyways."

"But Ben's not showing up, not answering his phone . . . that looks suspicious."

My worries about what else his nonappearance could mean escalated once more. Then again, knowing Ben, he *could've* latched on to a pretty girl during the flight home and conveniently forgotten about his commitments. I squeezed Dad's hand. "Let's wait to see what Ben says when he shows." *Please, Lord, let him show.*

"Will you stay until after the funeral?" Dad sounded beyond tired.

"Yes. I'll call the office once the details are settled and ask for extra time off if I need to." Aunt Martha and my parents had booked their return flights for ten days from now, but I'd planned to fly home Monday night. "I better call Nate and make sure he's okay with watching Harold longer." I pulled out my cell phone. "No reception. Remind me to call him when we return to the road."

Dad about-faced. "We can go now. I should get back to the house before it gets any darker and your mother starts worrying about me." I could tell Dad was trying to make light, but he couldn't mask the heaviness seeping through his words.

"I'll walk with you partway," I said. "Ashley's already asleep. She wore herself out crying." Instead of following the trail back to Jack's, I steered Dad across the field to cut the corner and intercept the road farther up.

My call to Nate connected just before we reached the road.

Nate picked up on the third ring. "Hey, Serena. How's it going? You missing Harold already?"

"Um." I fumbled my way through telling Nate about Uncle Jack's death and swiped at a tear that managed to leak out despite my vigorous blinking. "So I was wondering if you could—"

The roar of an engine jerked my attention to the road. Blinding headlights suddenly burst on. I vaulted backwards. "Dad, watch out!"

4

The vehicle clipped Dad and sent him flying.

I scrambled to my feet. "Dad! Dad!" In the deepening darkness, I couldn't make out his form amidst the scrub brush. I ran blindly in the direction his body had flown. "Dad, where are you?" I paused to listen.

The mournful sound of a distant foghorn was the only reply.

Panic squeezed my throat. My eyes took a while to adjust to the darkness after being blinded by those headlights, but finally I spotted a dark mass the size of a man. "Dad!" I raced toward him.

He didn't move. Didn't speak.

I dropped to my knees at his side and pressed my fingers to the pulse point on his neck. His pulse was weak, but there, his breathing ragged. "Dad, can you hear me?"

Did I imagine that hitch in his breath?

I reached in my pocket for my cell phone but came up empty. I'd been talking to Nate when the vehicle roared up.

I must've dropped it when I vaulted the ditch. "Help! Help! I need help!" I shouted.

For a second, I thought I heard the low purr of a motor and wasn't so sure that was a good thing. What if it was the maniac driver coming back?

With no moon or stars, I couldn't see if Dad was bleeding, and I didn't dare try to move him. I pressed my hand to his cheek. "Dad, everything's going to be okay. Stay with me."

Blood, warm and sticky, trickled over my fingers. I carefully probed to find the source—a gash on the side of his head. I whipped off my sweater and pressed it to the wound. "Dad, can you hear me?"

The wind picked up as fog slinked around us, circling like sharks at the smell of blood.

Preston's porch lights blinked on in the distance.

"Help! Someone help me!" I shouted. I palpated Dad's torso and limbs, found a probable fracture in his ankle. Even if he regained consciousness, there was no chance I'd be able to walk him back to the house.

"Dad, talk to me." I felt in his pockets for a cell phone but found only his wallet. "Listen, I'm going to have to go for help. I won't be long." My voice faltered. "I promise." Standing, I looked for some way to mark where he was lying. I didn't dare take the sweater back from his bleeding skull, but I only had a T-shirt and jeans left on me, and . . . socks. I dropped to the ground to pull off a shoe and sock.

"Serena? Ward? Where are you?" Mom's voice whispered through the mist.

Had I imagined it? "Mom?"

A pair of flashlights bobbed through the darkness.

"Mom! Over here!" I yanked my shoe back on and frantically waved my arms.

"Serena, keep calling. I can't see you," Mom shouted.

"Call an ambulance. We need an ambulance!"

One of the spots of light halted, the other continued its headlong dash toward the sound of my voice. I kneeled at Dad's side and rechecked his pulse, his breathing, and whispered soothing words between shouts of "over here."

Eternal minutes later, Mom joined me. She muffled a gasp and immediately repeated the checks I'd already done, all the while begging Dad to talk to her.

Aunt Martha jogged into view, puffing loudly. "The ambulance is on its way." She surveyed the situation, then added, "I'll stand at the road and wait for them, or they'll never spot us in this fog."

An image of the speeding vehicle returning bombarded my thoughts. "Be careful," I warned.

Dad roused under Mom's insistent pleading. She held his hand until the paramedics arrived, then Aunt Martha pried her away to give them room to work. As they put a C-collar on him and secured him to a backboard, the police questioned me.

"It was a bigger vehicle, an SUV of some kind, but I couldn't tell you the color," I said.

"And he didn't stop?"

"Didn't even slow down," I clarified, although I was sure the other officer scrutinizing the road with his flashlight could tell that by the absence of skid marks.

He took copious pictures, then pulled out a measuring tape and sketch pad.

The paramedics loaded Dad into the ambulance.

"You ride with them," I told Mom. "Aunt Martha and I can get Ashley or Preston to bring us."

"But you should be checked too."

"I'm fine. I jumped out of the way." A throb in my ankle flared, asserting otherwise, but I ignored it for the moment.

"Well, I guess that's all for now, Miss Jones," the officer said and then handed me a card. "If you think of anything else that may be useful, give me a call. I hope the rest of your visit to the island is more pleasant."

"Thank you"—I glanced at the card—"Officer Lennox."

"What are you thinking?" Aunt Martha asked as the officer returned to his partner.

She could read me too well. "I'm not so sure the accident was an accident."

"Why's that?"

"Dad and I were in Uncle Jack's house just before it happened."

Aunt Martha nodded. "You think his murderer may have come to scrounge for incriminating evidence and spotted the two of you leaving?"

Sometimes it was downright scary how much alike we thought. "Yeah, that pretty much sums it up."

"Of course, you know how youth like to party at the beach. One of them could've had too much to drink and not even seen you," she said, as if it should make me feel better.

It didn't. I couldn't even identify the vehicle. Some FBI agent I turned out to be. I nixed the impulse to fill Tanner in on the new development. I didn't have my phone anyway.

An SUV pulled to a stop at the roadblock set up by the officers examining the crime scene. Preston burst out of the vehicle and raced toward the officers. "What's going on? Was anyone hurt?"

Officer Lennox caught him by the arms to stop him from trampling the evidence at the same time Preston spotted me. He shot a frantic glance back toward Ashley's cottage. "Where's Ashley? Is she okay?"

"Where was Preston all this time?" I asked Aunt Martha as we closed the distance between him and us. "Wasn't he at the house with you?"

"He went out for groceries."

"Who's Ashley?" Officer Lennox asked.

"The owner of the cottage I'm staying at," I explained, then to Preston added, "She's fine." I squinted back at the cottage, void of lights. "Slept through it all." *Apparently*.

Aunt Martha sidled around the roadblock and surreptitiously examined Preston's front bumper. An uneasy feeling churned my stomach as I kept his attention in the opposite direction. Not because I suspected Preston but because Aunt Martha's sleuthing could put her in the line of fire of the same creep who'd taken Dad out.

She flicked off her flashlight and gave me a solemn nod a nanosecond before Preston glanced her way.

"Do you mind giving Serena and me a lift to the hospital?" Aunt Martha covered, reaching for the passenger door handle. "I hate for her mother to be sitting there alone while the doctors treat Ward."

Officer Lennox took down Preston's name, address, and whereabouts at the time of the accident and then gave us all permission to go.

I took the backseat, which I shared with three bags of groceries, confirming that Preston had gone where he'd said.

He stopped for a minute at his house to put the perishables in the fridge. I was surprised that I could scarcely see the flashing cruiser lights from here. It was a wonder Aunt Martha and Mom had heard me shouting. I breathed a silent prayer of thanks for that mercy and another for Dad's recovery.

"You know," Aunt Martha spoke from the front seat, "I wouldn't put it past that Carly woman to try to take out Ashley and Ben out of spite. Maybe she mistook you and your dad for them."

"Her car is a lot smaller than the vehicle that hit Dad." My thoughts veered to Ben and Carly's allegations about him. I hadn't mentioned to Aunt Martha that he arrived in Boston a day earlier than Ashley thought, might already be on the island. Considering the information might tempt Aunt Martha to do more sleuthing, I'd sleep better if she didn't know just yet. The driver could've been Ben as readily as anyone else. And if he mistook Dad and me for Ashley and Preston, then he would've had a strong motive to run us down. With Ashley out of the way, he'd inherit everything.

My stomach churned at the realization that theoretically, Ben could've arrived on the island early enough to kill Jack too. His plane had landed in plenty of time.

Preston returned to the vehicle. "I texted Ashley to let her know what's going on in case she wakes up."

* * *

It was after 1:00 a.m. by the time we pulled back into Preston's driveway. Dad had been admitted for observation. He had a concussion, four stitches on his head wound, and a broken ankle. Mom had insisted on staying with him, and Preston had suggested I stay in my parents' room at his place for the rest of the night so as not to disturb Ashley. I was too tired to argue.

Hours later, I woke to the sound of Ashley's caustic tone.

"Wait," Ashley said, "aren't those Serena's shoes? She's *here*?"

My heart dove. What did she think? That I snuck over here for an illicit rendezvous with her fiancé? She knew me better than that.

"Didn't you check your messages?" Preston asked calmly.

I threw Mom's bathrobe on over the T-shirt and shorts Preston had lent me to sleep in and reached for the bedroom doorknob. *On second thought.* I quickly changed into the clothes I'd been wearing last night so as not to fuel any more mistaken assumptions.

I emerged from the bedroom as Preston relayed the events Ashley had slept through.

She looked irritated and skeptical until her gaze dropped to the bloodstain on the front of my T-shirt. She gasped. "Preston just told me what happened." She pulled me into a hug. "I'm so glad you're okay." She clearly hoped I hadn't overheard their conversation, so I let it go. The last thing I wanted was a repeat of the cold-shoulder treatment she'd given me at the end of my previous trip.

"You have company waiting for you on the veranda," Preston said.

"I do?" I slipped out the patio door and startled at the sight of Nate and Aunt Martha sitting on the veranda overlooking Tisbury Great Pond.

Nate stood and a pained look crossed his face as his gaze tripped over my bloodied clothes.

"Nate?"

He drew me into his arms and hugged me tight. "It almost killed me to hear you screaming for help and be helpless to do anything."

His heart was pounding against my ear. And he smelled nice. *Really nice.* Like laundry fresh from the line with a hint of a distinctly masculine spice. He eased his hold just enough to cradle my face in his hands.

My breath caught at the tortured look in his pale blue eyes.

His thumb lightly brushed over my bruised cheek, and he muffled a guttural groan. "I had to see for myself that you were okay."

I gaped at him, stunned.

"He called my cell phone last night as soon as he heard you scream and couldn't raise you again," Aunt Martha explained. "That's how your mother and I knew to go out and look for you."

"Oh." With all that happened, I'd forgotten that I'd been on the phone with him. "Thank you," I whispered, tears pricking my eyes. "You may have saved Dad's life."

His gaze searched mine as his thumb whisked a tear from my cheek. "I'm glad you're *both* okay," he said, his voice a tad wobbly.

My mind flailed about for a quip to lighten the moment. I mean, we watched a lot of old movies together, shared more than a few dinners . . . but we'd never even kissed. Not that the urge to hadn't crossed my mind. So what was I supposed to make of his dropping everything to fly halfway across the country in the middle of the night to check on me? Wait a minute . . . "How did you get here so quickly? Even the red-eye wouldn't have gotten you into Boston early enough to catch the first ferry across." I stepped back so I could think straight.

His hands dropped to his side, and his lips tipped ever so slightly downward. "I flew into the island's airport. I would've been here earlier, but they don't allow night landings."

"No, not since the Kennedy accident."

"So I learned."

"You're telling me you *flew*, as in piloted the plane yourself?"

His cheeks colored.

"You never told me you had your pilot's license!"

He shrugged. "It never came up."

"He hasn't flown since—"

Nate cut off whatever Aunt Martha had been about to divulge with a sharp look. Clearly she not only knew about his ability but also knew the reason he didn't want to talk about it.

Ohh-kay, then. Since I preferred to avoid talking about the cause of my claustrophobia, I knew how he felt and didn't press. I was sure Aunt Martha would fill me in on the juicy details later anyway. Instead, I asked, "Where'd you get the plane?"

"Oh, that part was easy," Aunt Martha piped up again. "He borrowed it from a friend of mine."

"Malgucci?" Whether her newest friend was actually a mobster was still up for debate, but either way he had uncomfortably close ties to the mob in St. Louis, and I sure didn't like the idea of Nate owing them a favor on my account.

"No, one of my *old* friends."

Aunt Martha had traveled so many places for work before she retired that it didn't surprise me she had a friend with a plane. But a friend that would lend it to a complete stranger on her say-so?

Aunt Martha clearly knew how to turn on the charm, and I couldn't help but think that Mom had read Martha's so-called spinsterhood all wrong. I was beginning to think she could've settled down with her choice of men . . . if she'd been so inclined.

"Nate's was the first flight to land this morning," Aunt Martha said with a healthy dose of admiration, or maybe it was pride, since I had her to thank for the surprise visit. "Preston called a friend with one of the rental agencies to make sure there'd be a car ready and waiting the second the airport cleared Nate for landing."

"Wow, you thought of everything"—I tugged my bottom lip between my teeth, not wanting to sound ungrateful—"only, who's taking care of Harold?"

A "meow" sounded from under the veranda.

Chuckling, Nate tugged at a leash I hadn't noticed anchored under a leg of the chair he'd been sitting on. "He came along too."

My black-and-white cat emerged rather reluctantly from under the veranda, looking indignant about being harnessed and leashed, which had been a smart move on Nate's part. Who knew where Harold would've gotten to otherwise. I reached down to make a fuss over him, but a fluffy white, no doubt female, cat poked its head over the step, and Harold gave her his attention instead.

"Already making friends, I see," I said wryly.

Aunt Martha grinned. "Nothing like the ocean breezes to put a little romance in the air."

5

Preston and Ashley joined Nate, Aunt Martha, and me on the veranda, breaking the awkward silence that followed Aunt Martha's whimsical statement on romance and ocean breezes. "Breakfast is ready," Preston announced, setting a tray laden with muffins and jam on the table.

"Is that my phone?" I snatched up the smartphone also on the tray.

"I hope so. Officer Lennox dropped it by. Found it in the ditch after we left the scene last night."

I thumbed in my password and the home screen appeared. "What a relief!"

Nate leaned over and glanced at it. "Only *four* missed messages."

"All from you, I suppose?" I said with an I'm-on-to-you smirk.

He held up his hands in surrender. "Not me."

I tapped the icon to bring up the messages.

Tanner.

My heart stuttered.

He couldn't have heard about the hit-and-run. Could he?

Oh, he'd be so ticked at me for not calling him right away. He liked Dad a lot. Squirming, I schooled my expression and scrolled through the messages.

Thankfully, they were all of the cajoling please-tell-me-you're-staying-out-of-trouble variety. I texted back a cheeky:

You know me.

He instantly texted back a wry:

Too well.

Nate leaned over and squinted at my phone screen.

I muffled my chuckle and quickly clicked back to the message list.

"Tanner, Tanner, Tanner, and . . . *Tanner*," Nate read aloud, then exchanged a look I couldn't quite read with Aunt Martha—exasperation, maybe. "Doesn't the guy know you're on vacation?"

"I—" I pursed my lips closed again, not ready to have Ashley hear I'd called an FBI agent to look into Ben's whereabouts, especially when I still didn't know the answer to that and what I did know didn't look good for him.

"Oh, I almost forgot to tell you that I heard from Ben," Ashley blurted, as if she'd read my thoughts. "He texted me earlier this morning." She flashed Preston a sheepish look, probably because if she'd seen a message from Ben, she had to have seen Preston's message explaining why I was here this morning instead of at the cottage. A message she apparently hadn't believed until she saw my state. "He said he missed his flight. And since there was no way he could make it in time for the engagement party now, he decided to stay in South America until the wedding."

"Are you serious?" I exclaimed, stunned by Ben's outright lie. To think I'd feared he'd been a victim too. "Did you call him back to tell him about Uncle Jack?"

"I tried but he didn't pick up."

"Did you text him the message then?"

"Do you think I should? It seems like such a horrible way for him to hear the news."

Somehow I doubted it would be the first he'd heard of it. Nausea roiled my stomach.

Preston gave Ashley's hand a tender squeeze. "I think you should. Phone service can be hit and miss in the places your brother travels. It could be days before you catch him, but he can retrieve the text as soon as his phone connects again."

"Preston's right," Aunt Martha said gently. "Under the circumstances, it's the best you can do. I'm sure he'd want to be here."

Tearing up, Ashley blinked rapidly and thumbed the message into her phone with shaky hands.

I gritted my teeth to contain my anger at Ben. I could think of only one reason why Ben would lie to Ashley about missing his plane—to avoid being a suspect in Jack's murder.

I excused myself to use the restroom and took the opportunity to put in a call to Agent Jackson.

He picked up on the first ring. "Jones, what part of—?"

"I think whoever killed Jack tried to kill my dad and me last night," I interjected before he could finish his rant.

"What?"

Preston and Ashley's voices drifted through the bathroom door.

I turned on the faucet so they wouldn't hear me talking and filled Jackson in on last night's hit-and-run.

"So you think the alleged killer spotted the two of you snooping in Jack's house?"

"It's a little too coincidental, don't you think, that Jack would accidentally fall to his death at Menemsha Hills and the next night we'd be run off the road outside his house?"

"Did you relay your suspicions to the police?"

Examining the state of my clothes in the mirror, I pinched my blood-encrusted shirt away from my skin. "Right, and paint an even bigger bull's-eye on my back." Jack had clearly confided in someone he shouldn't have. My breath snagged. *Isaak?*

"Point taken. When are you returning to St. Louis?"

"I'm not going anywhere until Jack's killer is behind bars," I said, mentally replaying yesterday's conversation. What had Isaak really been doing when I surprised him at Jack's house?

"Hey, trust me, I'm going to turn over every stone I can find that'll shed any light on this antiquities smuggling ring Jack called about."

"Have you even tried to locate Ben yet?" Isaak had claimed Jack said his nephew was the one with the information, so tracking down said nephew should've been at the top of his agenda.

"Yeah, I know he flew into Boston the day before yesterday." His grim tone sounded empathetic, as if he knew I was thinking what Ben's nonappearance could mean.

Okay, so maybe I could trust him. My personal connection to the case was clearly hampering my objectivity. Dad's suspicions of Jack's business partner flitted through my mind. If Dad was right, Jack's call to the feds about an art crime might not even have anything to do with his death.

"Have the police run down alibis of everyone who stood to benefit from Jack's death?"

"They haven't located the nephew yet, but Jack's niece and his business partner both had solid alibis."

Which left the person Jack intended to expose as our prime suspect.

I paced the bathroom floor. *Do I tell Isaak about Ben's text?*

I couldn't believe Ben was capable of murder, but I wouldn't have believed he'd lie about missing his plane either. "You wouldn't happen to have a friend at the phone company who could look up where a call originated, would you?" It'd be a whole lot quicker than trying to get the information through official channels.

Agent Jackson let out a sigh. "I may."

I updated him on Ben's text to his sister claiming he was still in South America, then recited his number from what I'd memorized off Ashley's phone screen.

"You think Ben is our smuggler."

Whoa. "No, he's a freelance writer. I just—" Ben wouldn't. Would he? *Listen to me.* I speculate about him being capable of murder but balk at the idea of him looting burial sites? "You know what stinks about our job?"

"You have to suspect everyone."

My heart sank. "Yeah." I shook my head, not that Isaak could see me. Knowing Jack, if he'd figured out that Ben was smuggling antiquities into the country, he would've tried to convince him to turn himself in. Which meant either Ben didn't come on board with Jack's plan or someone higher up the food chain caught wind of it.

"I'll call my friend at the phone company," Isaak said softly, then clicked off.

By the time I returned to the veranda, only Nate and Aunt Martha were still there. "Where'd Ashley and Preston disappear to?"

"They went for a walk," Aunt Martha said. "And your mother called. She said your father will get a cast put on his ankle this morning and then she'll call when they're ready to be picked up. I figured you and Nate could fetch them in his rental car."

"Yes, of course. Although before I do anything, I need to head back to the cottage and shower and get into some clean clothes."

Nate pushed a muffin on a plate in front of me. "Have something to eat and then I'll drive you down there."

The tenderness in his voice rattled my already shaky grip on my emotions. Not trusting myself to meet his gaze without falling apart, I tore a bite from the muffin and popped it into my mouth. Falling apart was so not me. It was the one trait I was happy to share with my very-British, stiff-upper-lip nana.

Nate's masculine scent tangled with the aroma of coffee and salt air, teasing my senses and compelling me to glance his way.

A wave of warmth washed over me at the concern shadowing his eyes. The eyes of a man who flew through the night to make sure I was okay. It felt pretty nice to be worried about. In a nonmothering way, of course.

And from the intensity in those darkening eyes of his, it was a good thing my mother wasn't here.

My heart did a silly little flip as I forced my attention back to my muffin.

"Leave Harold with me," Aunt Martha said. "He and I are going to do some fishing."

"I think you need to go out a lot earlier in the morning or wait until evening if you want to catch anything."

"Don't you worry about me. I've been fishing since long before you were born." She shot Nate a wink as she pushed up from her chair, then she gathered Harold's leash and led him down to the water.

"Mind telling me what that wink was about?" I said to Nate, not entirely sure I was ready for the answer.

"*Fishing?*" His lips twitched into a smile. "Wow, and here I thought *I* was sleep-deprived."

"Oh no, who does she think she's going to interrogate around here?" I twisted in my chair to see which direction she'd headed.

"She'll be fine," Nate reassured. "She has a gift for extracting information with no one the wiser."

"It's the British accent."

He chuckled. "You're probably right."

Maybe. But it didn't make me worry any less. I scooped up the remnant of my muffin. "Let's go. I'd like to talk to Jack's business partner and start trying to retrace Jack's steps for the past week or so before Mom calls." And what did it say about me that talking to Jack's business partner felt safer than talking to Nate about . . . anything else?

■■■

"Hey." Nate banged on the washroom door. "There's some guy hauling a big iron sculpture off your uncle's front yard."

"What? Stop him. I'll be right out."

I quickly rinsed the shampoo out of my hair and jumped out of the shower. It had to be the neighbor. Unbelievable.

By the time I raced outside, Nate was helping a spectacled, slick-haired twerp lay Jack's sculpture behind the shed in the backyard. I stalked over, my jacket flap open, the butt of my gun visible above my waistband. "What's going on?"

"The sculpture was blocking his view," Nate explained.

"So?"

"So in the interest of keeping peace between the neighbors, I helped him move it out of sight until whoever inherits the house decides what they want done with it."

"Seriously?" I said to the weasel-eyed twerp. "You couldn't even wait until Jack's body was in the ground?"

"I'm sorry for your loss," he said.

"No, you're not. You probably jumped for glee when you heard. I hope you wind up with an even worse neighbor!"

"Serena, come on." Nate clasped my elbow and steered me back toward the cottage.

"He's been harassing Jack over his lawn ornaments for years," I hissed, ripping my arm from his grasp. "For all we know, he pushed Jack down those stairs just so he could get rid of the sculptures himself."

Nate stopped and faced me, clasping both my arms. "Do you really believe that?"

I glared at him for three full seconds before realizing how crazed I must've sounded. I ducked my head. "No, I guess not."

Nate pulled me into his arms. "It's okay. Grief makes us all a little crazy sometimes."

The steady thump of his heart calmed my riotous emotions. "It's easier to be angry than sad," I admitted.

"I know," he whispered, and I knew he did because he'd lost his parents in a car accident when his younger brother was still a teenager. "You want to blame someone," he said softly, "but what if there's no one to blame? What if Jack really did just trip and fall?"

I pulled away enough to look him in the eyes. "Do you think I'm crazy trying to prove he was killed?"

"No, of course not."

"It couldn't have been an accident."

"Why is it so important to you to believe that?"

"Because it's not fair!" Oh, great, how totally irrational did that sound?

Nate's expression was empathetic.

I couldn't handle it. It made me want to cry. And I didn't like to cry. Crying didn't help anything. It just gave me a headache.

"You're not going to believe this," Ashley said and stormed across the yard toward us, Preston trailing her. "We just called the funeral home to make arrangements, and they said it could be days before Uncle Jack's body is released to them. The police sent it to the Chief Medical Examiner's Office in Sandwich."

"Sandwich?" Nate asked.

"A city off-island," I explained.

Preston stopped at Ashley's side and stroked her back reassuringly. "I told her it doesn't mean they think he was murdered. The police probably just decided that with Carly screaming murder, they'd better do their due diligence."

"Preston is right," I said to Ashley because I saw no point in stressing her more with my unsubstantiated suspicions.

We walked back to the cottage together. Once inside,

Ashley sank into a corner of the sofa, pulled her knees to her chest, and buried her head in her arms. "What are we supposed to do until the body's released?"

"Did the funeral director mention anything about Jack's personal effects?" I asked.

"You mean like his camera and wallet? The officer left those yesterday."

"You have them?" I glanced about the room. Every tabletop and bookshelf was decorated with dishes of sea glass. Over the years, I'd logged countless hours combing beaches with her for the colorful treasure.

"They're on the desk."

Spotting Jack's decades-old beat-up leather camera case tucked between the CD rack and computer monitor, I exchanged a hopeful look with Nate, then sprang up to fetch the camera.

But Preston was standing next to the desk and scooped it up first. "You should see the gorgeous pictures Jack took of the island," Preston said to Nate. He lifted his chin to the framed sunset photograph hanging over Ashley's fireplace. "That's one of his." Preston flicked the back-cover switch.

"No!" I lunged for the camera, but the back had already popped open, exposing the film.

"What's wrong? I'm pulling the card reader"—he looked down—"oh, shoot." He snapped the cover closed. "I forgot Jack still used film."

I took the camera from him and manually rewound the film. "We might be able to salvage the first few pictures. Is there a place on the island that still develops 35mm film?"

"Yes, Mosher's on Main Street in Vineyard Haven," Ashley said.

"Hey." Preston joined Ashley on the sofa. "We could take them to Jack's and show Nate some of the albums."

"Could we take a rain check?" Nate asked. "Serena was going to give me a bit of a tour of the island before we pick up her parents."

My breath caught in my throat. What if they volunteered to take us around? I couldn't exactly justify stopping at Uncle Jack's office and talking to his partner as a must-see sight.

"Good plan," Preston said enthusiastically. "You've got a beautiful day for it." He jotted down an address on a slip of paper and passed it to me. "Take a drive by this place. It's the most recent completed house Jack designed. Quite a sight." Preston held my gaze. "The owner's an avid antiquities collector too."

Catching his hint, I telepathed my thanks and glanced at the address near the West Chop Country Club. "We definitely will."

"If you want to leave the film with us, we can take it in," Ashley volunteered.

"That's okay. We'll be driving right by when we go to the hospital," I said.

"What was that about?" Nate asked a moment later as he held open the rental's passenger door for me.

"What?"

"That look between you and Ashley's fiancé."

Wow, Nate was perceptive.

"Because in case you didn't notice, Ashley thought it was a come-on."

My heart hitched at his sour tone. I teasingly arched an eyebrow. "And you?"

He shrugged, but I didn't miss the way his lips tipped

up at the corners. Nate rounded the car and climbed in the driver's side. "Well?"

I filled him in on Jack's suspicions about the antiquities smuggling. "I confided in Preston about Jack's call to the FBI and this"—I held up the address—"is a lead."

"Excellent." Nate started the car. "So where to first?"

"Edgartown. I want to talk to Jack's business partner. I'm kind of surprised he didn't call Ashley first thing to pay his respects. He had to have heard the news by now."

"May I make a suggestion?"

"Sure."

"We should check out the scene of the accident before the curiosity seekers get there. We may find something the police missed."

"That's a great idea." I gave him directions to Menemsha Hills. Between the comfortable seventy-degree temperature, the still air, and the clear skies, the conditions were perfect for surveying the scene.

When we arrived at the trailhead, there was only one other car in the parking lot, although curiosity seekers could also walk to the stairs connecting the forest trail to the rocky shore from either direction along the beach. Nate grabbed his camera from the trunk. "Ready?"

I tucked the bottoms of my pants into my socks. "Yes, follow me and try not to brush against the bushes. The ticks are bad this time of year." It was a thirty-five-minute uphill walk on a sandy path through an airy forest of oak trees. We crossed a back road I'd forgotten about but from the look of all the tire tracks was where the police had parked yesterday.

I stopped at the top of the hill overlooking the ocean and silently motioned Nate to stop too.

A silver-haired man was hunched over examining something halfway down the weathered cedar steps.

Nate took a picture of him, then whispered close to my ear, "That guy's clearly scrutinizing the scene of the accident. What's our story?"

"Let's play dumb tourists. Might learn more."

Nate nodded, then took a steady stream of pictures of the path and surrounding area, even though there'd be no easy way to discern which footprints belonged to emergency responders and which might belong to a killer.

"Hello," I called to the man on the steps and started down. "Beautiful day."

The man sprang up and spun around to face me. He had a black-and-white cat in his arms and looked as if he was trying to take something from its mouth as the cat struggled to break free.

The cat wore a red harness and lead just like Harold had had on earlier. I blinked.

The cat *was* Harold. "Hey, what are you doing with my cat?"

6

Harold sprang from the stranger's arms and streaked toward me. Correction—past me and straight to Nate.

"Catch him!" a female voice rose from below the steps.

"Aunt Martha?" I bent over the handrail to see for myself. "How on earth did you get all the way over here?" Last I saw her she'd been strolling toward Tisbury Great Pond on the other side of the island.

"Did you get it away from him?" she asked the man who'd been holding Harold, totally ignoring me.

"No." He hurried past me up the stairs.

Nate had Harold cuddled in his arms and held up a piece of blue sea glass. "Was this what you were after? Harold had it in his mouth."

The man's shoulders slumped. "It's not a button," he called back to Aunt Martha, who'd already rounded the bottom of the stairs.

She harrumphed. "And here I thought Harold had found a clue."

"What's going on?" I asked, although I had a pretty clear idea of what my Aunt Martha had been doing. "Who's this?"

Her cheeks colored as her gaze lifted above my head to the man now standing a few stairs above me. "Winston. He's a dear old friend."

Dear? I glanced from one to the other, stifling the urge to ask why this was the first I'd heard of him. "Do you live on the island?" I asked instead.

"Yes, didn't I tell you I'd planned to look him up?" Aunt Martha asked, closing the distance between them. "I called him after you and Nate went to Ashley's, and he came straight to fetch me."

Not surprising given the way he looked at Aunt Martha as she hugged his arm. I had the feeling they'd been *more* than friends. Grinning, I extended a hand. "Nice to meet you, Winston. It isn't often that we get to meet one of Aunt Martha's old friends."

Winston's eyes twinkled as he slipped his hand around her waist and gave me a solid handshake. "I'm surprised. I heard tell she had a man in every port."

Plenty of acquaintances, that was for sure. And more than a few in high places. But no one she'd ever called *dear*.

Aunt Martha swatted him, her cheeks flaming. "Off with you." Sobering, she returned her attention to Nate and Harold, then me. "I suppose it was silly to hope we might spot some telltale evidence the police missed."

"I did find a few stray blue threads caught in the cedar handrail"—Winston pointed to what looked like a piece of fabric torn from a lightweight jacket caught on a splinter of wood—"but it looks as if he toppled down the steps, not over the rail, so they may not be connected."

"There are traces of blood on the rocks at the bottom of the stairs," Aunt Martha interjected. "And lots of footprints in the sand at the top. From the emergency personnel, I imagine."

"When Harold scurried off with what looked like a button in his mouth," Winston went on, "we thought Jack might've grabbed his attacker's clothes and popped a button."

"Alleged attacker," I corrected out of habit.

Winston acknowledged the semantics with a nod, then pointed out the pros and cons of the three approaches the alleged attacker could have made.

"You sound as if you've worked in law enforcement," I said.

"Been in real estate for the last fifteen years." He glanced at Aunt Martha.

She collected Harold from Nate. "I guess we should leave the sleuthing to the younger folks." They headed back up to the trail.

"What do you make of that?" I asked Nate.

"You know your aunt. She likes to be mysterious."

Hmm, but I had to wonder what Winston had been into before real estate. We descended the steps and scouted the rocky area beneath. I forced myself to ignore the bloodstain because, despite months of training and more than a year on the job, it was still hard to forget that this was where a family friend had met his end.

"I don't see any clues. How about you?" Nate asked.

Teetering around on the ocean-smoothed rocks, scrutinizing the ground, reminded me of the hours Ashley and I had spent combing for sea glass as kids. But never at this beach. Uncle Jack had said sea glass never seemed to wash up around here. "Oh! It's a clue."

"What's a clue?"

"Can I see that piece of sea glass Harold found?"

Nate handed over the fingernail-sized chip of smoky blue glass.

I turned it over between my fingers, tracing my thumb over the rounded edges. "Whenever Ben used to complain about not being cute enough to get the girls to notice him or Ashley used to complain about being mediocre in everything she tried, Jack would show us a piece of sea glass. He would remind us how it had once been ugly and unwanted—useless— but in being pushed around by the waves and roughed up by the rocks and sand, it was transformed into a beautiful, sought-after treasure."

"He sounds as if he was a pretty amazing uncle," Nate said.

"He was. And I think this piece of sea glass could be a clue."

"How so? Sea glass shows up in pretty random places along the beach."

"But never on this beach."

Nate scrutinized the ground. "You sure about that?"

"It's what Uncle Jack once said. At the very least, it'd be rare. It's far more likely this piece fell from the attacker's pocket."

Nate shook his head, not looking nearly as excited as he should. "Or from one of the emergency personnel's. Or even Jack's pocket. Maybe he picked up pieces he found to add to his niece's collection. Or maybe he noticed the sun glint off this rare find and came down the stairs to investigate."

"You think I'm creating a crime where there isn't one."

"No! Someone ran you and your father off the road. We know that for a fact."

"And we can't ignore that it may be connected to Jack's death."

"Exactly. So let's question his partner."

■■■

I gave Nate directions to Edgartown, where Jack and Frank had a small storefront on Winter Street. Nate snagged a curbside parking spot right in front. "It doesn't look like he's in."

I squinted at the sign. "It says closed due to a death in the family. Maybe we can catch him at his house." I plugged his name into the search app on my phone and came up with the address, then pinpointed the location using the map app. "You're not going to believe this. He lives up the road from Menemsha Hills."

Nate pulled back onto the street. "Do you want to call him first?"

"No. I'd rather not give him advance warning. I'm not buying the cops' finding." I caught Nate's arm as he turned onto Church Street. "Stop."

"What is it?"

"I thought I saw Carly."

"The fiancée's daughter?"

"Yeah. Talking to Gaudy Souvenir Guy."

"Huh?"

I searched my memory for the name Aunt Martha had spied on the guy's luggage tag. "Charles Anderson. I saw him at the Boston airport yesterday with a replica of a Maya god that he looked pretty edgy about being discovered with in his luggage."

"Okay, but if he arrived in Boston at the same time as you, then you know he didn't kill Jack."

"Sure, but maybe that souvenir I saw was really a disguised artifact. Maybe he's the smuggler Jack was on to."

"What are you saying? You think Carly killed Jack because she's souvenir guy's girlfriend or something?"

"It's possible." I snapped a photo of the pair on my cell phone. "Okay, go, go, before they see us."

Nate hit the gas, and I put in another call to Isaak.

"Tanner ran a background check on Anderson for me yesterday and nothing popped," I explained to Nate as I waited for Isaak to pick up. "But maybe Anderson just hasn't been caught yet." I signaled Nate to hold his thought as Isaak came on the line. "Hey, could you run a background check on Carly Delmar for me?" I explained my suspicions about Anderson and her possible relationship to him.

"Sure, I'll get back to you," Isaak said and hung up.

As Nate and I headed back to Menemsha, he asked, "If Jack was about to add Carly—or at least her mother—to his will, you really think she'd pop him before the ink was dipped?"

"Jack was about to spill whatever he knew to the FBI. And he wasn't scheduled to sign his new will until next week."

Nate's forehead scrunched, as if he was trying to make sense of it. And couldn't. "But Martha said Carly accused Ashley and Ben of killing Jack, right?"

"Yes."

"Why would she do that? If the police weren't calling Jack's death a homicide, why risk sparking an investigation?"

I shrugged. "Criminals aren't always the brightest bulbs in the box. Besides, she spouted the accusation the instant she jumped out of her car. A guilty conscience would make her assume the police found the death suspicious."

"Hmm."

"I'm not saying she did it. I just want to know what Gaudy Souvenir Guy does for a living and what their relationship is." I thumbed a text message to Tanner, asking if his check on Anderson turned up an employment history. "Hey, the Lord must've nudged me to notice the guy for a reason, right? I don't believe in coincidences."

"But they do happen. Sometimes."

"Turn here," I said, spotting Frank's road. "It's that house on the left." Frank was washing his car in a baggy sweat suit. His hair had grayed significantly since I'd last seen him, and he'd put on a few extra inches around the middle.

Nate parked in the driveway behind him.

I hopped out of the car, and three strides from coming nose to nose with the guy, I suddenly realized that I didn't have a clue how to question him. "Uh, hi," I stammered. *Oh, really smooth.*

He stopped chamoising his rear panel and squinted at me. His eyes were red, his face haggard. "May I help you?"

I introduced Nate and myself.

His expression turned sympathetic. "Yes, I remember you from the summer barbecues Jack used to throw." His voice caught. "You and Ashley used to race around with those identical pigtails flopping behind you both. The two of you were inseparable. It's been a long time."

"Yes, it has," I said softly.

Frank's gaze dropped to the ground. "I can't believe Jack's gone."

"Have the police talked to you?" I asked.

74

His attention snapped back to me. "Why would they?"

"The state police always investigate an unattended death," Nate explained. "To help them rule out foul play, they'd want to know if you were aware of any enemies Jack may have had. Disgruntled clients perhaps."

I found myself staring at Nate. He was amazingly familiar with the procedure for a civilian.

Frank nodded. "That makes sense. But that kind of talk must be killing Ashley and Ben. How are they holding up? I was going to head over there after I finished up here."

"Ashley is as well as can be expected," I said. "We're still waiting for Ben to return from his trip."

Frank clenched the rag he was holding, the color seeping from his fingers. "It's high time that kid stopped gallivanting around and took some responsibility. Doesn't he know his sister needs him?"

"I guess he'll have no choice now," Nate said. "I assume he and Ashley will inherit Jack's share of your architect firm?"

"I'll buy them out," Frank muttered. "I'm sure they'd rather have the money." He rubbed at an invisible spot on the trunk of his car, his trembling jaw betraying the emotional storm he was battling. "I can't imagine foul play being involved. Jack didn't have any enemies. Our clients all loved him."

"A few weeks ago Jack mentioned to my dad you'd made an offer to buy out his share of the business," I said offhandedly, watching his reaction carefully.

He didn't appear fazed. "Yes, I wanted to give him more time to enjoy with his new wife."

"Did you have partnership insurance?" Nate asked.

"Excuse me?"

"You know . . . life insurance on each other. So that the business wouldn't be jeopardized if one of you had to buy out the partner's share to settle the estate?"

"Oh, yes, we did."

"So now you'll own the whole business without being a cent out of pocket," Nate mused.

Frank's face reddened. "What are you implying?"

"Nothing at all," I interjected, pretty sure Frank was three seconds away from kicking us off his property. I shot Nate a stop-goading-him look.

He just shrugged.

"Jack and I were friends," Frank insisted. "Yes, it drove me crazy that he refused to get with the times and carry a cell phone and work on a computer, but"—he sent Nate a heated glare—"I didn't want him dead."

"Of course not," I said with more conviction than I felt and mentally scrambled for another approach. "Um, the family needs information I suspect Jack would've recorded in his planner, but we haven't been able to locate it at his house."

My conscience twanged, even though I was sure the fabrication was true on some level. Eventually they'd need to know a lot of information that was probably in Jack's date book. And Frank didn't need to know why *I* wanted it. "Do you know if Jack kept it at the office?"

"Everything from the office is right here." Frank popped his trunk hood and lifted out a cardboard box.

My heart did a lopsided somersault in my chest. On the one hand, if Frank had something to hide, he'd hesitate to hand over Jack's stuff to perfect strangers, right?

On the other hand, his partner had been dead less than

thirty-six hours, and he'd already cleaned out the man's office?

That smacked of I-want-to-make-sure-no-one-finds-anything-incriminating.

The image of the perforations left behind by the page torn from Jack's message book rose to mind, and I scanned Frank's trunk for telltale signs of the same.

The trunk was immaculate. I mean, just-vacuumed immaculate. Of course, he was out here cleaning his car, but suddenly I had to wonder what had prompted the urge to do that.

I glanced inside the box. It contained framed photographs of Ben and Ashley and of Marianne, as well as a paperweight that looked as if it'd been made by a three-year-old, a pen set, miscellaneous sundries—I dug deeper through the box—and a planner!

"I was going to ask Carly to give the box to her mom, then figured it should go directly to Ashley since Marianne technically wasn't next of kin yet." Frank pushed the box into my hands. "Could you take it to her?"

"Don't you want to see her?"

"Of course, but—"

"Don't you need to go through Jack's planner so you can be sure to follow up on client appointments he had scheduled?" Nate interjected.

I kicked his shin. Discreetly, of course. He was supposed to be helping me. And I wanted a look at that notebook!

"Already did. Thanks."

Okay, that was helpful. Not that I'd think for a second Frank hadn't combed every single page of the book before tossing it into the box. "How do you know Carly?" I asked before Nate could interrupt me again.

"She's our receptionist."

"Your receptionist? I didn't know she worked for you and Jack. Was that how he met her mother? Carly introduced them?"

"That's right."

"Carly dating anyone?" Nate asked, as if he was interested.

The instant twinge in my stomach irritated me. Not that I thought Nate was actually interested. It had to be a ploy.

"I wouldn't know," Frank responded a tad warily.

Nate grinned as if that was the best news he'd heard in weeks. "What are her interests?"

"Interests?" Frank repeated, and I had to admit I was just as confused.

"You know, does she like to go for long walks on the beach? Collect sea glass? Meander antique shops?"

Ooh, clever man. Although did he *really* think Frank would buy that Nate was shopping for tips on how to win Carly while I was standing right beside him, from all appearances looking as if *we* were a couple?

"I couldn't tell you," Frank said. "I don't see her outside the office."

"Well, thank you very much for your help. We'll see that Ashley gets this box." I handed it to Nate, then pasted an urgent uncomfortable look on my face and turned back to Frank. "Could I use your restroom before we go?"

"Sure, it's inside the door on the right."

"I'll just be a minute," I said to Nate, hoping he got the keep-him-occupied message scribbled between the lines. I scurried inside, ignoring my niggling conscience. Sure, this wasn't a legal search. And if I found anything incriminating, I wouldn't be able to use it, unless the evidence happened to be lying out in plain view somewhere between the front door and the restroom.

My breath caught the instant I stepped inside the front door. Frank was an antiquities collector. African masks dotted the walls. An ancient vase sat on an antique table in the front hall. A breathtaking mosaic was visible through the archway leading to the living room. I slipped into the restroom. A chipped, clay watering jug, the kind extracted from an Egyptian excavation I'd once studied, filled half the counter.

My pulse suddenly thrummed my ears like a tribal drumbeat. Ben had been in Egypt. But the 1951 Antiquities Law had declared all Egyptian antiquities the property of the state. Export without a permit was strictly forbidden, which begged the question—did Frank ask Ben to smuggle something out for him? Just how legit was Frank's collection? I scrutinized the jug more closely, then the mask on the wall above it.

The mask could easily be a fake. Duplicating and aging ancient wooden objects was relatively easy. But Egyptian pieces were another ball game altogether.

Even cautious collectors could inadvertently acquire illegally obtained artifacts. One dealer had gone so far as to launder artifacts by placing them on consignment at Sotheby's and then buying them back himself, to provide his pieces with a provenance that appeared legitimate.

Then again, Frank had clearly been building his collection over years. So . . . what might Ben have discovered about Frank that would prompt Jack to turn him in and risk untold damage to their company's reputation?

I hurried out of the bathroom, my mind reeling, as Frank and Nate came in the front door.

"Wow," I enthused. "You have an amazing antiquities collection."

"Thank you. It's probably time I donate it to a museum so more people can enjoy it. My great-grandfather was an archeologist. Most of the pieces are souvenirs from his excavations, from the days when that kind of thing wasn't illegal."

"Hmm." So Frank was savvy of the laws.

"Could we have a tour?" Nate asked, and I silently cheered when Frank agreed. Except Nate seemed to be glancing everywhere but at the antiquities as Frank led us from room to room.

"What were you looking for?" I asked when we were back in the car.

"Signs of a houseguest. I thought Ben might be hiding out here."

Of course! I couldn't believe the possibility hadn't occurred to me, given Ben's recent trip.

"Didn't look like it though," Nate went on. "All the shoes by the door were the same size. The sink and tub in the guest bathroom were dry. And only one cup sat by the kitchen sink."

"Wow, I'm impressed you noticed all of that. You'd make a great detective."

"Your Aunt Martha will be tickled to hear that." He grinned and headed toward the address Preston had given us. "What do you think of Frank?"

"I'm not ready to trust him. His explanation sounded too rehearsed—and clearly intended to silence questions."

"But easy enough to verify."

"Yeah." I thumbed through Jack's planner, starting at today's date, and carefully scrutinized each page. "He didn't have any notes about his calls to the FBI in this book. Only client appointments and the occasional lunch date with Marianne seemed to rank."

"How many different clients did Jack see in the last two weeks?"

"Three. The one we're headed to now. A celebrity who's taking bids for an indoor pool design. And a church planning an addition."

"So we can probably rule out the church?"

"Not necessarily. A lot of the antiquities smuggled out of South America these days are religious artifacts and paintings stolen from small rural churches. A minister ignorant of the artifact's provenance may eagerly accept such a donation for the church."

"Sure, but a donation doesn't make the smuggler any money."

"True." I tilted my head to look at Nate's profile as he drove. "You planning on asking Carly out?"

He laughed. "You didn't think I was really interested in her, did you?"

I don't know why, but I shrugged as if it didn't matter to me one way or the other. Maybe I wanted to see how he'd react. See if he'd know I was teasing the way I teased Tanner.

His eyes twinkled. "She's not my type."

"What's your—"

A text alert from Tanner interrupted the question: *Any new developments?*

I glanced at Nate and then thumbed in *Not sure yet* and hid a smile.

7

No one answered the door at the West Chop address Preston had given us—a two-story mansion perched on a hill overlooking the ocean.

Nate stepped back and lifted his gaze to the second story. "Your uncle had a real gift for design."

I pressed my nose to the front window and cupped my hands around my eyes. "Doesn't look like the owner has moved in yet. There are only ladders and paint tarps inside." My phone rang and I glanced at the screen. "It's the Boston FBI agent I told you about." I clicked the phone to connect. "What did you find out?"

"Ben Hill's call came from the island," Isaak said without preamble.

"He's here?" Ben was Ashley's only living relative. If he killed Jack, she'd be deva— My throat constricted, choking off my breath. Was that why he didn't want her to know he was here?

It could've been a perfect alibi if he hadn't made the mistake of using his phone once he got here.

"Can't say for sure if he's still here," Isaak went on. "The phone is no longer emitting a signal."

"Maybe his battery died, or he just got smart and turned off his phone," Nate said, apparently listening in.

"Have you read any of Ben's articles?" Isaak asked.

"No, why?"

"I scanned some this morning to see if anything popped. He's written at least two articles on Maya sites in South America. And from the details he included, he's clearly talked to looters firsthand."

"Did you tell the state police?"

"Not yet. Lying to his sister about his whereabouts isn't a crime. And if he decides to turn up and play innocent, it's probably better if he doesn't know we're on to him. In the meantime, I'll run a more thorough background check. Check out his acquaintances. You know the drill."

"Yeah, well, I'm sure he's met Carly, given his uncle was going to marry her mother. Did her background check turn up anything?"

"Haven't heard back on that one yet."

"Okay, keep me posted."

Nate opened the car door for me. "What do you want to do?"

I climbed in, then twisted around and snatched the photo of Ben from Jack's box in the backseat. "Let's go to Vineyard Haven and see if anyone remembers seeing him."

As we drove into town, Nate spotted Mosher's. "Let's drop the film off now. Then the photos may be done by the time your parents need to be picked up."

We made quick work of dropping off the film, and while I was at it I made a copy of Ben's photo, so Nate and I could split up. A few minutes later we parked across the street from the dock. A ferry was approaching, so the timing was perfect to catch all the waiting cabbies. "You start at that end. I'll start at this end."

Most of the cabbies scarcely gave the photo a glance before saying something along the lines of "I see too many faces a day to remember." When the next cabbie in line responded with "Why are you looking for Ben?" my stomach dipped.

"You know him?" Are you helping him? Will you tell him people are looking for him? The questions piled up in my mind so fast I almost missed his answer to the one I'd uttered aloud.

"Sure, we went to high school together. I read about his uncle on social media this morning. That's rough."

"Have you seen him? His sister can't get a hold of him and is super worried."

The guy chuckled. "Knowing Ben, he probably hooked up with a girl and is oblivious to the news."

"You've seen him, then," I pressed, since he hadn't exactly answered my question.

"Yeah, he came in on the ferry the night before last. I spotted him hitchhiking to his uncle's out on State Road and stopped to say 'hi.' I had a full van or I would've given him a lift myself."

"Do you know what time that was?" The ferry's horn blew and all the cabbies straightened, their gazes streaking toward the gangplank. "It's important," I added.

Ben's friend dragged his attention back to me. "Yeah, sure. Not long after the six fifteen ferry got in."

"Thank you. Ashley will be relieved to hear it. And please, if you see Ben again, let him know his sister needs him."

"Of course. Give her my condolences. My name's Dan. Dan Reece."

"I will."

Nate squeezed my shoulder. "You're not going to believe this."

"Did you hear that?" I whispered. "I have an eyewitness that puts Ben on the island before sunset the night Jack died."

"Is that good?"

"Well, not if I want him to be innocent, I guess."

"Okay," Nate said. "I'm thinking we might have a more urgent issue to handle."

"What?"

"I spotted Carmen Malgucci on the gangplank and he's headed our way."

I tracked the direction of Nate's gaze. Carmen looked like one of those iconic Italian actors who always played a mafia character—dark hair, slightly overweight, bulbous-nosed. He first met Aunt Martha when she mistook him (whether rightly, the jury was still out) for exactly that. "Does Aunt Martha know?"

The night they met, she'd asked him if he could "get her a kidney" . . . the transplant kind, for the wife of a museum security guard; a security guard who also happened to be a suspect in one of my cases. As luck would have it—not that I really believed in luck—Carmen had lost his wife to kidney failure and was so moved by Aunt Martha's story that he offered to be tested as a donor. The rest, as they say, is history.

"Do you think she would've been renewing acquaintances with Winston if she knew?" Nate said as he thumbed a message into his phone.

"Sure, why not? It's not as if she and Carmen are exclusively dating or anything."

Nate slipped his phone back into his pocket, his gaze returning to Carmen. "Hate to break this to you, but when a guy drops everything to get on a plane to make sure his *friend* is okay, he's thinking otherwise."

I think my chin might've dropped, because it sounded as if he wasn't just talking about Carmen. But Nate's phone chose that moment to ring.

The instant he clicked to connect, Aunt Martha's voice rang out. "Very funny, Nate."

Apparently his feverish texting a moment ago had been a warning message to Aunt Martha, because he said firmly, "I'm not joking."

"Oh dear. What was Carmen thinking? I just called to tell him Ward and Serena had had a bit of trouble. Nothing that should've prompted him to hop on a plane."

"Clearly he's fonder of your family than you realized."

Huh, that was pretty sweet.

"I'm guessing he'll want to rent a car," Nate said. "Do you want us to give him Preston's address or suggest he follow us home? It'd buy you more time since we still have to pick up the photos and her parents."

"Don't be silly. Give him the address. He won't be jealous of Winston."

"Yeah, he will."

"Okay, okay, thanks for the heads-up."

I couldn't help giggling. "Mom won't believe it. Shoots a few holes in her 'do you want to end up a spinster like your great aunt?' arguments."

We greeted Malgucci and helped him sort out a car rental,

then gave him directions to Preston's. Nate added the address of the bed-and-breakfast he was staying at near there.

Oh, wow, I hadn't given any thought to where Nate would be staying or that he likely hadn't slept in the past twenty-four hours.

"You must be beat," I said to him after Malgucci drove off. "Did you get any sleep last night?"

"Sure. I had a power nap while the plane was on autopilot." He winked and my stomach did the kind of whoop-de-whirl I imagined his unattended plane doing.

"Uh . . . how about we grab a bite and eat at the beach? Give you a chance to close your eyes for a few minutes before we have to pick up my dad?" He looked like he could use more sleep, despite what he'd said.

He grinned. "I never say no to the beach."

We picked up a couple of sandwiches and water bottles from a nearby coffee shop, and as we returned to the car, I noticed a black sedan idling at the curb a few cars behind Nate's rental. I wouldn't have thought anything of it, except that it pulled out a heartbeat after we did and trailed us to Owen Park. The sedan parked at the road, but the driver didn't get out. I climbed out and peered over at it but couldn't make out the driver or get an angle on the license plate.

"What's wrong?" Nate asked.

I skirted Nate's rental to come up on the back of the sedan. "I think that car is following us." Now that I thought about it, I'm pretty sure the same car had been idling across the street from where we'd spotted Carly and Gaudy Souvenir Guy.

The sedan took off before I could get close to it.

Nate squinted after it. "Probably just a tourist who doesn't know where he's going."

"Hmm." After what happened to Dad, I was probably being a little paranoid.

Nate spread out a big beach towel he'd pulled from his car, and we sat down and ate.

The sky was blue and the ocean even bluer. "This is gorgeous," Nate said.

"Yeah. Too bad the water's still way too cold to swim. Although, I've got to say that I prefer the relative quietness of the island this time of year to the wall-to-wall tourists I used to see during my summer visits."

"Would you want to live in a place as isolated as your friend Ashley does?"

"I don't know. In any other part of America, probably not. Between lowlifes and the aggressive strains of wildlife, I wouldn't feel safe going out for a morning run. But here, there are no bears—"

"No? Your aunt mentioned polar bears." The sparkle in his eye gave away that Aunt Martha must've also informed him the so-called polar bears were a group of women who gathered each morning to exercise, sing spirituals, and swim at Inkwell Beach.

I laughed. "No furry bears with sharp claws and even sharper teeth. And people don't even worry about locking their doors. At least, they didn't when I used to come here as a kid. I guess maybe that's changing these days."

"So you feel safer living in a city that has over a hundred murders a year?"

I shrugged. Sure, it didn't make sense, but . . . "The only place I'm likely to run into a bear is if one escapes from the zoo. How about you? Could you see yourself living in the countryside?"

"Sure. As long as I have a wife and kids to share it with."
He held my gaze, not in the teasing way Tanner might have
after saying something like that, but in an open this-is-my-
dream-any-chance-you'd-want-to-share-it kind of way.

My pulse tripped. I told myself I was imagining things and
turned my attention to my sandwich, which had somehow
spilled over my hand.

"My grandparents had a farm when I was a kid," Nate
went on. "I used to love to visit. There was so much more
for a boy to do and to explore."

"Better than loitering at the mall or going brain-dead playing video games," I said, recovering my equilibrium.

"Exactly."

Starting to get a little anxious that I hadn't heard from
Mom yet, I tried reaching her by phone. She didn't answer,
so I suggested we pick up the photos and then head to the
hospital.

I thumbed through the photos as Nate drove. "Well, this
was a dead end. Only six pictures turned out. All of them
ocean sunsets." No murderer that I could see lurked in the
foreground.

"You'll figure this out," Nate said confidently, pulling into
the hospital parking lot.

I tucked the envelope into my purse, not feeling nearly as
optimistic. "Why don't you wait here and catch a few winks
while I find out what's going on."

I found Dad test-driving a pair of crutches in the lobby
as Mom cheered him on. He grinned when he saw me. "Not
bad for an old man, huh?"

"You're not old." I kissed his cheek. "You've already been
released? Why didn't you call?"

"I did," Mom said. "Got your voice mail."

I checked my phone and a missed-message alert lit the screen. "I'm sorry. It looks as if it just came in. I must've been in a dead zone."

"Well, you're here now. That's all that matters." Mom held open the door for Dad as I led the way to the rental.

Ten feet from the car, Mom gasped. "What's Nate doing here?"

"Didn't Aunt Martha tell you? After hearing about the accident, he flew through the night to come to make sure I was okay."

"Oh."

Oh? This from the mother who was after me at every opportunity to settle down and give her grandchildren. *Oh* was all she could say?

"That's great," Dad said. "Isn't that great, June?" he prodded.

Mom's enthusiasm livened up a fraction. "Yes, *yes*, of course. I'm sorry. I'm just tired, I guess."

Nate woke up when I opened the passenger side door. He jumped out and helped Dad ease in.

"What a nice surprise," Mom said to Nate. "Are you planning to stay long?"

He must've heard the same odd note in her voice that I had, because he shot me a questioning look, to which I shrugged. "As long as I'm needed," he answered chivalrously.

"That's nice," Mom murmured and climbed into the backseat. Only she didn't sound as if she thought it was nice, and an ominous foreboding swept over me like the darkening clouds swallowing the sun.

I joined Mom in the backseat. "Are you feeling okay?"

She glanced toward the front of the car, her gaze gliding off Nate's in the rearview mirror, before returning to me. She squeezed my hand. "Yes. Sad, of course, for Ashley and Ben and Jack's fiancée, but grateful that you and Dad are safe. Have they set a date for the funeral?"

"Not yet." I explained the reason for the delay, then we traveled in silence the rest of the way back to Preston's. I debated taking the opportunity to fill Dad in on our visit with Frank Dale, but I suspected Dad might not want Mom to know about his suspicions of Jack's business partner. As we turned into Preston's driveway and I spotted Malgucci's rental, I opened my mouth to explain, but Mom spoke first.

"Oh, look, someone else has arrived," she sing-songed. "Who do you suppose that could be?"

"I forgot to mention Carmen Malgucci also flew in. He wanted to make sure Aunt Martha is safe too."

"Oh dear," Mom fretted. "What will the police think if she shows up at Jack's visitation with a mobster on her arm?"

"He's not a mobster." At least, not that anyone had proved. It was more a case of guilt by association. Or perhaps in Malgucci's case, by bloodline. Personally, I'd never seen any evidence he was into anything illegal, and I was grateful he didn't have any qualms about donning the family facade if it meant keeping the people he cared about out of trouble. As he'd proved a few months ago, when a couple of lackeys for the Russian mob threatened to take out Aunt Martha and me.

Carmen and Aunt Martha yoo-hooed from the veranda, where they were sharing afternoon tea. Aunt Martha, like my grandparents and parents, was born in Britain. Naturally, their immediate response to the arrival of company was to brew tea. We'd never gotten into crumpets, but oh, how I loved it when Aunt Martha made her scones with Devon-shire cream.

"Earth to Serena." Nate nudged my shoulder with his.

Somehow, everyone else had already congregated on the veranda, but I was still standing at the bottom of the steps. Only *everyone* didn't include Ashley and Preston. I asked where they were.

Preston emerged from the house carrying a tray with more teacups and a second teapot. "Ashley has a migraine. She went back to her cottage to sleep it off."

"I let Harold go with her," Aunt Martha added, "to keep her company."

I showed Preston the picture I took of Carly and Gaudy Souvenir Guy. "Do you know this guy?"

"Sure, that's Carly's brother, Charlie."

"Charlie and Carly?" Nate asked, disbelief modulating his tone.

Preston chuckled. "Charles is his given name. Why?"

"Wait a minute. Don't they have different last names?" According to Aunt Martha, Charlie's luggage tag had said Anderson.

"Carly's an Anderson too. Their dad died when they were little, and neither of them took their stepdad's last name when Marianne remarried."

"What happened to her second husband?"

"He died."

"The poor woman. She must've been crushed."

"She was really depressed for a few years afterward, Jack said. Did a stint in the hospital. It's probably what made Carly and Charlie so close. He was out of high school but apparently stuck around to take care of her."

"What does Charlie do for a living?"

"I don't really know. He travels a lot. You could ask Marianne. She wants to meet with Ashley and the funeral home director tomorrow morning. Ashley was hoping you'd accompany her."

"Of course I will. Maybe I should go down to the cottage and check on her."

"No, when she gets like this, she just needs to sleep."

"Did she hear from Ben?"

"Not that she mentioned."

Nate shot me a silencing look. I helped myself to a cup of tea from Preston's tray and meandered over to Nate's side at the railing. "What was that look for?"

"I don't think you should tell him what you know about Ben," Nate whispered.

"Why?"

Nate urged me to stroll with him to the farthest end of the veranda. "Mind if I look at Jack's photos?"

I handed him the packet and then texted Isaak the correction on Carly's last name.

Nate gave the photos a cursory glance without pulling them out, then studied the negatives. "There's another photo they could've printed. It's half over-exposed, but we may be able to see something in it."

Aunt Martha ambled over to us, apparently having eavesdropped on our conversation. "You could use Jack's darkroom."

"Sure, if I knew how to develop prints," I said wryly.

"Nate knows how."

I gaped at him. "Really?" Was there anything this man didn't know how to do?

He nodded and then shrugged, as if he'd also heard my unvoiced question.

"I don't know," I wavered. "We probably should ask Ashley if she minds."

Dad waved us back to the group. "What are you all whispering about over there?"

"Using Uncle Jack's darkroom. Do you think Ashley would mind?"

"I wouldn't bother her now," Preston said.

"What's this about, sweetheart?" Dad probed.

"The last photos Jack took before he died." I slanted a wary glance at Preston, but it wasn't as if he didn't already know we were looking at Jack's film. He'd probably just been trying to make sure we didn't disturb Ashley unnecessarily. "We thought they might offer a clue to what happened."

"Then of course you should use his darkroom," Dad said.

I gulped down my cup of tea, then turned to Nate. "Okay, let's do this."

Nate drove us the half mile back to Jack's.

"Park next to the cottage," I said, reaching for my door handle. "I want to check on Ashley before we go in and let her know what we're up to so she doesn't panic over the strange car in the driveway." I hurried into the house, being careful not to let the screen door slam.

All the curtains were drawn, but Ashley's bedroom door was ajar. I poked my head inside. "You awake?" I whispered, only to see she wasn't in her bed. I checked the connected bathroom. Empty.

A sound came from my room. What was she doing in there? Did she fake the migraine to buy time to search my stuff?

My stomach knotted. This was her house. She had every right to be in whatever room she wanted. But that didn't mean I had to knock. I quietly clasped the doorknob and jerked it open. "What are you—?"

Harold burst from the room and wound around my legs, purring loudly.

"It was *you* making that noise?" I scooped him up and scratched the back of his neck, the tension in my gut easing. Until . . .

"What were you doing locked in there? Where's Ashley?" I checked the kitchen. The living room. The laundry room. The second bathroom. "Ashley, you here?" I asked, louder this time, my mind flashing to Ben as I raced from closet to closet, checked under beds, behind sofas. Would Ben take out Ashley?

It wouldn't be too smart since clearing the way for him to be the sole beneficiary would also make him the prime suspect in their deaths.

My throat constricted. *Ashley can't be dead!*

At the sound of the front door opening, I spun around. "Ashley, thank—"

"No, it's me." Nate came in with the box of Jack's personal effects Frank sent home with us and set it on the desk in the living room. "Isn't she here?"

"No! She's gone."

8

Nate steered me out Ashley's front door, then took Harold from me and dropped him back inside. "Her car is here, so she couldn't have gone far. Probably just walked to the water to clear her head."

"But Preston said she had a migraine. She can't stand the light when she gets them."

"Do you think she lied about that? That she went off with someone? Or that she was kidnapped?"

I strode to the middle of her front yard and turned 360 degrees, scanning Jack's neighboring property, the trees behind the house, and the scrub brush across the road. Then I raked my fingers through my hair. "I don't know what to think."

"Maybe she felt better and walked back to Preston's."

"We would've seen her."

"Did you see that?" Nate squinted. "Someone's in Jack's house."

We hurried across the yard and peeked in the living room window. Inside, Marianne was standing at Jack's desk and shoving something into a small backpack.

"What do you think she's doing?" Nate whispered.

"I'm going to find out." I stormed to the front door, then knocked and pushed it open at the same time. "Hello? Ashley? Are you in here?" I feigned surprise at the sight of Marianne. "Oh, it's you. I'm sorry. I didn't see a car outside, so I . . ." Feeling a twinge of remorse that my pretense was bordering on an outright lie, I let the explanation trail off.

She jerked up the flap of her backpack and yanked on the zipper.

"I found a couple more." Ashley emerged from a back room carrying a pair of framed photos. "Oh, Serena, hi."

My heart jumped with relief she was okay. Then wariness over what the two of them were up to instantly morphed the feeling.

Nate stepped inside behind me. "Hey, what's going on?"

Marianne took the photos from Ashley, not bothering to add them to the backpack she'd already swung over her shoulder. "Thanks. I should get going now. I think I have plenty."

"Marianne wants to scan a bunch of Uncle Jack's photos and put together a slide show for his funeral," Ashley explained. "I was helping her pick some."

"How'd you get here?" I asked.

Marianne fluttered her hand toward the window. "I parked at that little lot on the bend. Went for a walk through the meadow first."

To sneak up to Uncle Jack's house from the back? Where no one would see her?

Only, Ashley did. Had Marianne come up with the photo story so Ashley wouldn't suspect why she was really here? Whatever reason that might be. I glimpsed the photo

Marianne had tucked under her arm of her and a clearly smitten Jack, and my conscience twinged. But only for a second. After all, I didn't know Marianne from a hole in the ground.

And I was feeling so punchy, I wasn't even sure if that was a mixed metaphor, but the point was . . . what if she was better than me at coming here under false pretenses?

"Can I see the photos you chose?" I asked, angling for a look inside the backpack.

Marianne tightened her grip on its straps. And that wasn't just my imagination, because her fingers actually turned white. "You'll have to wait for the funeral. I want it to be a surprise."

I wanted to believe the tearstains on her cheeks were from genuine heartache. Not to mention that I couldn't imagine Jack asking her to marry him, planning this engagement party, and then turning around and calling the FBI on her.

Nate elbowed me and whispered, "You're staring."

I shook away the suspicious thoughts, and offering her a smile, stepped aside from the door. "I'm sure the slide show will be beautiful."

Fresh tears dribbled down her cheeks.

Maybe Mom was right about me. Maybe I did stare too much. Some people were exactly what they seemed. The challenge was deciphering which ones were and which ones weren't.

"I think I'll go back to lying down," Ashley said, also moving toward the door. "I'm sorry I haven't been good company."

I waved off the apology as unnecessary and asked her about using Jack's darkroom.

"Now?" She sounded as if the idea bothered her. And despite my recent staring-is-rude pep talk, I took that to mean that what really bothered her might be what we'd *find* in the picture we wanted to develop.

"Is there a problem?" I asked ever so casually, because I couldn't help myself.

"No. Of course not. Go right ahead," she blurted in a staccato that belied the invitation. "Come over and get me when you're finished. Preston's going to order pizza for supper."

Nate flicked on the red light hanging over the table in the darkroom and locked the door. His arm grazed mine as he turned toward the enlarger, and I think I might've gulped out loud, because he looked at me with concern. "You going to be okay in here?"

"Sure." I offered a wan smile. Who was I kidding? Yes, I was claustrophobic, but the room wasn't *that* small. My cubicle at work was smaller. Of course, I didn't have to *share* my cubicle.

Nate's throaty chuckle sent unexpected tingles skittering down my spine. "If you want to wait in the living room, I understand."

"No, no. I'm fine."

"You're sure?" He caught my wrist and pressed his fingertips to the pulse point. "Because your heart is racing."

"Uh . . . locked in a dark room with a handsome man?" I quipped.

He squeezed my hand, grinning. "We'd better get this photo developed before . . ."

"Anything *else* develops?" I said ever so innocently.

Nate kissed the back of my hand before releasing it. "Exactly."

Ooh, the room suddenly felt a whole lot smaller and a

whole lot warmer. I edged into the corner to give him room
to work.

"Before we set up the chemicals, I want to put the nega-
tive in the enlarger and make sure there's something worth
developing." He snapped it into place, then peering through
the eyepiece, adjusted knobs. A moment later he stepped
back and invited me to take a look.

I gasped. "Are those Jack's legs?" The part of the photo
that hadn't been overexposed by Preston's faux pas depicted
the upper thighs and knees of jean-clad legs.

"That's what we need to figure out. The photo's blurry,
as if the camera went off accidentally. It could've happened
when he fell, or it could've happened if he'd been startled
and turned suddenly. Do you know what Jack was wearing
at the time of his death?"

"No, but I can call the police department and find out." I
pulled out my phone, then glanced at the enlarger. "Is turning this on going to wreck anything?"

"Not until I take the photo paper out. Go ahead."

I put in the call.

"I'm sorry, ma'am. I'm only free to discuss the information provided in the press release," the person on the other
end said.

"May I speak to the chief?"

"He's not in right now."

"Okay, never mind."

"Marianne would know," Nate suggested, "since she found
him."

I cringed. "I don't want to have to explain why I'm asking,
especially if she has reason to be suspicious of my motives."

"Good point. Okay, turn off your phone and we'll get this

100

developed. We can worry about figuring out whose legs they are later." Nate selected several brown bottles from a shelf on the wall, then poured the different chemicals into a series of trays on the counter. "Ready?"

I nodded.

He slipped a piece of photographic paper from a black sleeve he'd pulled from a box on the shelf and lined it up in the holder on the base of the enlarger. Glancing at the clock, he snapped the enlarger light on and off again. "Let's see what we've got." He put the paper in the developer bath and swished it around with a pair of plastic tongs.

Slowly the image began to emerge.

"The fit of those jeans looks too tight for Uncle Jack," I commented. "It's been a few years since I've visited, but if he was anything like Dad, he'd have favored a more relaxed fit."

"When we're done here, we can check what's in his closet. But yeah, I see what you mean. We're definitely looking at a guy who favors tight jeans."

"Or a woman." I nibbled on my bottom lip, hating myself for thinking it, but I couldn't shake the image of Marianne's bloodless fingers as she clutched that backpack, refusing to let me see the photos—and whatever else—she'd helped herself to.

Nate moved the photo on to the stop bath, then jerked up his head and turned his ear toward the door. "Did you hear that?"

I stilled, but couldn't hear anything beyond the sound of our breathing. Then I heard it too. The creak of a door. Footsteps. If it was Ashley, why didn't she announce herself? Was it Marianne back to look through more of Jack's stuff? Ben?

Someone here to put an end to my sleuthing?

The doorknob rattled and I pulled my gun.

Nate slid the photo out of the stop bath and into the fixative, then whipped out a gun too.

"Where did you get that?" I whispered as the sound of footsteps grew faint.

He looked at me as if I'd grown a third eyeball. "I came to Martha's Vineyard because someone tried to run you off the road. What did you think I'd bring? My boxing gloves?"

"No, I . . ." *He boxed?* I shook that wayward thought from my head. "I meant I didn't know you owned a gun."

"There are a lot of things you don't know about me."

Evidently. I hoped he knew that a St. Louis carry permit wasn't any good in Massachusetts. "Kill the light," I hissed, figuring red or not, I didn't want whoever was out there seeing it.

"We're in a darkroom. If no light gets in, no light gets out either."

Right.

Something crashed. "That sounded like a lamp." I turned the lock and using the wall as a shield, swung open the door, my weapon braced between my hands. "Freeze!"

The intruder, his back to me, set the lamp—minus its mangled shade—back on the table.

Nate dropped to one knee, his body partially shielded by the wall on the opposite side of the opening, and raised his gun. "She said 'freeze.'"

The intruder raised his hands. "Okay, okay, take it easy."

My breath hitched at the familiar voice. "Tanner?" How'd I not recognize that dark head of hair and those broad shoulders on sight?

Because he's supposed to be in St. Louis, that's why. I

holstered my gun and grinned as he slowly turned around, his hands still raised in surrender. "Your breaking-in skills could use some practice," I teased.

"Yeah, well, it's not as bad as the time you fell in the water in front of those Russian mobsters."

"That was your fault!"

Tanner shrugged, a grin tugging at his lips, although he still hadn't lowered his hands.

"What are you doing here?"

"You mind calling off Dudley Do-Right there?" Tanner chucked his chin in Nate's direction. "So we can have this conversation without a gun pointed at my head."

I glanced at Nate, who hesitated another second or two, looking as if he'd rather shoot him.

9

"I can't believe you didn't warn me Tanner was coming," I whispered to Aunt Martha as we set out plates and napkins for dinner. After Nate finally holstered his weapon, I'd managed to convince him to finish in the darkroom without me so I could figure out why Tanner was here. But two hours later, I still wasn't sure of the answer.

"I *did*. Your phone went to voice mail," she hissed into my ear as we returned to the kitchen.

Oops. I'd forgotten I'd turned it off so the light wouldn't corrupt the photo development.

"Trust me," Aunt Martha went on, "I know exactly how you feel."

Of course she did. She'd been enjoying a perfectly pleasant day renewing acquaintances with Winston when Carmen steamed into port.

Mom stopped stirring the lemonade she was making at the kitchen sink and let out a contented sigh. "It's so romantic, to think you have not one but *two* handsome young men fly across the country to come to your aid."

"Tanner came because you begged him to." I'd gotten that much out of him. It explained why Mom had been so unenthusiastic about Nate's presence. I waited for her to deny it.

She didn't, and my heart inexplicably dipped.

Okay, not so inexplicably. A silly part of me had fantasized Tanner fabricated the fictitious summons to save face. After all, Nate *had* beaten him here. I muffled a groan. "Mom, with all that's happened, I'm not exactly thinking romantic thoughts."

Butterflies twirled in my stomach at the sudden memory of the kiss Nate had pressed to my hand in the darkroom. Would he have tried for an even sweeter kiss if Tanner hadn't shown up?

I shook my head. Listen to me. We'd just lost a dear friend. And I had an art crime case that was clearly important to him, not to mention his probable murder, to solve. I didn't have time to be twitterpated over a couple of guys bent on role-playing knights in shining armor.

I set down the napkins I'd been, um, mutilating and turned back to the cupboard to get out glasses. Mom and Aunt Martha were leaning against the counter, smiling at me.

"What?" I barked, annoyed they'd clearly caught me daydreaming.

"Nothing. Nothing," Mom and Aunt Martha sing-songed, busying themselves with nothing.

Ashley came into the kitchen carrying Harold. "Your friend wants to see you outside."

He'd sure taken long enough to finish up at Jack's and fetch Ashley. I slipped out the side door so Tanner wouldn't spot me leaving. Nate stood by his rental, watching a couple of birds glide on the thermals. "Hey. I'm sorry about the surprise visit," I said.

He gave me an it-happens shrug. "I found some stuff after you left, and I didn't know who else you wanted to hear about it." He handed me the photo he'd developed. "I checked Jack's closet. You were right about him favoring relaxed-fit jeans."

My breath stalled in my chest. "So we're looking at the legs of his murderer."

"Or at the very least, perhaps the last person to see him alive." He beeped his trunk unlocked and rounded the back of the car. "I also snooped around the dresser, desk, and tabletops a bit. No sign of any sea glass."

I nodded, not wanting to trace the potential implications of that find at the moment.

"But I did find this." He opened his trunk and motioned to the contents—a large backpack, the kind twentysomethings used to travel Europe or Australia.

"Whose is it?" Even as the words passed my lips, I knew the answer. "Ben's?" I added in a whisper, flipping over the luggage tag to confirm it. I untied the top. "Where'd you find it?"

"It was propped against the front wall of the house, behind the porch rocker to the right of the door."

"You're kidding. I can't believe we didn't notice it before now."

"Maybe it wasn't there earlier."

My heart thumped. So Ben had come looking for Ashley like I'd feared?

"Or no one thought to pay attention to what was on the porch," Nate added.

I rummaged through the bag's contents. "Nothing here but clothes and shoes and"—I leafed through the leather-bound book tucked in an outside pocket—"a new journal."

I skimmed the six pages he'd written on. There was nothing about art or antiquities or Jack, merely notes on the places he'd visited and ideas for articles.

Nate unrolled the designer jeans that had been stuffed into the top of the bag. "These are a style people usually wear tight."

My head started pounding. "This doesn't look good for him."

Preston trotted down the stairs, probably off to pick up the pizzas. I quickly stuffed the journal and jeans back into the pack, but not quickly enough. "Hey, isn't that Ben's?" Preston joined us and peered into Nate's trunk. "It is. Where'd you find it?"

"On Uncle Jack's porch."

Preston looked around. "Ben's here?"

We didn't respond.

"He's *not* here?" Preston tugged on his ear, a habit I recalled from our brief dating stint. "You think he was connected to the art crime Jack called the FBI about?" Preston hissed out a long sigh, his gaze drifting to Tisbury Great Pond or maybe the ocean beyond. "Makes sense, I guess. A few years back he showed me an artifact he'd picked up on one of his trips. Asked what I thought it would be worth."

And you're only telling me this now? The sound of the pounding surf suddenly grew thunderous, or maybe that was the blood rushing past my ears. I took a deep breath to calm my rioting thoughts. "What did you tell him?"

"That it was illegal to take cultural artifacts out of most of those countries without the government's permission. I told him to turn it over to the authorities and plead ignorance."

"Did he?"

"I thought so. I mean, I assumed he did." The muscle in his jaw flinched. "I'm sure he did. Ben's a good guy. He even wrote an article about antiquities smuggling not long after that." Preston's tone and expression didn't match the certainty of his words. I could understand him wanting to cover for his fiancée's brother, but what if Ben was also Jack's killer?

Preston excused himself and returned to the house.

"I don't trust that guy," Tanner said from behind me, making me jump.

"You can say that again," Nate agreed.

"Wait!" I patted my pockets. "Either of you got a pen and paper?"

"What for?" they both asked.

"The two of you agreed on something. This is an occasion for the history books. I think you're both wrong, but that's beside the point."

Nate chuckled and said to Tanner, "They used to date."

"Wait, how'd you—?"

Before I could ask him how he'd found that out, although I was sure I had Aunt Martha to thank for the disclosure, Tanner said, "Ahhhh," as if the detail explained everything.

"What's that supposed to mean?" I demanded.

Tanner graced me with an unnaturally patient look, as if I might be too simpleminded to understand. "You have blinders on when it comes to guys you date." His gaze shifted pointedly toward Nate.

The corners of Nate's lips twitched into a grin. Apparently, he'd rather let Tanner think we were dating than take offense at what I was supposedly blind to in him.

Preston came out with Ashley. Malgucci and Aunt Martha bustled out behind them.

I slammed the trunk shut. What was Preston doing?

"Ben's here?" Ashley said, her voice verging on hysteria. "You found his bag?"

I glared at Preston.

"She's my fiancée! I couldn't *not* tell her."

Ashley frowned. "Why wouldn't you tell me Ben is here?"

"Ben?" Malgucci said. "Isn't that the guy you think killed Jack?"

Aunt Martha swatted him in the gut with the back of her hand, and he let out an "ooomph."

"What was that for? That's what you said, isn't it?"

The shock on Ashley's face hit me like a roundhouse kick to the chest. I hadn't voiced that particular suspicion aloud. But that didn't make me feel any less guilty.

"Uncle Jack wasn't killed," Ashley said adamantly, looking from face to face but finding little reassurance. She looked as if she wanted to stomp her foot like a toddler. "He wasn't. The police said so. This is because of what Carly said, isn't it? I can't believe you believed her!"

I dug my teeth into my lower lip, wondering if Ashley might have trusted Carly's statement if she knew about Jack's call to the FBI asking for a deal on Ben's behalf in exchange for information.

"You heard her mom," Ashley rushed on. "Carly over-reacts all the time."

"Then why did Ben lie about missing his plane?" I asked softly. "Why didn't he want us to know he was already on the island?" I hated to compound her loss, but the can of worms had been opened. Putting off facing the situation wouldn't make it any easier to deal with.

"What are you talking about? Preston said you found his

backpack on Jack's porch. He'd hardly leave it sitting in plain view if he expected us to buy his missed-plane story."

"She's got a point," Tanner said.

Of course she had a point! But that didn't stop me from wanting to smack him for poking me with it, as if that little incongruity hadn't already occurred to me too. I already felt bad enough for grilling her.

Ashley whipped out her phone and madly thumbed a message—no doubt along these lines: *I know you're here, so explain yourself.*

Only . . . What if Ben didn't send the text? "Wait," I blurted.

"Too late," Ashley said smugly. "I told him we're having a memorial service Saturday night and he'd better be here."

"When did you decide that?" I asked.

"With Marianne this afternoon," Aunt Martha said softly.

"Maybe Ben got hit by a car or something," Malgucci suggested, "and sent the bogus text so you wouldn't worry about him."

Ashley burst into tears.

Aunt Martha swatted Malgucci a second time. "You're not helping."

"Ashley, it's okay. I'm sure it's nothing like that. But I'll call the police and the hospital right now." Anything to mitigate how awful my questions about Ben must've sounded. Whatever she'd been mad at me about as a teenager wouldn't hold a candle to my all but flat-out saying her absentee brother looked guilty of murder.

Preston wrapped his arm around Ashley and coaxed her toward his car. "We'll go pick up the pizzas while you take care of the call."

I opted to check in with Special Agent Jackson first since I hadn't updated him on the latest news.

He advised me to sit tight and said he'd talk to the police.

"What now?" Nate asked when I disconnected.

"We wait."

"Maybe Ben will show up," Aunt Martha offered, "now that he knows Ashley knows."

"I'm not so sure he'll get the text," I replied. "Isaak said Ben's cell phone wasn't showing up on the grid anymore."

Tanner arched an eyebrow, which loosely translated meant: *You don't saaaay? Well, well.* Trouble was, I didn't know if he was goading me because I'd referred to the agent by his first name or because Isaak had managed to get the information without nearly enough evidence for a search warrant.

I opted to go with the latter. "He called in a favor."

Malgucci snorted. "The American legal system hard at work protecting its citizens."

Aunt Martha slipped her arm through the crook of his. "You won't get any empathy from this lot." She winked at me, or maybe Nate, then coaxed Malgucci back inside as I stewed over how to mend my relationship with Ashley.

"Gotta like her," Tanner said, snapping me out of my thoughts.

"Yup, Martha's one of a kind," Nate concurred.

I swayed sideways and they each caught an arm. "You okay?" Tanner asked.

"No, my world is utterly off-kilter. The two of you have agreed on two things in the span of less than twenty minutes."

Nate chuckled. "If it bothers you that much, I'm sure we can find something to disagree about." He looked to Tanner. "What do you say?"

"You're a toad."

"See," Nate said, "we're disagreeing again already. Feel better?" He tapped his forefinger to his chin as if suddenly deep in thought. "Then again, when a princess kisses a toad, he turns into a handsome prince, right? So the comparison may not be so far off."

I giggled. I couldn't help it. The giggle earned me a mock scowl from Tanner, which made me giggle even more. I wasn't sure if it was intentional or not, but they'd succeeded in distracting me from how much I'd upset Ashley with my suspicions, and I loved them for it.

I abruptly stopped giggling. *Love?* Did I just say—*love?* Oh man. Oh man, oh man, oh man. All Mom's talk about me settling down might have started to seep into my psyche. I didn't *love* love them. I admired them. I enjoyed spending time with them. I appreciated their concern for my well-being. That wasn't the same as love, right? Not in the romantic sense.

Not that romantic thoughts toward them hadn't crossed my mind . . .

"Serena? Are you okay?"

"Huh?" I wasn't sure who'd asked, so I glanced from one to the other and smiled reassuringly. "Yes, of course. I'm fine. I'd better get back to the kitchen and see if Mom needs any more help." I raced inside before either of them could question me further.

"Nice to see the boys getting along," Mom remarked as I meandered into the kitchen. She nodded toward the window, where outside Tanner and Nate seemed to be chatting amiably.

"Why wouldn't they?" I said. My first mistake.

She looked at me with that head tilt that meant *You seriously have to ask?* "I understand what you're going through," she said consolingly. "You have a shift husband and a house husband and you're confused."

"What? I'm not the one confused here, Mom. I'm not married."

"Not in the biblical sense, of course, but I read about this very thing online. Well, it was about male officers and how they have a 'shift wife'—a partner or co-worker or waitress at a coffee shop they frequent while on the job—who they can share all their work stresses with, who gets the humor they need to stay sane. That kind of thing."

"Mom, working for the FBI isn't the same as being a first responder."

"Let me finish. Then you go home and you have Nate to hang out with. And you can forget about your work when you're with him."

That wasn't exactly true. My mind slipped back to my undercover visit with Nate, at his invitation, to a bar frequented by artsy types when I'd been searching for a forger.

"But now you're on vacation," Mom went on. "And working"—she scowled—"and they're both here with nothing to do but be with you. So, you'll have to decide which one you most want to be with."

No, I don't. I mentally stomped my foot, feeling as if I were three and Mom were telling me I *had* to do something and I were yelling back *you can't make me.*

Tanner poked his head into the kitchen. "Pizza's here."

"Thank you, Tanner." Mom hurried past him. "I'll help Preston set it on the dining room table."

I made a move to follow, but Tanner sidestepped and

blocked the door. "Hey, I'm sorry your trip isn't shaping up to be much of a vacation."

I nodded. I mean, what could I say?

"How about we get dinner at one of the island's seafood restaurants tomorrow night?" he suggested. "Take your mind off things for a little while at least."

I didn't immediately answer and his eyes dimmed a fraction.

"Or did you already have a date with Nate?"

"We're not dating."

"A guy you're *not* dating doesn't borrow a plane and fly halfway across the country to make sure you're okay."

"He cares about me."

"I'll say. The man hasn't been in a plane since the last one he piloted was shot down over Yugoslavia!"

"What?" My voice must've spiked a tad too loud, because the next room suddenly got quiet. I hauled it down a few octaves. "What are you talking about?"

Tanner rolled his eyes. "Don't you do background checks on the guys you date?"

"No. Do *you*?"

"That would be illegal," he said, with a smirk that said he had.

I refrained from grilling him for details, not wanting to give him the satisfaction, even though I was desperate to know why Nate had been flying over Yugoslavia in the first place. *Pilot Nate* was not the mild-mannered, tea-loving, cat-adoring, film buff I knew.

Then a hole in Tanner's argument hit me like a bolt of lightning, and I could scarcely contain my own smirk. "If Nate flew here because we're *dating*, how do you explain your being here?"

Tanner grinned. "I'm your shift husband."

I dragged my hand down my face and muttered, "You heard that?"

"Serene-uh," he drawled. "It's o-kay."

With a Spanish lilt, I said, "I don't think that word means what you think it means."

Tanner smiled, but I wasn't sure if he'd clued in that I borrowed the line from one of my favorite movies. *Nate would have.*

What was I supposed to think of Tanner's supposed interest in me?

I mean . . . my parents begged him to come. And asking me out on a date? That was the kind of thing he'd do to irritate Nate.

Mom's voice drifted into the kitchen. "Come, you two. We want to say grace before we eat."

Tanner didn't move, just lifted that infernal eyebrow of his to say he was still waiting for an answer.

"Yes, I would love to go to dinner with you. Thank you for asking."

He stepped aside and with a gallant bow motioned me to go first.

Nate stood on the other side of the door, frowning.

10

The next morning, thanks to my promise to accompany Ashley to the funeral home for her appointment with the director and Marianne, I was spared from facing Nate and Tanner.

Then again, Nate was probably grateful for the extra sleep time given the all-nighter he'd pulled flying here. Which reminded me . . . I still hadn't asked him about Yugoslavia.

Since Ashley and Marianne had seemed pretty chummy yesterday afternoon while searching for photos at Jack's house—if that's what Marianne had really been after—I wasn't sure why Ashley still wanted me to come along. Maybe because Ben still hadn't responded to her text, and she was starting to worry that I might've been right about him. Although, after the silent treatment she'd given me last night, despite my apologies, I was surprised she'd resumed talking to me.

"You ready?" Ashley asked as I emerged from her guest room. "I still haven't heard from Ben, so I want to stop at the police station on our way and file a missing persons report."

My phone vibrated in my pants pocket. I lifted a single

finger to signal her to give me a minute, then pulled it out and glanced at the screen. Special Agent Isaak Jackson. "I need to take this." I retreated to the guest room and closed the door. "What did you find out?"

"Would you believe there are eight different police departments on this little island? Not to mention a sheriff's office and a state police office?"

"The population does swell to more than a hundred thousand people in the summer."

"Yeah, well, unfortunately that grant they implemented to centralize record keeping hasn't finished the job yet. I called every single office, but none have a record of an interaction with Ben in the last seventy-two hours. The last officer I spoke to suggested we file a missing persons report."

"Yeah, we were about to do that."

"Good. Now, I do have good news. I got a lead on the antiquity Jack called me about."

My pulse quickened. "Go on."

"The chief disclosed that a photo of an old clay vase was found in Jack's jacket pocket."

My fingernails dug into the palm of my hand. I forced myself to relax. I wasn't up on the retail value of antiquities, but it was hard to fathom a single vase being worth a man's life. Maybe the police were right and Jack's death was an accident. Or . . . maybe the vase was the tip of the iceberg—a lead on a bigger operation.

"The chief will have a copy ready for one of us to pick up any time after 10:00 a.m. Can you handle that? I promised the wife and kids we'd go out on the boat this morning."

"Absolutely. Thanks, Isaak."

I quickly rang up Aunt Martha. "It's Serena. I don't have

time to explain, but I need you and Carmen to meet us out-side the funeral home after our appointment."

"Sure, we can do that."

I could always count on Aunt Martha to be up for an ad-venture. "Then I'll need you to accompany Ashley wherever she needs to go after that so I can pay a visit to the state police office."

"You don't want Ashley to know where you're going?"

"It would avoid a lot of questions I don't know the an-swers to just yet."

"Leave it to me," she chirped. "I have the perfect cover story."

My heart flip-flopped. What had I done?

"Serena," Ashley called. "We need to leave now or we won't have enough time."

"I've got to go," I said to Aunt Martha and hurried out to Ashley's car.

"You're wrong about Ben," Ashley said. "And I have a bad feeling your aunt's boyfriend is right."

There was no good way to respond to that. Neither sce-nario was good for Ben.

We stopped at the Chilmark police station to file the miss-ing persons report. The sergeant who took the information must've been the same officer Isaak had spoken to, because he didn't waste our time asking all the "could he just be . . ." questions that likely accounted for a good number of the non-emergency missing persons reports they took down.

Ashley gaped at me when I filled in the approximate date and time of his arrival by ferry and the fact he'd been hitch-hiking. "How do you know that?"

I shrugged as if I hadn't canvassed every cab driver at

the ferry to find out. She didn't need to know how deep my suspicions about his *nonappearance* ran. "I got talking to an old friend of Ben's when Malgucci's ferry came in. He mentioned seeing him."

Thankfully, she didn't question how I'd recognized a friend of Ben's.

By the time we reached the funeral home, Jack's fiancée was waiting for us at the door. Her eyes were puffy, and dark circles had settled beneath them. Thankfully, her daughter Carly hadn't joined her.

Ashley apologized for being late and launched into the reason why, right down to finding Ben's backpack on Uncle Jack's porch. The color drained from Marianne's face, and I couldn't help but question if it was for fear of what might've happened to Ben or for fear of something else. A side effect of spending almost two years interrogating suspects who rarely spoke the truth in the first round.

The meeting with the funeral director proved to be easier than I'd expected. As it turned out, Jack had long ago made his own funeral arrangements, and Ashley and Marianne needed only to be informed of his requests and update the information for the obituary. Jack had stipulated a closed casket and no visitation times before the service, which I'm sure was meant to spare Ashley and Ben from added emotional strain.

The director confirmed with the police that the body would be released tomorrow at the latest. Marianne and Ashley agreed on Saturday evening for the service, and I expressed confidence that Ben would turn up by then. If he wasn't in jail.

We stepped outside at 9:53, and Aunt Martha toodle-ooed us from the far end of the parking lot.

As we meandered over to ask what brought her into town, a distinguished-looking older man jumped up from a garden bench and intercepted us. He wore a slightly outdated business suit that tugged at his midriff and scuffed leather shoes, tempering my first impression when I'd glimpsed his graying sideburns and well-trimmed salt-and-pepper hair. He grasped Ashley's hand. "I was grieved to read in the paper this morning about your uncle's accident."

"Thank you." She disentangled her hand from his grasp and kept moving toward Aunt Martha.

The man didn't take the hint. He trailed us across the lawn, and Carmen—scratch that—Nate opened the driver's door.

"Where's Carmen?" I blurted.

"He went bass fishing with Preston before dawn this morning. When we left, they'd just finished cleaning their catch, and he was headed back to his B&B for a nap," Aunt Martha said.

Which she'd probably already anticipated when I called this morning. I should've known she'd pull something sneaky to ensure I spent time with Nate over Tanner. Not that I was complaining. But Tanner would be.

"Jack and I are old friends," the man behind us said a hair too desperately to the back of Ashley's head, then rambled on about their mutual interest in art and antiquities.

That caught my attention, but before I could quiz him further, Marianne, who wasn't even driving with us, interjected, "I'm afraid you must excuse us. There is much to do."

"Of course, of course." The man pressed his business card into Ashley's hand, reminding me of a circling vulture. "The name's Joe. I'd be interested in purchasing some of your uncle's pieces once the estate is settled."

Uncle Jack had an art collection? Where did this guy get that idea? Enlargements of his own photographs were the only decorations gracing his walls.

"I'd give you a good price," the man added.

Ashley stared at him mutely, but after a moment, managed to nod.

The instant he climbed into a faded car close to the door, Marianne snatched the card from Ashley's hand and ripped it in two. "He and Jack were old friends, my eye. He's one of those flea market vendors that hawks whatever he can get his hands on from people's estates."

Aunt Martha toed the discarded pieces of business card toward her, then reached down and picked them up. Pocketing them, she tossed me a wink.

As sidekicks went, she was the best. If I ever decided to quit my day job and become a PI, I'd hire her in a flash. Well, except for the fact that Mom would kill me.

I winced at the poor taste of my own mental quip, considering we were standing outside a funeral home. I watched the man drive away and wondered if Marianne was right about him or if he knew something she didn't want Ashley and me to find out. I texted Isaak Joe's name and business address and suggested he run a background check.

"What are you doing here?" Ashley asked Aunt Martha.

"Oh, honey, I got to thinking you'd want to choose floral arrangements for the service, and Serena is hopeless with things like that."

"Hmm, thanks Aunt Martha," I said.

"Nonsense, you know you are. You can't even keep houseplants alive."

Nate chuckled. "Yeah, criminals fare far better with her."

Great, now they were ganging up on me. "I'll have you know that the dieffenbachia you left in the apartment is still alive, and I've been its guardian for over a year."

Aunt Martha gave me an odd look. "That plant's fake, dear."

No way. It looked so real. Guess that explained why it survived months at a time without water.

"Besides," Aunt Martha went on, discreetly slipping the business card into my hand, "Serena loathes shopping. You should've seen her poor friend trying to get her into bridal shops to choose a maid-of-honor frock last year. And this way she and Nate can have a bit of time alone to sightsee."

Ashley met my gaze and smiled, seemingly catching on to Aunt Martha's *true* motive. Probably truer than the fact I'd asked her to come.

Somehow I was sure the fact I'd inadvertently caught the bouquet at the wedding last month loomed larger on Aunt Martha's mind than my deficit in the shopping-gene department. Mom had ramped up the matchmaking hints ever since Zoe's wedding, and from the assist Aunt Martha gave Nate to get him here, he was clearly Aunt Martha's front-runner.

Thankfully, Ashley thought flower shopping with Aunt Martha was a wonderful idea since she hadn't even remembered that it was something she should do. I gave Ashley a hug and mouthed "thanks" to Aunt Martha, then turned toward Nate's sporty yellow rental car—different enough from Malgucci's that I should've clued in it was his long before he'd stepped out.

But Nate didn't follow me. "I meant to ask," he said to the women in general, "what's the best beach around here to hunt for sea glass?"

122

"Oh, Eastville is good," Ashley said.

"What about at Menemsha Hills? The hunting any good there?"

"Not at all. I don't know anyone who's ever found any sea glass at that beach. Do you, Marianne?"

Marianne had one foot in the red sports car her daughter had been driving a couple of days ago, and her gaze jumped from Nate to Ashley. "No. Never." Her attention returned to Nate. "Why do you ask?"

"Just curious."

As he reached to open the passenger door for me, I whispered, "I'm not so sure that was smart."

"Told us something. Don't you think?"

"Yes, that I can't trust you to be discreet."

"Trust me. I can be discreet when it matters." His light touch at the small of my back sent tingles dancing up my spine as he smiled down at me. "I hear I'm playing chauffeur."

Okay, that wrangled a smile out of me. "Yes, I appreciate it. Thank you."

He scooted around to the driver's side. "Where to?"

"The state police headquarters. It's practically across the road."

He drove slowly down the funeral home's long driveway. "What did you think of Marianne's reaction?"

"Curious. The police already know she was at the crime scene, so she had no reason to be worried she might've dropped something incriminating there."

"Exactly, so why did she look so unnerved?"

"Good question."

He turned onto the road and almost immediately into the

small lot behind the police station as I filled him in on the photo I needed to pick up.

A text message came in from Tanner: *You almost done at the funeral home?*

My thumb hovered over the screen.

"You feeling guilty?" Nate asked.

I shoved the phone back in my pocket. "What are you talking about?"

"Tanner flew all this way to help you with the case, and here I am, the 'non-'agent, driving you around."

"Well, you flew here too, and no, I wasn't feeling guilty, but thanks so much for giving me something else to angst about." I meant it to sound wise-cracky, but I don't think I managed to pull it off.

"Hey, I've got to respect any guy who has your protection at heart, even if he beat me to the draw on inviting you for dinner." Nate winked at me. "Got lunch plans?"

"Why'd you stop flying?"

His smile dropped. "Will it make a difference to your answer?"

Oops. With all the talk about flying, my brain had gotten stuck on wondering about why he'd stopped and hadn't registered his lunch invitation. "Yes."

"Yes, it'll make a difference?"

"No, 'yes, I'll have lunch with you.'"

"Ah, good." He opened his door. "Shall we go in?"

"Wait. First I want to know why you stopped flying."

"Because my parents died in a car accident and my brother needed me," he said matter-of-factly.

"What does your brother needing you have to do with giving up flying?"

"I was a courier, flying all over the place and never home."

"So, you flew cargo planes."

"Yeah."

I flicked to the webpage I'd saved on my phone of a cargo plane shot down over Yugoslavia. "Was this your plane?"

Pain flickered across his face as he nodded. "For three days, my brother thought I was dead."

"That must've been scary. I can understand why you never wanted to fly again."

"I love flying. I'd forgotten how much until I came here. I could take you up if you like."

Reflexively, I gripped the armrest and gritted my teeth, already feeling claustrophobic. "I don't know. I have a hard enough time with the big planes."

"It has lots of windows. It's not much different than driving in a car, only it's in the air." His voice took on a hint of a pretty-please tone that made me want to acquiesce.

"We'll see."

A trooper swaggered out of the two-story white clapboard building and headed straight for us.

"I guess our sitting back here made him antsy," Nate said.

"Wait here." I climbed out of the car.

"May I help you?" the trooper asked.

"I'm Special Agent Serena Jones, here to pick up a photograph."

"Right. I'll get that for you." He returned within a minute and handed me a manila envelope. "You just caught me in time or you may've been waiting hours. Have a good day."

He drove out of the lot in a state trooper cruiser before I had the picture out of the envelope.

Nate took one look at the photo and said, "No way, that looks like the Fenton Vase."

"*The* Fenton? Are you sure? I thought it looked Mayan, but . . . if it'd gone missing from the British Museum, we would've heard about it." The Fenton Vase was discovered around the turn of the twentieth century, in Guatemala, if I remembered correctly, and purchased by C. L. Fenton, hence the name. Given Ben's article on Mayan antiquities smuggling, I wanted to believe that he was on board with Jack to expose a smuggling ring. But he wouldn't have been asking for a *deal* if his hands were totally clean. I blew out a breath. At least we weren't looking at Middle Eastern antiquities, which might've tossed terrorist ties into the mix.

"It looks like the one I saw as a kid when my family visited the British Museum," Nate said. "But there are others around, only not with as pristine provenances."

"Because Fenton exported his before Guatemala's post–World War II decree declaring all artifacts the property of the state."

"Exactly. It's one of the few Mayan pieces in foreign collections with a legal provenance."

"I'm impressed. You know your antiquities."

"I did a massive project on the Maya when I was in grade school. My grandfather had a piece at the time, and the iconography had always fascinated me. It's what made the artifacts so popular on the international market in the '60s."

"What happened to your family's artifact?"

Nate's gaze drifted to the windshield, and his eyes crinkled as if inside he was smiling at some memory. "My project convinced him to return the piece to the Guatemalan government."

I laughed. "So you were already playing art crime detective a couple of decades ago!"

He let his grin show. "Gramps was horrified to learn how destructive the looters are. We're talking sawing the stone monuments to make it easier to get them out of the jungle and tunneling into temples and pyramids to access the pottery buried with the dead. So many sites were looted long before they were discovered by archeologists that it became an unrecoverable loss to our understanding of the Ancient Maya."

I studied the picture. "What do you know about the look-alike vases?"

"Can't help you there. But check out the British Museum's website. They may have more information that will help."

I did a search for the website on my phone and sure enough, there was a write-up for the vase along with several photographs of the piece. "It's remarkable how similar they look. It says four other pots by the same artist, likely looted and trafficked in the 1970s, exist in foreign collections."

"It doesn't say which collections?"

"No." I input the description into the FBI art crime database to see if anything came up. Not a single record for the Maya time period.

"The vases must be in public museums if they're known to the British Museum. But then, you'd think they'd be more delicate about declaring them essentially stolen from the state."

I did an online search for *Fenton vases*. "If museums repatriated every antiquity they owned that didn't have pristine provenance, there'd be a lot of empty spaces. And as some curators have pointed out, they are often preserving what would've long ago been destroyed or irretrievably lost to looters or the elements, if not for their investments." I scanned the options and clicked on a reputable looking one. "Huh, this article says there are six known vases. Three are in American museums, the one in Britain, one in Berlin, and one in Guatemala City. But none have been reported stolen."

"So this could be a reproduction."

"Or one that's recently surfaced from a private collection." I couldn't help the excitement that trickled into my voice. It would be an amazing recovery.

"So what do we do now? Retrace Jack's appointments from the time he called the FBI? See if we can spot this vase?"

"Its owner isn't likely to be foolish enough to have it in view. Not if he's connected to Jack's death. And especially if he's clued in that I'm a friend of the family. We need someone who has no apparent connection to Jack's family to check out the homes."

"How about Martha's friend? He said he was in real estate."

"Winston? Yes, he'd be perfect." I phoned Aunt Martha.

After I got off the phone with Aunt Martha, I called Tanner to enlist his help too. I gave him the address of Winston's realty office and five addresses Jack had visited in the previous two weeks—three clients, two potential clients. The plan was Tanner would pretend to be a business tycoon, shopping for real estate. With Jack's clients, he would say he was thinking of hiring the Hill and Dale architect firm and wanted to see some of their designs for himself first. With the other two addresses, Winston would say their houses were exactly the size and location his client was looking for and ask if they would be interested in selling.

"Are you sure using Tanner is smart?" Nate asked after I hung up. "Ashley and Preston know he's helping you."

"Do you really think either of them are connected?" I snapped a picture with my phone of the vase and forwarded it to Tanner and Aunt Martha.

"Preston seemed too ready to cast Ashley's brother in a questionable light last night."

"That's just the way he is. He spouts out everything he

thinks you'll want to know, on just about any subject you bring up."

Since we didn't want to risk being spotted anywhere near Tanner and Winston, I suggested we test Nate's theory by gauging Preston's reaction to the picture of the vase. But halfway to his house, I got a call from Isaak Jackson. "Hey, that was quick. Did you find something interesting on Joe?"

"No. Get over to Lucy Vincent Beach. I'll be there as soon as I can."

"Why, what's going on?" I pulled out the island map Nate had tucked between the seats and pointed to the beach.

Isaak's response was in such a hushed voice, I couldn't make out what he said—except it sounded like *a body*.

"What? I couldn't hear you."

"I can't talk right now. Just get over there."

Nate had already pulled a U-turn and was racing that direction.

I turned the phone over and over in my hand. "This isn't good. This is so not good. I can't believe this is happening."

"What are you talking about?"

"The body. He said *body*. It's got to be Ben." My voice cracked and I looked away, watched the scenery whiz by without really seeing it. "This is how it always happens. If Aunt Martha were here, she'd tell you."

"*It?*"

"In the mysteries she's always watching. Just when the sleuth is sure she knows whodunit, the suspect dies. How could I have suspected him? He'd always been a good kid. When we found his backpack last night, I should've known something happened to him. Just like Carmen said. Only worse."

"Take it easy."

"I can't! You heard Isaak. He told me to get over there. That means he's got to believe it's Ben too. To think I spent the last two days harboring suspicions about him. Imagining him smuggling antiquities. Imagining him actually killing Uncle Jack rather than risking going to jail. Imagining he'd tried to do the same to Dad and me.

"Poor Ashley, how can she survive losing both her uncle and brother in the span of three days?"

"Serena, listen to me. You don't know it's Ben. Don't borrow trouble."

Logically, Nate was right, of course. But deep down, I knew it must be Ben. It explained why Ashley hadn't been able to reach him—and much more. "He probably came home early to surprise Jack and ended up surprising whoever had been searching Jack's house. A killer who didn't see a problem with killing one more person to avoid getting caught. Only whoever that person was didn't know Ben had dropped his backpack behind the chair on the porch before letting himself in."

Nate didn't say anything.

Because he knows I'm right. I needed air. I lowered the window. "It makes sense. Doesn't it?" I let my drive for answers blind me to my faith in my friends. My mind flashed back to long-ago trips with Ashley to the beach and Ben's skinny little legs always trying to keep up with us. Why were we always so mean to him?

"Or Ben's cohort decided he was a liability," Nate theorized.

My stomach fell. "I like my theory better." One that kept his reputation untarnished. Ashley deserved that much.

"You know if the police wind up ruling Jack's death a murder, with Ben dead, Ashley would become their prime suspect since she'd stand to inherit everything."

"One more reason we need to find that vase."

By the time we neared Lucy Vincent Beach the sky had darkened to steel gray and a fine mist had started. Police cars and other vehicles jammed the parking area. My gaze skittered over a black sedan, and my heart missed a beat. "That looks like the car I thought was following us yesterday."

"It's a rental. There are probably dozens just like it on the island."

I jumped out of the car and squinted at the driver. He was wearing jeans and a dark green sweatshirt and flashed an official-looking ID to the officer manning the entrance to the beach. "He looks familiar." I started after him.

"Probably because he looks like that actor," Nate said, trailing after me. "Hey, we're on Martha's Vineyard. Maybe he *is* that actor from *The Italian Job*. What's his name?"

"Mark Wahlberg," I mumbled, remembering now where I'd seen the guy before.

"Yeah, that's it."

"It's not the actor. It's the guy who was watching me in the airport."

"Serena, I hate to break this to you. You're beautiful. A guy would have to be in a coma to *not* watch you."

My heart did a silly pirouette in my chest. We were definitely treading beyond neighbors-watching-old-films-together-and-sharing-pizza territory. "That's sweet. Thank you." I stopped and, half-turning, pressed my palm to his chest. "I need you to wait here." I pulled my FBI badge from my purse and hurried over to the officer who'd just let the

Wahlberg look-alike through. The officer didn't look as if he was old enough to shave yet, so with any luck, he was a rookie who wouldn't question a fed's interest in a floater.

I flashed my badge, and he lifted the tape for me to duck under.

"I'm with her," Nate said, on my heels.

The rookie didn't balk.

"I can't believe you did that," I hissed at Nate.

"Why? You'd rather I flash my *Secret Service* ID?"

"Ha ha. C'mon."

Once we cleared the trees surrounding the parking lot, the wind picked up, whipping us with sheets of rain. It slicked right off Nate's jacket, but my windbreaker was drenched within seconds. As we approached, the group of first responders gathered around the body opened for a stretcher to pass through.

Nate, a good six inches taller than me, craned his neck and said, "It's not Ben."

I tried to see. "How do you know?" I maneuvered through the group to catch my own glimpse and muffled a gasp. Gaudy Souvenir Guy—Charlie? The relief that I wouldn't have to tell Ashley her brother was dead was dwarfed by heartache for Marianne and Carly.

I forced my mind to detach itself from the emotions. The cops were talking as if his death was a boating accident—out fishing without wearing his life jacket. But I wasn't buying it. Not on the heels of Uncle Jack's death. Then again, could the killer be stupid enough to not think that two deaths within a few days of each other wouldn't raise a boatload of red flags?

Nate elbowed me and pointed my attention toward Wahlberg, who was staring at me from the fringes of the group.

I walked over to him. "Watching me is becoming a bad habit. Mind telling me why?"

"Let me guess. A fed?" he said.

"That's right, and you?"

He scrutinized Nate.

"He's okay," I said, to reassure him he could talk freely, and showed him my ID. "He's a friend from St. Louis."

Wally nodded. "I'm with the state police."

I pointedly let my gaze sweep his non-uniform.

He flicked his badge. "Drug task force."

"So that's why you were standing around the airport the other day?"

"We got a tip."

My mind zigzagged from the memory of Wally watching me in the airport to the K-9 officer and drug-sniffing dog checking out Charlie's souvenir. . . . *And now Wally was here.* "A tip about Charlie?" It explained why Wally followed me—he probably saw me snap Charlie's picture on my cell phone when he and Carly were having that argument on the sidewalk yesterday.

"What can you tell me about him?"

Are you kidding me? What can you *tell me?* I squashed my rampant thoughts. If I wanted Wally to divulge useful information, I'd have to lead him to it. "He caught my eye in the airport because there'd been a case where a dealer dipped priceless artifacts in resin to disguise them. I'm with the FBI's art crime team. I came here to celebrate a friend's engagement, and Charlie turned out to be the future stepson."

"Jack Hill," Wally said.

I should've known that any detective doing a half-decent job would've already made that connection. "That's right."

Emergency workers manhandled the gurney holding the body bag off the sand and into the back of a waiting ambulance.

"Do you think Hill's death was an accident?" Wally asked as we headed back toward the parking lot.

"Why ask me?"

Wally nodded toward the departing ambulance. "I don't like coincidences."

"That makes two of us. What can you tell me about Charlie?"

Wally scrutinized me for a long moment and seemed to decide his chances of coming ahead in the information trade would fare better if he loosened his lips. "He was spotted having lunch with one of South America's wealthiest drug lords. We think he's connected to a local drug ring. Maybe the kingpin."

"Then maybe we should get a closer look at those souvenirs he brought home with him. He could be using antiquities as currency to pay for drugs." If we followed the money, maybe we'd find Jack's killer.

Wally shook his head. "Currency's going the wrong way. Americans pay the South Americans for the goods, not the other way around."

My chest deflated.

"When you looked at the body, you seemed surprised it was Charlie. Who were you expecting?" Wally asked me.

I glanced at Nate to buy me an extra moment. On the drive here, while believing I'd find Ben, I'd convinced myself he was innocent. Now . . . I couldn't be sure. But Wally didn't need to know any of that. "A friend of the family is missing. I was afraid he might've been the victim."

Wally's interest piqued, just as I'd feared. "A drug user?"

"No." Never mind that I hadn't seen him since he was sixteen. If his sister were concerned his disappearance was connected to a drug problem, she would've said something.

With an acknowledging nod, Wally pulled out his wallet, pried out a business card, and handed it to me. Real name Alan Moore.

I stifled a frown. I'd grown kind of fond of thinking of him as Wally.

"If you hear anything that may be of help, give me a call," Wally, I mean Alan, said.

"Will do." I texted Isaak to let him know our floater wasn't Ben, then climbed into the car beside Nate. "Head to Preston's?"

Nate glanced at his watch. "How about we have lunch first?"

I plucked at my jacket that had already dripped a puddle onto my pants. "Can we swing by Ashley's so I can change into dry clothes first?"

"No problem."

We passed Preston's on our way and seeing that Ashley's car still wasn't there or at home, I didn't feel as bad about taking Nate up on his lunch offer. And with Tanner busy playing newcomer-interested-in-property, I wouldn't have to worry about what he might say or feel guilty about ignoring him.

The instant Nate pulled to a stop, I told him to give me five minutes and ran inside. I quickly changed into my black jeans and a lightweight, soft pink, cotton sweater, pulled a comb through my drenched hair and looped it into a ponytail, then borrowed one of Ashley's jackets hanging on the row of hooks by the door. An umbrella hung beneath it, so I grabbed that too.

As soon as I stepped onto the porch, Nate rushed out of the car, then relieved me of the umbrella and holding it over me, escorted me to the car.

My heart did another silly dance at the attention.

Fifteen minutes later when he parked outside Lucky Hank's, he said, "Stay right there," then grabbed the umbrella and rounded the car to open my door for me once more.

Okay, I was impressed. Sure, over the years guys had opened doors for me, but Nate was the first to actually ask me to wait so he could. And for some reason his attention was starting to make me nervous.

As Nate ushered me inside, a familiar voice made me jump.

"Well, well, well," Tanner said, sounding all jovial. But his eyes weren't smiling. "So now we know why you really sent Winston and me out on this wild goose chase."

12

"Hey, guys, you stopped to grab lunch? Any leads yet?" I asked in my brightest voice.

"Sure," Tanner said. "I've got my eye on a house that would be an amazing summer home if I ever decide to go on the take."

I laughed. Tanner was the most passionate and hard-core FBI agent I knew. He knew every last dot and dash of the FBI book, and the only reason he'd so much as bend the rules was if it helped him get the bad guys faster.

But perhaps glimpsing a sales lead, Winston declared in true realtor form, "The homes can be pricey, but they're great investments."

Tanner patted him on the back. "Let's keep our eyes on the goal and let these two eat." He offered Nate a terse nod as he passed him out the door. So much for not feeling guilty.

The unfortunate meeting put a damper on our lunch. I chattered on about what I'd come to think of as Jack's case, and Nate didn't attempt to steer the conversation in any other direction. By the time we headed back to Preston's, I wondered what I'd been so nervous about.

Then it hit me like a two-ton truck. I was afraid this transformation in our relationship or aberration or whatever I should call it wouldn't work. I couldn't remember the last guy I'd dated more than a few times. And I really, really liked my *friend* Nate. I didn't want to lose that because I . . .

I what? I slanted a glance across the car at Nate, straining to keep my pounding heart from matching the staccato of the rain spattering the windshield. I didn't even know why I always cut bait. The bad habit, topped only by turning down dates in the first place, had always been my friend Zoe's favorite topic of conversation since it exasperated her to no end. I'd told myself that a serious relationship could wait until after I found the art thief that killed my granddad.

Of course, I'd been a naive rookie at the time.

After more than a year and a half on the job, I knew in my head that finding Granddad's killer was more a question of "if" than "when."

But I wasn't ready to give up.

"A penny for your thoughts?" Nate asked, and spotting Preston's driveway, I suddenly realized we'd driven the whole way in silence.

"I'm sorry. Just mulling." What if my unfinished business with Granddad's killer had skewed my perspective of Jack's death? "Um . . . do you think I'm letting my imagination get the best of me? Maybe Jack did just fall. Maybe Charlie's and Jack's deaths aren't connected. Maybe that guy who swerved at Dad and me the other night on the road was just a drunk kid. It's not as if any more attempts have been made on our lives. Whoever 'owns' that vase might not even know Jack was about to report it." I stopped for a breath, and Nate's expression grew even more empathetic.

"I think you need to follow your heart *and* the evidence and see where they lead."

My *heart* did a somersault, because I was pretty sure that Nate wasn't just talking about Jack's case.

Nate parked behind Preston's car, and we let ourselves inside. "We'd better not mention Charlie's death," I whispered, "just in case the police haven't notified Carly and Marianne yet."

"Whatever you say."

Ashley and Aunt Martha weren't back yet. Mom and Dad were reading quietly in the living room.

"Where's Preston?" I asked

"In his workshop downstairs," Dad said.

Downstairs was a basement, built into the side of the hill with a walkout on the back. From my recollection, Preston's father had had a woodworking shop on the far end. On sunny days, it'd been bathed in natural light from the sliding-glass doors and multiple windows. But Preston had always favored the fine arts, so I suspected he'd converted the workshop into a studio.

He must've heard the stairs creak as Nate and I padded down, because he appeared at the door of the workshop as I reached the bottom stair and pulled the door closed behind him. "You're home. How'd you make out with everything?"

"Good." I filled him in on the arrangements, then asked for a tour of his studio.

"Actually, I can't right now. I'm working on something personal, and I want Ashley to be the first one to see it when it's finished."

"Of course. I understand." Although I had a twinge of doubt when he didn't meet my eyes as he said it. Then again, maybe he'd just remembered the last time he'd given me a tour of the workshop . . . and presented me with a heart pendant he'd carved for me. I unfolded the photocopy of the photo of the Mayan vase. "I was wondering if you've ever seen a vase like this on the island?"

He studied the photo. "A Fenton Vase?" He shook his head. "The closest one I know of is in the Boston museum. Why?"

"Uncle Jack had this picture in the jacket he was wearing."

Preston's eyes widened. "So you think this might be what he was on to?" His voice rose with excitement, and he studied the photo more closely. "There was an article about these vases in a recent edition of that *Arts and Antiquities* magazine your uncle gets. Nothing about a discovery of another one though."

"Jack never mentioned seeing one to you?" Nate spoke up.

Preston glanced at him. "Me? No." He rubbed his fingers and thumb over his forehead as if deep in thought. "I can't recall visiting any collector on the island who has Mayan artifacts, and when people learn I'm an art history professor, they're usually eager to show off their collections."

"Okay. Thanks anyway." We'd have to wait and see if Tanner and Winston came up with any leads. I excused myself and slipped into the basement bathroom. Preston had a stack of reading material in a holder next to the toilet—a crossword puzzle book, a couple of fishing magazines, a home improvement magazine. Looking for the trash can, I opened the cupboard under the sink. "What do we have here?" I pulled a rolled-up magazine from the otherwise empty can—the December issue of *Arts and Antiquities*, the very issue I'd noticed missing from Uncle Jack's collection. I checked the mailing label. Jack Hill.

My thoughts rioted. Why would Preston have taken it? And thrown it in the trash can? I scanned the table of contents. Not a single article pertained to Mayan vases.

By the time I exited the bathroom, Nate and Preston had wandered back upstairs. I glanced at the closed door to Preston's workshop and engaged in a mental tug-of-war with my conscience. I had no right to invade his privacy, and no permission to search the premises. But finding that magazine had me—

A disgruntled "meow" came from the other side of the door, then frantic scratching.

"Harold, did you get yourself shut in Preston's studio?" I turned the doorknob, but the door wouldn't budge.

"Everything okay?" Preston called down the stairs.

I turned the knob again and this time added a shoulder bump against the door. It still wouldn't budge. "No, Harold's locked in your studio."

Preston hurried down the stairs and pulled a key from his pocket. "Sorry about that. I should've remembered he'd followed me in there. I coaxed him downstairs because your Dad's allergies were acting up." Preston opened the door the tiniest crack and Harold bolted out and straight up the stairs. Chuckling, Preston reached in and flicked the lock on the back of the doorknob once more, then pulled the door closed and actually tested it.

Did he really think I'd be that desperate to peek at his project? Or was he hiding something else in there?

Nate appeared at the top of the stairs, cradling Harold. "Where was he?"

Preston headed back up the stairs. "My workshop."

Something about Nate's quiet acknowledgment suggested there'd been more to the question, but first things first. I hurried up after Preston, my hand fisting tighter around the rolled magazine. "Hey, I found one of Jack's magazines in your trash can. Did you mean to throw it out?"

Preston didn't so much as flinch at the question. A few steps into the kitchen at the top of the stairs, he turned. "Sure, one less thing for Ashley and Ben to dispose of, right?"

"Why did you have it?"

He shrugged. "Jack often passed along issues with articles he thought I'd be interested in."

A car pulled into the driveway and Preston excused himself.

Nate, with Harold still in his arms, tossed me a skeptical look. "You believe him?"

I pulled Nate into the dining room so we wouldn't be overheard. "I want to, especially after all my fretting in the car about suspecting Ben."

"Uh, yeah . . . but we still don't know what to think of him either," Nate reminded me.

I rolled the magazine back up in my fist. "I know. I know. And I got to thinking that the night the car ran down Dad and me, Preston was the only person, besides Isaak Jackson and Tanner, who knew I wanted to figure out what Jack had called the feds about."

I gave my head a mental shake. Listen to me—half an hour ago I was questioning whether the whole thing was a figment of my imagination. What must Nate think of my yo-yoing theories? Still . . . "Preston could've watched Dad head to Jack's house and made that excuse about picking up groceries to Mom and Aunt Martha."

Voices I didn't recognize drifted in from the living room.

I lowered my own. "I mean, Preston had groceries in his vehicle when he gave me a ride later, but he could've picked those up after the hit-and-run. He didn't show up until after the ambulance had already left."

A dark-haired, middle-aged woman poked her head through the doorway and beamed at me. "Remember me?"

"Diana! It's so good to see you."

She pulled me into a warm hug. "I wish it were under happier circumstances. I was just bringing a meal over for the family, and when I didn't find Ashley at home, I figured I'd find her here."

"She'll be back soon." I introduced Diana to Nate. "When I visited in the summers as a teen, Diana was the youth group leader."

"Have you met Marianne?" Diana asked.

I nodded.

"The poor woman. She's inconsolable."

I sucked in a breath, about to say I'd heard about Charlie, only to realize that wasn't what she was talking about.

"Marianne blames herself for Jack's death," Diana went on.

"What?" A triple jolt of caffeine couldn't have kicked my brain into high gear faster. "Why?"

"She and Jack had a fight over something silly that night. You know the way couples do when wedding jitters build."

I pictured the argument taking place at the top of the steps to the beach. Marianne shoving him . . .

"It was just before her book club was due to start, so he left before they had a chance to make amends," Diana went on, snapping me out of my wild imaginings. "She's convinced he tripped and fell because she'd made him so upset. She can't forgive herself that the last words between them had been harsh."

"Oh. Yes. That's got to be hard." Could the cause of death have been that simple? But then, how do we explain the picture of someone's jean-clad legs on Jack's camera?

Ashley rushed in, her face flushed. "Have you heard anything about Ben?"

I glanced past her shoulder to Aunt Martha's shadowed face. "The radio had something about a young man found on the beach. A possible boating accident," she said softly.

"I checked. It wasn't Ben," I reassured her, hesitant to admit who it was. If the radio announcer withheld the information, the police may not have had a chance to notify Marianne and Carly yet.

Ashley collapsed onto a kitchen chair. Her coat flapped open and three bits of sea glass tumbled from one of the pockets.

Harold leapt from Nate's arms and pounced on the blue one.

Nate lowered his head and whispered in my ear. "That's what I wanted to tell you before. When Harold darted out of Preston's studio, he had a piece of sea glass in his mouth."

My gaze lifted from the pieces Ashley was scrambling to rescue to her jeans. Her skintight jeans.

13

After Diana left, we congregated in Preston's great room, which overlooked Tisbury Great Pond. Preston stood at the window in his crisply pressed chinos and silk shirt. I didn't think I'd ever seen him in jeans.

"We can't just stand around and do nothing," Ashley said, sounding more worried about Ben than I would've expected if she were responsible for Jack's death.

"We should be out looking for him," she went on. "He's always hitchhiking. He probably started off to a friend's place when he didn't find me or Uncle Jack home. He could've been hit like Mr. Jones and be lying in the scrub brush somewhere."

"Good idea," Aunt Martha chimed in. "Now that it's stopped raining, we can fan out from Jack's house in pairs."

Mom set aside the crossword puzzle she'd been working on. "That's a great idea."

"Carmen's on his way over, so he and I can walk east down the road," Aunt Martha said.

"Ashley and I can go over the dunes to the water and comb the shoreline," Preston offered.

"Nate, you and Serena can walk west down the road," Aunt Martha said. "The rain will have washed away any footprints, so you'll have to pay extra close attention to any sign the grasses have been flattened."

My phone hummed the *Get Smart* theme song—code for Tanner's calls. I excused myself and slipped into the kitchen for privacy.

"Hey, we found something you'll want to see," Tanner said, only he didn't sound as if I'd be happy about it.

"What did you find?"

"Where are you?"

"At Preston's."

"I'll pick you up in ten minutes."

"Pick me up? Where are we going? We were about to search the roadsides for signs of Ben."

Nate must've been half-listening from the other room, because he stepped into view, his expression concerned.

"Somewhere where we won't be overheard." Tanner hung up before I could get in another word.

"I need to go out for a bit," I said to Nate. "Tanner wants to show me something."

"I can search with Nate," Mom volunteered. Whether to make it easier for me to spend time with Tanner or to have an opportunity to vet Nate, I wasn't sure. Maybe she just wanted to help. Of course, I'd have an easier time believing it wasn't all about me if she didn't remind me every other week that over a year ago, I'd said I'd been thinking about settling down—which in her mind meant giving her grandchildren. Since I made the mistake of saying as much in front of a roomful of women at my cousin's baby shower, and *said baby* had just turned one, I clearly hadn't been thinking straight at the time—side effect of being clocked with a can of peas by a fleeing suspect.

Nate had a hangdog look as I climbed into Tanner's car ten minutes later. Keeping the two men in my life separate was so much easier back in St. Louis, where I saw Tanner at work and Nate at home and the two rarely crossed paths. Mom's shift-husband/home-husband theory niggled my thoughts.

I pushed it aside and focused on the *Arts and Antiquities* magazine Tanner slapped onto my lap a second before backing out of the driveway. The cover image was of a Mayan Fenton Vase. "Where'd you find this?" I squinted at the mailing label—Frank Dale. "At Jack's business partner's? What were you doing there?"

"No, at the potential client's house Jack visited ten days ago. It was sitting on his coffee table."

"Is he a collector? Did you see the vase? Did he have other Mayan artifacts?"

"Uh, you're missing the big picture here," Tanner said as if I were more than a little slow on the uptake. He tapped the cover. "Look at it."

"I am looking at it," I snapped back, not bothering to keep the irritation from my voice. He *could* be more forthcoming. It was the April issue. Frank must've lent it to him. I checked the index and flipped to the article on the vase. "If Frank knew him well enough to lend him a magazine, why'd Jack take the appointment to pitch their services?" To think if I'd done more than scan the spines of Jack's magazines, I would've seen this issue two days ago. And picked up whatever clue Tanner couldn't believe I wasn't not seeing.

Tanner reached across the seat and closed the magazine, then pulled to the shoulder and shoved the car into park.

"You're not looking." He yanked the copy I'd given him of Jack's vase photo from his pocket a nanosecond before I saw it.

"No way!" I grabbed the paper from him and compared it to the image on the cover. It was the exact same vase, oriented in the exact same position, sitting on the exact same surface. "It's a picture of the magazine cover."

Tanner made the ka-bing sound of hitting a target in a shooting gallery. "The pretty girl gets the prize."

Sometimes he could be really irritating. "Uncle Jack couldn't have made this. The words have been edited out. Jack doesn't even have a computer, let alone a digital camera."

"So who'd he get it from? And why?"

"Maybe someone gave the photograph to him and claimed he had the genuine article, asked what it would be worth to him," I theorized, as I punched the state police chief's number on my phone. "Hello, this is Special Agent Serena Jones again. That photo found in Jack's pocket. Was it dusted for fingerprints?"

"Yes." An eruption of computer keys being tapped sounded over the phone. "Here it is. In addition to the deceased's prints, there was a thumbprint on the front of the photo and two fingerprints on the back that didn't match his. We're running them through NCIC to see if we get a hit."

"Okay, thanks."

"There is another possibility," Tanner said as I clicked off.

"What's that?"

"Someone planted the photo to rabbit trail anyone tempted to link Jack's death to his call to the FBI."

"Yeah." I let out a self-deprecating snort. "And I fell for it hook, line, and sinker." I shook my head. "I even knew there were only six known vases in existence, all accounted for in various museums."

"Hey, I taught you better than that." He looked at me intently, clearly waiting for me to connect a few more dots I'd apparently overlooked.

I gasped. "Whoever printed the photo had access to a copy of the magazine!" I called Isaak and explained what we had discovered. Then I asked him to request that computer forensics check the original photo to determine if it'd been doctored from an online image of the magazine cover or was scanned from a hard copy. If it were the latter, it would narrow down our suspects considerably. "See if you can get a list of the magazine's subscribers living on Martha's Vineyard too."

"I'll make the calls," Isaak said. "Good work."

"I had lots of help." I smiled at Tanner and clicked off. "Okay, so until we hear otherwise, we can assume that our man photographed or scanned the magazine cover."

"Frank could've done it. You said your father suspected him, right?"

"Yeah, and apparently he lends out his magazine."

"Actually, he puts them in his waiting room. The client said he picked it up from there. You can ask Carly who else has been in for appointments since the April issue was put out."

"I don't think Carly will be in any condition to give us that kind of information." I winced at the memory of Charlie's ashen face. "Her brother's body washed up on the beach this morning."

"No way. What happened?"

"The operating theory is a fishing or boating accident."

"But you think the two deaths are connected?"

"Charlie was about to become Jack's son-in-law!" I blew out a sigh. "He was also under investigation for possible involvement in a drug ring." Pieces started to fit together in my head. "Maybe Jack caught wind of the suspicions. He and Marianne had a fight before he headed to Menemsha Hills. They could've argued about Charlie, because Jack wouldn't tolerate anything illegal going on and Marianne would naturally be defensive of her son."

"So you think we're talking drug dealers—not art smugglers—now?"

I massaged my fingers over my throbbing temples. "I don't know." I hated how hopeless I sounded. "How are we supposed to investigate when we don't even know what we're supposed to be investigating?"

Tanner suddenly pulled a U-turn.

"Where are you going?"

"Back to Preston's. Seems to me Jack's missing nephew could be the key to unlocking everything."

I splayed my fingers over the magazine still lying on my lap. "Jack subscribed to this magazine too. And Preston would borrow them."

"Did you show him the photo from Jack's pocket?"

"Yeah, but nothing about his reaction struck me as suspicious."

"All the same, let's not tell him we've figured out it's a copy of a magazine cover."

I rolled the magazine and shoved it in the glove box. As we rounded the corner back onto Jack's street, Aunt Martha burst out of the bushes flanking the road.

"Stop!" I grabbed the door handle and jumped from the car the instant it stopped. "Did you find something?"

Malgucci caught Aunt Martha's hand and smacked a kiss on her cheek. "She was chasing a butterfly."

Aunt Martha spouted a Latin name I didn't catch. "I haven't seen one since I visited Mexico," she added breathlessly.

Malgucci gleamed at her, looking as smitten as—

"Hey, does Ben have a girlfriend on the island?" I blurted.

"Ashley called every friend of his she could think of after we finished at the florist," Aunt Martha said. "No one's seen him."

"At least not that they're admitting to," Tanner said, joining us outside the car.

I called Ashley's cell phone. "Hey, who was that girl Ben always hung around with during high school?"

"You mean Lisa?"

"Yeah, that's the one." I could still picture her long corkscrew blonde curls flapping in the air as she raced Ben into the water and nine times out of ten beat him. "Is she still around?"

"Yes, the same place she's always lived, but I already called her. She said she hasn't seen him."

I got the directions, then motioned Tanner back into the car. "C'mon, we need to visit Lisa." The house was less than two miles away—nothing to a guy who backpacked across half the world.

"What makes you think she's lied about seeing him?"

"Lisa was Ben's best friend growing up," I explained as Tanner drove. "She always turned down his requests for a romantic relationship because she said she didn't want to lose his friendship if it didn't work out."

Tanner glanced at me, his eyebrow raised curiously. "Sounds like the kind of friend who'd cover for him."

"Maybe. Ben could be a little wild sometimes, and Lisa was kind of his Jiminy Cricket."

"His Jiminy what?"

I rolled my eyes. "You know? *Jiminy Cricket*. Pinocchio's conscience?"

He chuckled. "Pinocchio I know."

"Oh, that was her house," I said as we passed it.

Tanner backed up and into the driveway, and at the sight of the dark blue Jeep Patriot sitting there, my heart missed a beat. The vehicle looked uncomfortably similar to the size and shape of the SUV that clipped Dad Wednesday night.

I jumped out of Tanner's rental and examined the Jeep's front and passenger side. The vehicle appeared to have been recently washed and waxed . . . to remove blood? "Do you think hitting my dad would've left a dent in a vehicle this size?"

Tanner rapped his knuckles against the bumper. "Not necessarily. More likely crack the plastic bumper."

Lisa's wasn't cracked, but that didn't stop my stomach from churning as I strode to her front door.

"You know that every third person on this island seems to drive a vehicle like that," Tanner said.

"Yeah, I know. But every third person isn't also an old friend of Ben's." I hated that I was back to suspecting him, but there it was.

Lisa opened the door only a crack in response to my knock. "May I help you?"

"Hey, Lisa, remember me? Serena Jones."

"Oh yes, Ashley's friend from St. Louis." She opened the door a fraction more, filling the gap with her body. Tanner's gaze flicked from me toward the drawn drapes at the living room window, but I'd already noticed. "I was so sorry to hear about Jack."

"We're pretty worried about Ben, actually. His friend said he saw him hitchhiking this way the same night Jack was killed. Has he been in touch?"

Her gasp didn't strike me as all that genuine. "Jack was *killed*?"

Okay, the quaver in her voice sounded pretty real.

"The news report said it was an accident," Lisa added, sounding desperate for me to confirm it.

"We suspect otherwise."

From the other side of the door, out of Lisa's line of sight, Tanner smiled at my obvious appeal to her Jiminy Cricket reputation.

I furrowed my brow and lowered my voice. "And now a second body's been found."

"It's not Ben," Lisa said as if she knew it for a fact, then quickly added, "is it? I mean"—she danced her fingertips through a lock of hair, across her reddening cheeks, then over her lips—"clearly you wouldn't be asking about him if it was . . . right?"

Tanner cocked his ear toward the corner of the house and signaled he'd check the rear—standard procedure when arriving to apprehend a suspect. A little more difficult to explain when paying a neighborly call. Then again, everything about Lisa's body language suggested she was hiding something and maybe buying time so someone could slip away.

"May I come in?" I asked.

Lisa glanced over her shoulder. "Let me put my bird away first. He likes to fly out whenever he gets the chance." The door closed.

I darted to the corner of the house, but Tanner had already disappeared around the next one. I returned to the door at the same time it opened. As Lisa motioned me inside, Tanner finished his three-sixty of the house and climbed the porch steps in one long stride.

I quickly apologized for not introducing him earlier and remedied the oversight.

Lisa welcomed us both inside. "Please excuse the mess," she said, discreetly pushing a couple pairs of shoes into the closet before closing it. "I've been on nights at the hospital."

"Your parents still live here?" I asked.

"No, they moved to the mainland three years ago." She picked up a mug and a discarded chip bag from the coffee table. "Can I get you something to drink?"

Dropping onto the sofa, I declined, but Tanner said, "A coffee would be great, thanks." The instant Lisa was out of earshot, he informed me that the curtains had been drawn on the windows of the three rooms at the back of the house, but he'd seen movement in the room on the left. Then he tilted his head toward a pair of drinking glasses on the end table. Not that that was conclusive proof she was hiding Ben. I'd been known to collect a few glasses in my living room—all my own—before catching up on dishes. But the men's watch sitting beneath the lamp . . . that looked suspicious. Like maybe our Jiminy Cricket wasn't walking the straight and narrow herself these days. It hadn't exactly escaped my notice that she'd avoided my "has Ben been in touch" question.

Tanner strolled in the direction Lisa had disappeared and asked if he might use the restroom.

Nervous energy shuddered across my shoulders and down my spine. Whoever owned that watch could be hiding at the back of the house, waiting for us to leave, or . . . to make a wrong move.

Lisa strode into the living room carrying a tray with two mugs and a glass. "I thought you might like water."

A strange thud drifted from the hallway Tanner had disappeared down, followed by a strangled cry.

14

Reaching for my gun, I raced toward the hallway.

A cockatiel swooped past me, flapping wildly. At the other end of the hall, Tanner grumbled about "stupid birds."

Laughing, I slid my gun back into its waistband holster. Okay, so apparently she hadn't been feeding us a line with the "let me put my bird away first" excuse. Only . . .

Lisa's ashen complexion suggested I wasn't the only one who'd assumed Tanner was tackled by something bigger than a pint-sized parrot.

"What did you do?" I asked, looking from Lisa to Tanner.

Tanner smoothed his hair. "I opened the wrong door." He shuddered. "Sorry, I have a thing about birds."

Interesting. I'd have to ask him about that sometime. At the moment, the feather-ruffled cockatiel sat perched on the top of the drapery rod, eyeballing him. Concern over the bird escaping could've prompted Lisa's suspicious behavior at the door earlier.

"I'm sorry," Lisa stuttered, "Grayson doesn't have the best manners. Please, won't you sit down?" She sank into a plush armchair without waiting for us to sit first and expelled a distraught sigh. "I don't understand. Why would anyone want to kill Jack?"

"He was privy to information someone didn't want out," I said, figuring I had nothing to lose by admitting that much. If by chance Ben were listening from a back room, at least he'd know that he couldn't get away with whatever he thought hiding out would do for him. I sat on the sofa while Tanner, who'd apparently decided to forgo a visit to the little boy's room, held up the far wall, arms crossed, one eye on Grayson.

"And . . . and . . . ." Lisa fussed with the hem of her sweater. "You said someone else close to him is . . ." Her voice trailed off, apparently unable to say "dead."

"Charles Anderson. His fiancée's son."

Lisa's face paled to a color even pastier than before. "How awful. And you think it's because he knew what Jack knew?"

"Clearly we're looking at someone who has no qualms with dispensing of whoever gets in his or her way," Tanner said, his voice deep and ominous.

"And Ashley is petrified he's gotten to Ben too," I jumped in. If Lisa believed our search was motivated solely by concern for his welfare, she'd have no justification to lie about seeing him, no matter what story Ben had fed her.

"Maybe this friend of Ben's mistook another hitchhiker for him," Lisa suggested.

"No, we know he's here."

She stifled a strangled sound, her gaze flicking to the tell-tale pair of drinking glasses on the end table.

By "he's here" I'd meant *on the island*, but clearly Lisa's guilty conscience assumed otherwise. And I was losing my patience. "Could you ask him to come out and talk to us?"

She gulped loud enough for me to hear. "He's not here."

I gave her a skeptical look.

"I swear he isn't. You can search if you want. I don't know where he is."

I signaled to Tanner to take her up on the invitation, then refocused on Lisa. "But you have seen him?"

She twisted her hands in her lap and nodded sheepishly. "I found him wandering along the road with a head wound Tuesday night."

"I thought you were working nights."

"Not that night."

I nodded. "Go on."

"He said someone hit him with a rock. I offered to drive him to the hospital, but he refused to go. I tried calling his uncle's and Ashley's, but there was no answer at either place. I let him sleep in the spare room so I could keep an eye on him. Concussions can be dangerous."

Tanner rejoined us with a miniscule shake of his head. "When did he leave?"

"He slept until past noon the next day, which could've been partly jet lag."

From my experience, when witnesses offered unrequested information, they were usually compensating for what they didn't want to divulge. I simply nodded and looked at her expectantly, as did Tanner.

She sighed. "He walked down to Jack's in the afternoon, shortly before I left for work. He didn't want a ride."

Okay, if Lisa drove her Jeep to the hospital, that ruled out Ben using it to take out Dad and me on the road. But . . . "Did Ben have his backpack when you picked him up Tuesday night?" I asked.

Lisa shook her head.

So, he could've presumably left it on Jack's porch Tuesday night and never made it back on Wednesday. Which meant whoever got to Jack and Charlie could've already gotten to Ben, too, and used his phone to send that bogus text so we wouldn't go looking for him. My heart raced. "Did he say who hit him?"

"He said he didn't see who it was. He thinks he may've been knocked out for a few minutes."

Tanner's eyes narrowed. "Has Ben returned since Wednesday afternoon?"

"I haven't seen him again."

"Is that a *no*?" I pressed, since she was far too adept at equivocating.

She shrugged. "Like I said, I've been working nights. He may've come back when I wasn't here." She glanced up at a clock on the wall. "Oh no, I've got to go or I'll be late. I'm sorry I couldn't be of more help."

Tanner handed her his business card. "If you see him again, please call us immediately. You could be in danger."

"Ben would never hurt me." The certainty in her voice made it clear she wasn't scared of him and confirmed, more or less, he wasn't threatening her.

Tanner helped himself to the coffee he'd been ignoring and finished it in three gulps. He set down the mug with a loud clomp. "I meant danger from the man who already failed to kill him once."

A healthy dose of panic flickered in Lisa's eyes before they dropped to Tanner's card. "Yes, I see what you mean."

We let ourselves out, leaving her to stew on that thought. "Do you think she'll call?" I asked Tanner as we climbed back into his rental.

He spun out of the driveway and peered past me into the woods surrounding Lisa's house. "I'm counting on catching him sneaking back before her shift ends." He flashed me a grin. "How's a stakeout dinner sound?"

"Not as appetizing as Lucky Hank's," I teased, ridiculously more comfortable with the prospect of eating takeout in his car while watching Lisa's house than eating in a fancy restaurant with him. A stakeout dinner was status quo. Not a date.

"But worth it if it means finding Ben, wouldn't you say?"

"Absolutely."

We checked in with the others already congregated back at Preston's house but opted not to tell them Ben had been at Lisa's or about his injury. While we'd been questioning Lisa, Carly had called Preston and Ashley and told them about her brother's death, so between that news and not having found any sign of Ben in their search, Ashley was frantic enough without adding another reason for her to be concerned. I excused myself from the group to grab a bottle of water, hoping Nate might follow.

Mom cornered me between the refrigerator and the sink. "Nate really cares about you. All he did was talk about you the entire time we were searching. And being an apartment superintendent isn't such a terrible job. He seems very intelligent. Given the right encouragement, he could probably do well in whatever he put his mind to."

I gave my head a mental shake. Was that why Mom had been favoring Tanner over Nate? Because he had a better job?

"Don't you shake your head at me," Mom scolded, because apparently I didn't even have to do it for Mom to know what I was thinking. "You could do a lot worse."

"Mom," I hissed, "this is not the time or place."

"Are you still going out to dinner with Tanner?" Mom asked, "because Aunt Martha just invited Nate to join her and Carmen at a seafood place in town."

"Yes. I said I would. I can hardly back out now."

Nate poked his head around the doorway. "Everything okay?"

"As well as can be expected. Could I have a word with you?" I shooed Mom out and waved Nate away from the doorway.

"Did your mom tell you we took Harold down to Ashley's house?" Nate asked. "Your dad's allergies were acting up."

"Do you think he'll be okay alone there until I get back?"

"Sure. Ashley gave him a couple pieces of sea glass to bat around."

My thoughts veered to the piece he'd found at Menemsha Hills, and I reminded myself again that Ashley had an alibi.

"You wanted to talk to me?" Nate prodded.

"Oh." I snapped my attention back to Nate. "Yes, I wanted to fill you in on what Tanner and I are doing tonight." I explained what had happened at Lisa's and about our plan to watch the house.

"Takeout, huh?" Nate broke into a full-blown grin. "Makes Lucky Hank's look pretty good."

My answering smile faltered a little at his words. Sometimes I didn't know what to think of these two guys. Were they really interested in me? Or just in one-upping each other?

Despite the twinge of self-doubt, I found my gaze lingering on Nate's smiling lips and remembering how soft they'd felt against my hand.

Tanner strode in, dark hair windblown, bringing the tang of sea air with him. "Ready to go?"

"Uh."

He cocked a single eyebrow at my eloquent response. "I'll take that for a yes," he said drily, his eyes flicking to Nate and then back to me.

I held up the water bottle I'd grabbed from the fridge, trying to squelch the awkward feeling that'd seized me. *It's not as if they can hear my thoughts*, I reminded myself. "All set."

Nate winked at me. "Bon appétit."

I glanced at the corners of the ceiling for hidden cameras. Completely irrational, I know. But I felt as if I'd been dropped in the middle of a reality TV show and all the juicy conversations were slated for Preston's kitchen.

Tanner guided me out to his car with a warm hand at the small of my back, which sent totally inappropriate sensations rippling through my belly. *He's your shift husband*, Mom's voice whispered through my thoughts, and I squirmed.

"Everything okay?" Tanner asked.

"Peachy, thanks," I said, as I pulled open the passenger door and got in the car.

The salty breeze coming through our open windows cooled my overheated cheeks, and I relaxed a bit at the familiar feeling of working a case with Tanner. "So . . . I've got to know. What do you have against birds?"

He groaned, clearly not eager to relate the story.

"Let me guess. You were picnicking as a little kid, and a seagull swooped out of the sky and stole your food right out of your hand."

"No."

"It let loose on your head?"

"Uh, no."

"Okay, your family had a pet bird and whenever it got out of its cage, it chased you around the house."

He chuckled. "Yeah, something like that. Only there were two of them. Lovebirds. And they'd dive bomb my head."

I grinned. "Lovebirds, huh? Explains a lot."

"You think?" He pulled up to the fish market at Menemsha and put out a hand to forestall me when I slid my seatbelt off.

"Ordered all your favorites ahead," he said, hopping out of the car. He stuck his head through the open window. "Prepare to be dazzled."

Ohh-kay. Not so familiar, this oddly date-like behavior. But . . . kind of nice. A pleasant warmth spread through me as I watched him pull open the door and disappear into the market. Being pampered now and then wasn't such a bad thing.

A few minutes later he strolled back out sporting three bulging paper sacks. He opened my door with a flourish, then handed me the bags one at a time. "Lobster salad. Lobster sandwiches. And—ta-dah!" He smiled before setting the last bag in my lap. "Lobster bisque."

"Oh." My warm fuzziness vanished. "Um, thanks."

Irrational disappointment churned through me. Okay, so Tanner clearly didn't remember the story I'd shared about my regrettable date with the guy who'd tried to impress me by cooking a big lobster dinner and then made me help with the dishes. After I'd thrown up. It was over a year ago, after all.

And Tanner was so clearly pleased with himself. He'd been trying to be nice, even if he'd missed the mark on the food. I guess it wouldn't kill me to do a stakeout on an empty stomach. Maybe there were some plain rolls or something.

I forced a smile as he slid into the driver's seat, then drew back in surprise when he burst out laughing.

"Aw, Jones." He gave my arm a mock punch. "That's so sweet. You were gonna spare my feelings, weren't you?"

"What?"

He checked for traffic, then pulled out, still chuckling. "I hope you weren't going to go so far as to actually *eat* the alleged lobster, so I wouldn't feel bad."

"Alleged lobster," I repeated blankly.

He turned and grinned at me. "Because vomit is seriously unromantic."

"What?" I said again, then turned the first bag around to look at the order receipt stapled to the top.

Fish tacos, crab enchiladas, clam chowder.

No lobster anything.

"Idiot," I said and turned to look out the window so he couldn't see the grin spreading across my face. I *loved* crab enchiladas. He did get all my favorites.

Wait. Had Tanner just said 'unromantic'? Like, as in . . . maybe he wanted this stakeout to *be* romantic? Then what did . . . ?

"You cold?" Tanner asked, interrupting my train of thought, which could only be a good thing. He cranked up the heat in the car as he turned back to Quansoo. "We'd better warm it up in here because once we park we won't want to turn it on again."

"Where do you plan to park?"

"Lisa's house is two in from another dirt road that winds behind her place. I figured we could park in the driveway of the house directly behind hers."

"A summer place?"

"I think so. It looked deserted this afternoon."

"With all the vacant summer houses on the island, Ben could easily be holed up somewhere else."

"Hey, what happened to the positive thinker I know and love?" Tanner flashed that teasing grin I'd seen a thousand times before, but my stupid heart kicked up as our eyes met.

Tanner turned his attention back to the road, and I mentally smacked myself.

These men were going to drive me crazy, if I wasn't already there. "I flew here for an engagement party and landed two murders, a missing person, and an antiquities smuggling case instead," I said, sharper than I intended.

Tanner sobered. "I'm sorry about Jack." He reached over and gave my hand a squeeze.

My befuddled thoughts skittered to happier times with Jack.

"Your dad was telling me stories this morning about all the people Jack helped over the years, donating his designs to Habitat for Humanity and for homeless shelters and for projects in developing countries, working on the crews, and even taking people into his home sometimes. Sounds as if he was a great guy."

"He was." *And he didn't deserve to die.*

But I kept that little rant to myself. Jack would be disappointed in me if he could hear it.

After my grandfather's death, Jack had been the one person who'd noticed that God and I were no longer on speaking terms. Only, Jack hadn't given me the usual pat answer about the price of free will. Instead, he'd shared the story of a family he'd met in Africa who'd lost two children to malnutrition and struggled to meet their daily needs. Then he said something to me I'd never forgotten: *Not one person in that family ever asked me how God could be so loving and still let them suffer.*

Jack figured it was because they'd always clung to God. And for them, God hadn't changed, only their circumstances had. Whereas I'd never really *needed* God, so I hadn't turned away from Him so much as I'd come to realize I'd never been all that close to Him in the first place.

These days . . . I still nursed the occasional dose of righteous indignation at the seeming randomness of it all. Yet, in my job, I'd seen good come out of the bad enough times to solidify my hope. "I saw the angel in the marble and carved until I set him free."

"Pardon me?" Tanner said, jolting me out of my thoughts that I'd apparently voiced aloud.

"Oh, sorry. It's something Michelangelo said." My heart felt surprisingly lighter at the thought.

"We're here." Tanner shifted into park and turned off the engine. "I'll take a quick scout around the perimeter to make sure Ben hasn't already returned."

It was 7:00 p.m., which meant it'd be close to an hour before sunset, although here in the woods, darkness was already creeping in.

Tanner returned inside of five minutes. "All clear. Let's eat."

There were enough trees between the two properties that Ben probably wouldn't look too closely at our parked car, but the foliage was still sparse enough that we'd have no trouble spotting his approach, unless he happened in from the northeast.

"Better food than our last stakeout," I complimented after polishing off the last crab enchilada.

"And better company than your lunch date," he teased. At least, I think he was teasing.

"I never kiss and tell," I said flippantly, trying to get back to our usual status quo.

His eyebrows lifted inquisitively.

Okay, wrong thing to say.

He relieved me of my empty container and spoon, his hand brushing mine as he handed me my chowder. "You kissed Nate?" he said, his tone even.

I rolled my eyes, acting as if his steady gaze wasn't making my heart pound like a jackhammer. "Public displays of affection aren't my thing."

"Hmm." He released me from his gaze and casually looked out each window, in turn, as if the foliage surrounding us was of the utmost fascination. "So, what if you were with an attractive, eligible guy in a . . . *private* setting?"

"Uh . . ." I stared into his chocolate brown eyes, looking for the hint of mischief that was surely there. "I, uh . . ."

A car door slammed and I jumped with relief.

"Did you hear that?" I hissed, my attention snapping to a black sedan whizzing past Lisa's house.

Tanner set down his dish, a small smile playing about his lips, then pulled out a miniature pair of binoculars. "Looks like we might be in business. Wait. Oh, for—" He lowered the binoculars, frowning.

"What?" I grabbed a napkin and wiped a dribble of clam chowder off my chin.

"Looks like we've been spotted." He plucked the chowder from my hand and set it on the dash. There was a gleam in his eye I didn't trust. "Sometimes you gotta take a PDA for the team," he said, leaning into my personal space.

168

"P. D. Wha—?"

His hands cradled my face.

"What are you doing?" I managed to squeak, attempting to pull back. But there was nowhere to go. My head was already against the back of the seat.

His gaze lowered to my lips, and my heart ricocheted off my rib cage.

"Making it look like we're just a couple out watching the submarine races."

"The submarine races?" I blurted, my voice rising a few more octaves. "We're half a mile from the ocean."

Laughter bubbled in his eyes. "Don't be so literal, Jones."

Tanner cut off my last squawk of protest with his lips. I vaguely sensed movement out of the corner of my eye, but . . . *whoa!* . . . this was no pretend kiss.

His lips were surprisingly soft and . . . thorough. My heart turned over, my squawk morphing into a sigh, and I found myself kissing him back, my hands creeping up to rest on his broad shoulders. *Wait!* What were we doing? We had to work together! This wasn't right.

With a herculean effort, I broke the kiss. For a second, we stared dumbly into each others' eyes, then my gaze skittered past his to . . . to . . . I squinted at his window. "Gun!"

15

Reflexively, I slammed Tanner to the seat even though it was impossible to get out of the shotgun's line of fire. At the same time, someone exploded from the woods and took a flying leap at our gunslinger.

Tanner did a hunkered-down one-eighty on his seat and kicked open the door, knocking the pair off their feet. I scrambled out the passenger side, pulled my gun on the lot of them, and shouted, "Freeze! FBI!"

Shotgun Guy, who already had his face in the dirt under the weight of Fly Boy, instantly unhanded his weapon and raised his hands. Fly Boy grabbed the gun and pushed to his feet, his back to me.

"I said *freeze*."

His hands shot up, the shotgun still in one of them.

Tanner snatched it away. "You can put down your hands."

The guy turned to face me, his hands still raised.

"Nate? What are you doing here?"

He stared at the gun I still had pointed at his chest.

Oops. I lowered it.

"Your aunt Martha and Carmen dropped me at the corner. I figured it was a nice night for a walk." He searched my eyes as he slowly lowered his hands.

Oh no! If Nate'd been out there, then he must have seen . . .

I looked away, feeling heat steal up my cheeks.

Leave it to Tanner to . . . wait a minute . . . *who* did Tanner see through those binoculars?

I glared at Tanner, who was patting down the guy on the ground. "You *knew* it was—" I bit off the accusation and stomped down the anger bubbling up in my chest.

Tanner had to have known it was Nate approaching the car. And that was the *only* reason he'd kissed me.

Tanner hauled the guy to his feet and propped him against the hood. "What's *your* excuse for being here, buddy?"

"I live over there." He pointed to the house next to Lisa's as I took a calming breath and refocused my thoughts. "I thought you were robbers casing houses."

"Have you seen anyone else sneaking around here the last few nights?"

His eyes lit and he looked from Tanner to me, clearly feeling vindicated for his paranoia. "Yeah, some guy showed up at Lisa's Wednesday afternoon. Was testing her doors and windows before I scared him off."

"What did he look like?" I pressed.

"About six feet. Dark shaggy hair and beard. Was wearing long shorts and a band T-shirt. Don't remember which one. But my wife called Lisa at the hospital, and Lisa said he was a friend."

So although Lisa may not have actually *seen* Ben again—if she hadn't been flat-out lying to us—she knew he'd been back.

"She mention his name?" Tanner cut in.

"Didn't ask. Hey, you mind if I see some ID?"

Tanner dug his badge out of his pocket to satisfy the alert neighbor, then emptied the shells out of the shotgun and handed it and the ammunition back to the guy. "Go on home."

"We might as well too," I said to Tanner after the guy was out of earshot. "If Ben was anywhere around here, he won't come back after that escapade until we're long gone."

"You're probably right." Tanner extended a hand to Nate. "Thanks for the assist. Sorry I nailed you with the car door."

"Not a problem."

"Get in, Nate," I said, opening my door. "We'll give you a ride back to the house." *And I'll just pretend this isn't awkward at all.*

"You heard him," Tanner countered. "He wants to walk. Nice night and all. Remember?"

I shot Tanner my light-saber glare.

"Okay, okay." He opened the rear door for Nate. "You better get in."

With a smile that didn't quite reach his eyes, Nate did as he was told. His gaze snagged mine in the rearview mirror.

"That was an impressive move you pulled out there," I said, giving him a determinedly upbeat smile.

He shrugged. "I just reacted."

Tanner climbed in, handed me the two containers of half-eaten chowder off the dash, then reversed out of the driveway.

"How was supper?" Nate asked.

"Dessert was pretty sweet," Tanner said cheerfully, and I nearly reached over to smack him before I thought better of it.

Instead, I shrank into my seat, trying to ignore the suddenly oppressive smell of uneaten seafood not mixing well with the overabundance of testosterone filling the vehicle. The rest of the ride passed in blessed silence, and I had Tanner drop me off at Ashley's before delivering Nate to his car at Preston's. Yeah, yeah, I'm chicken. What can I say? He who fights and runs away lives to fight another day.

Ashley wasn't home yet, which I was glad about. Harold was a much better listener. And nonjudgmental. Although from the way his purring got louder when I mentioned Nate's name, there was no mistaking where his allegiances lay. Lie? Laid? *Oh, brother. You know you're overthinking when you start questioning your own grammar.*

▪▪▪

I rose with the first glimmer of sunlight and dragged on my shorts, tee, and running shoes. Missing my morning run for three straight days had seriously messed with my peace of mind. Well, that and Uncle Jack's death and Ben's disappearance and . . . whatever was going on with Tanner and Nate.

Harold wound around my legs, purring loudly.

I cuddled him to my chest. "Sorry, buddy, you can't come. You be good, okay? Ashley's still sleeping. I'll feed you when I get back." I plopped him on the bed, and he curled into the warm spot I'd left behind.

I quietly let myself out the front door and savored a deep breath of tangy sea air. I pulled my right foot up until I felt a satisfying stretch in my quads and then let my gaze wander past Jack's house to the long stretch of field and ocean beyond. A smile slipped out at the memory of bygone morning runs with Ashley. As interesting as Forest Park in St. Louis was, running there couldn't hold a candle to running on the beach to the music of gently lapping water as the sun breached the horizon in glorious color.

"How long do you plan on stretching that leg?" Tanner's voice made me drop my foot like a hot potato.

I braced my hands on the porch rail and did a forward lunge to stretch the calf and buy time to hide what his appearance had done to my heart rate. His rental car sat in the driveway beside Ashley's. How had I not noticed it? "What"—I cleared my throat and tried again—"What are you doing here?"

"I thought you might like some company on your morning run." He bent his arm and nonchalantly tugged his elbow behind his head in an upper body stretch.

"You want to hu—" I choked off the word. *What was I doing?* Clearly operating on too little sleep. Because throwing out Sandra Bullock's singsong line, "You want to huuuug me, you want to kiiiiiiisss me" from *Miss Congeniality* was no way to get back to normal with Tanner. Not after—

I cleared my throat. "You want to hustle down the beach with me, do you?" I substituted lamely.

Tanner stopped stretching and looked deep into my eyes. "I do," he said solemnly.

Paralyzed, I stared back at his face for several excruciating heartbeats, then his dimples winked.

". . . want to 'hustle down the beach' with you," he finished.

I snorted, shaking off my stupor. "Try to keep up then, Special Agent." I skipped down the steps two at a time and took off across the field toward the water.

Tanner's long strides quickly eradicated my head start. "I thought you might want to talk."

My step faltered. "Talk?" Was he determined to keep me off balance this morning?

"Yep. Talk. Don't women always want to talk after . . . they nearly get shot?"

I huffed out a breath and rolled my eyes at him.

He didn't say anything more, and a less awkward silence settled between us as I slowed to a comfortable pace. But I still felt as if the ground beneath us was as precarious as the sand washing out with each lap of the waves, so I braced myself and blurted out the question that had been burning inside my head all night. "Why'd you come to the island?"

"To lend you a hand with the investigation."

Ye-ess. Obviously.

"Why?"

He didn't answer right away, seeming to actually give serious thought to his response. "Because it's important to you," he said finally.

My heart squeezed.

"And I knew you wouldn't be willing to leave it to the locals even though you're too close to the victim and some of the suspects to think straight."

Wow. There went my warm fuzzy. "Thanks for the vote of confidence."

"Have you questioned Ashley about her whereabouts the night Jack died?" Tanner asked pointedly, as if to prove his point.

My stride faltered. Nate must've told him about the sea glass the cat found at Menemsha Hills. "She was working."

"Have you verified that?"

"The police have . . . Special Agent Jackson said it was solid."

Tanner's silent censure irked. Did he expect me to duplicate the job of the entire police force? "If Ashley caught wind of me questioning her boss about her schedule, she'd never speak to me again."

"What if she's Jack's killer?"

"She's not."

"She has motive. She'll inherit half her uncle's estate, instead of the fractional amount she stood to inherit after he changed his will."

"She's engaged to Preston Sullivan Frasier III. Money is hardly a concern." We reached the sandy beach, and I veered right along the shoreline the opposite direction to Tisbury Great Pond and Preston's house.

"Nate tells me her fiancé 'accidentally' exposed the film in Jack's camera. Film that caught a picture of someone in tight jeans. The kind of tight jeans Ashley seems to favor. Or hadn't you noticed?"

Oh, so Tanner was noticing the fit of Ashley's jeans, was he? I picked up my pace again. "You and Nate getting chummy now?" I said, in a semi-sarcastic tone I immediately regretted.

Tanner gave me that single-raised-eyebrow glance as he ran alongside me in easy strides, scarcely breathing heavy. "Anything it takes to solve a case, right, Jones?"

"Right," I muttered. Definitely shouldn't have mentioned Nate. I slowed my pace and focused on the soothing streaks of orange coloring the horizon, the cries of the sea gulls swooping over the shallow waters. *Why can't I just let go and let God, instead of stressing over these two guys who are tangling me in knots?*

"Let's look at Preston," Tanner said, breaking into my

thoughts. "Maybe he's one of those Thomas Crown types who dabbles in antiquity smuggling for amusement, only Jack was on to him and Ashley's covering for him."

I attempted to slant him the one-raised-eyebrow look. "Thomas Crown?" I said, surprised he was familiar with *The Thomas Crown Affair* movie about a financier who steals a museum's painting. More likely, Nate fielded the theory after they dropped me off last night. Yes, it had to be Nate's idea. He was the movie buff.

"Yes, I watch movies too, sometimes, you know. I thought of it all by myself."

Huh.

"You ever think that Preston may be so rich because he is a criminal?"

"What about Ben? He lied about being on the island. And if it was his sister or Preston who assaulted him, why bother lying?"

"Hmm, good point. Maybe it was Preston but Ben figured the scumbag wouldn't tell Ashley because she might get all family loyalty on him. Whereas Preston would've figured letting everyone believe Ben's lie gave him time to hunt him down and silence him permanently."

"Preston is not a killer."

"Good-looking guys can be evil too, you know. I know it's hard for you to believe when you have a Paul Rudd look-alike as your partner."

I stopped dead in my tracks and burst into laughter. I planted my hands on my knees and gasped for breath.

"I know, I know. Rudd isn't nearly as toned. They just try to make it look that way with the ripples on the front of the Ant-Man suit."

I shook my head. "You're a nut. And I'm not telling you who I think you look like." A secret he'd been trying to weasel out of me since the first week we worked together.

Tanner grinned. "Because he's really hot, right? You're afraid it will swell my head."

I rolled my eyes and then took off at a fast jog. Tanner looked like Jeffrey Dean Morgan, but he watched so few movies, he probably didn't even know who the dark and handsome actor with the amazing dimpled smile even was.

Running along the beach, serenaded by the sound of the surf and the cry of the gulls, reminded me again of the many runs I'd shared with Ashley as a star-struck teen. She'd been the one who got me started comparing people to movie stars. Somehow I'd forgotten that over the years. With how many movie stars frequented the island, half the time the supposed look-alikes we spotted had probably been the real actors.

Tanner's voice interrupted my thoughts. "I'm trying to help you think outside of the box. Your aunt says Preston goes out in that fishing boat of his before dawn every morning."

"You talked to Aunt Martha about this?" Exasperation spiked my voice and sent a clutch of wading seagulls into flight.

"She mentioned Malgucci joined him yesterday morning. And by the time Malgucci got to the dock at 5:00 a.m., Preston had already done a loop around the pond."

"Are you saying you think Preston killed Charlie?"

"I'm laying out evidence. From the tidal wave maps, the coast guard figures the body floated to Lucy Vincent Beach from this direction."

"You talked to the coast guard?"

"I know a guy."

The narrow channel that connected the giant pond to the ocean had a deadly undertow. Anyone who toppled out of a boat there would get sucked under with little hope of survival.

"Nate mentioned Preston was cagey about what he was up to in his studio too."

My insides squirmed. The idea of Nate and Tanner bonding was just . . . wrong. I stopped and faced the glorious sunrise and willed the tension from my muscles. "We may know the smuggler's identity soon enough."

"How do you figure?"

"I searched eBay last night," I said. He didn't need to know it was at 2:00 a.m. because I couldn't sleep for thoughts of the kiss we shared and of Nate swooping to our rescue. I cleared my throat. "Found someone selling an ancient Egyptian amulet. Someone on the island."

"You think it's the guy Jack was going to turn in?"

"Wouldn't be the smartest smuggler, leaving his ads up on eBay after Jack alerted the FBI."

"But criminals aren't known for their smarts."

"Exactly." Then again, a mind-boggling number of antiquities had come up in my search— everything from a three-inch, carved-stone, fertility-goddess pendant to a two-foot, carved-wooden, anyone's guess what. I'd been one click away from calling it a night when I happened upon the jade Egyptian amulet being sold out of the United States. One more click told me the seller was from none other than Martha's Vineyard. Coincidence?

I didn't think so either.

"I contacted the eBay seller and explained I was visiting the island for the weekend and asked if I could see the item in person."

"What did he say?"

"Still waiting for a response." We ran in companionable silence for a couple of miles, with occasional interjections on my part of memories of my visits here as a youth.

"Wow," Tanner exclaimed as we neared the two-story-high pillars of sand left behind on the beach by the eroding clay cliffs.

"You've never seen them before?"

"I know you may find this hard to believe, Jones, but this is my first trip to the ocean."

"You're kidding me. All those weeks you trained at Quantico, you didn't take a weekend to drive to the beach?"

He fixed me with a look.

"Right. Hard core. Silly me. What was I thinking?"

He chuckled.

I pulled out my phone. "Here, let me snap your picture with the sand pillar."

As he hammed it up for my photo shoot, memories of doing the same with Ashley cascaded through my mind, followed by a deep sadness at how far apart we'd grown. I'd hoped that staying with her at the cottage would give us lots of time to reconnect, but she almost seemed to be avoiding me.

"What's wrong?" Tanner asked.

"What?" I glanced up, realized my smile must've turned upside down, and shook my head.

The uncertainty in his expression was so . . . sweet, my heart did a silly jig. I dropped my gaze to the sand. "Just remembering happier times with Ashley and wishing we could have them back."

"Why don't you just ask her why she got so mad at you that last summer you were here?"

I closed my camera app, regretting having mentioned that to him before I left St. Louis. I checked for messages, but the signal wouldn't cooperate, so I stuffed the phone back in its armband holder. "She just lost Uncle Jack. And Ben is hiding out on the island for who knows what reason." I refrained from adding if he was still alive. "It's hardly an appropriate time to bring up old hurts. Let's head back."

By the time we returned to the compound, Preston's car had joined Tanner's in the driveway.

Tanner was about to jump in his car to head back to his B&B to shower when a shriek rattled the cottage windows.

Ashley.

16

Ashley's shout of "That stupid cat!" had me scrambling up the front porch with Tanner on my heels.

I yanked open the door. "What's wrong? What did Harold do?"

Ashley and Preston were hunched over, picking colorful bits of sea glass out of the carpet. "He knocked my bowl of sea glass off the end table," Ashley complained.

The tip of his tail twitched into view from beneath the couch.

I bit down on a smile and stooped to aid the cleanup effort. Tanner's arm grazed mine, raising goose bumps, as he reached for a piece. *Oh man, was he doing this stuff on purpose?*

Harold eyeballed us from under the couch skirt, no doubt waiting for a chance to strike out a paw and claim a wayward piece.

"You two going out?" Tanner asked Preston and Ashley.

"Give it a rest," I muttered to him under my breath. Couldn't he see her bloodshot eyes? The dark bags beneath them? There was no way she had anything to do with Jack's death, and if Preston loved her, he didn't either. If they were going out it was because she'd want to spend every waking minute continuing the search for Ben. And I had a bad feeling when we found him, I'd have to arrest him. Because at this point, I didn't see how Ben could be both innocent and alive.

I didn't even want to think about how much Ashley would hate me for that, but it was better than the alternative—burying him.

"I have to work," Ashley said. "Catering a birthday party."

Stunned, I dropped back onto my heels and gaped at her. "They couldn't get anyone to take your shift?"

"The girl who was going to cover for me came down with food poisoning or the flu or something." Ashley didn't sound as if she minded, and her resignation niggled.

I'd half expected her to demand the police search every vacant summerhouse on the island. The way I figured it, Ben was either holed up in one, or best case/worse case, depending on how you looked at it, was being held hostage in one. Unless . . .

She knew more than she was saying.

"I'm here to fix Ashley's leaky faucet," Preston said.

Tanner emptied a handful of sea glass into the bowl and stood. "Well, I'd better get going."

Ashley suddenly looked worried. "You're not spending the day with Serena?"

He picked at the shoulders of his perspiration-soaked T-shirt. "Need to shower after that run."

"Oh, right, of course. Well, I guess we'll see you both . . . later?" Her voice trailed off.

"Absolutely." Tanner caught my eye and signaled me to join him outside.

I closed the door behind me so we wouldn't be overheard. "What now?" I hissed since I really, really didn't want to be told yet again that my childhood best friend might be a killer.

"I had the feeling if you stood next to Preston a second longer, Ashley's fellow employee wouldn't be the only one suffering from food poisoning."

"What?" I didn't bother to hide my exasperation at his cryptic gobbledygook.

"That summer after high school when Ashley got mad at you . . ." Tanner went on. "Did you date a guy Ashley was interested in?"

"No. Of course not. I would never do that."

Tanner cocked his head and looked at me with an irritating little smirk. "You sure you'd recognize the signs? You're kind of slow on the uptake when it comes to registering a *guy's* interest in you."

I gulped. Was he talking about himself? I'm pretty sure I felt the blood drain from my face and prayed Tanner wouldn't notice.

"There was Nolan in accounting." He counted off on his index finger and moved on to his second finger. "And that lawyer Jax and—"

I held up my hand like a traffic cop. "Okay, I get the picture. But this is different. Ashley and I used to talk about everything in those days. If she were interested in a guy, she would've told me. We talked about guys all the time."

"Yeah, but I'm guessing you turned a few heads in her direction that didn't normally notice." That little smirk quiv-

184

ered on the corner of his lips again. "Being a summer novelty and all to her classmates, I mean."

I rolled my eyes. "The population of this island explodes in the summer. I was hardly a novelty." Only . . . A memory flickered at the edge of my mind. An evening beach party. Ashley had pointed Preston out a few times over the course of the evening—as he was barbecuing, as he was playing volleyball, as he emerged from a swim—adding incidental facts about his family and college plans. The plans had included studying art, an interest I shared, so I'd just assumed . . .

My chest tightened. She hadn't been pointing him out for my benefit at all. Now her over-the-top reaction to finding me at Preston's house Thursday morning made perfect sense. "How could I have been so thick?"

Tanner chuckled. "You were a teenager. Blame it on hormones."

I cringed. No wonder Ashley had given me the cold shoulder after that night. She'd gotten all excited when Preston rounded the bonfire and headed our way. But then . . . he'd asked *me* out. Not her. Sure, I'd declined because I had only a few days left on the island to spend with Ashley, but he'd been insistent and scrounged up a guy to escort Ashley so we could go on a double date.

Tanner squeezed my shoulder. "I think my work here is done. Call me after you've showered. We should pay visits to Ben's other friends on the island."

"Uh, yeah, okay." Only, I still needed to talk to Nate too. As Tanner backed out of the driveway, I checked my cell phone for a message from Amulet Guy. Yeah, I was chicken. What was I supposed to say to Ashley now that I'd finally figured out why she'd probably been mad at me for the past ten years?

Amulet Guy's message appeared on my screen, inviting me to meet him at the open-air tabernacle in the center of Oak Bluffs at 11:00 a.m. I agreed and hit SEND.

"Now I have to figure out how to get there," I muttered to myself as I let myself back inside.

"I'm heading into town to get a replacement part for the faucet. Did you need a ride somewhere?" Preston asked.

"What?" It took me a moment to realize he'd been talking to me and to register what he'd asked. "Oh, that'd be— Uh, no. That's okay. Thanks anyway." I'd been about to say that'd be great, since asking Nate or Tanner for a ride would only irk the one I didn't call first. But the flare in Ashley's eyes had immediately nixed the option. It was too bad, too, because Preston would've been the perfect expert to evaluate the antiquity I was going to see. Then again . . . given Tanner's suspicions, maybe the less Preston knew, the better.

My cell phone chirruped the theme song from *Murder She Wrote*. "Oh, that's Aunt Martha." I scooped Harold from under the couch to take him to the bedroom with me, where he wouldn't cause any more trouble. "With more plans, I'm sure." And maybe I could finagle those plans to get me to Oak Bluffs without having to choose between Tanner and Nate for a ride.

I slipped into my bedroom and closed the door before clicking on the phone. "What's up?"

"Nate's talking about flying home. What did you do?"

"Nothing." Okay, there'd been that kiss with Tanner in the car that apparently . . . maybe . . . Nate had witnessed. I winced. "What did he say?"

186

"That he didn't want to get in the way of your job. Or whatever else you wanted."

"What's that supposed to mean?"

Aunt Martha let out an impatient harrumph. "He saw Tanner's car at Ashley's this morning."

Oh.

"He doesn't want you to feel as if you're caught in the middle of an old Peter, Paul, and Mary song."

"Huh?"

"You know. 'Torn Between Two Lovers.'" She sang a few bars and my heart hiccupped. "Nate said that? He feels like a fool?" *A lover?*

"Not in so many words, but clearly this island isn't big enough for the three of you!"

"What do you want me to do?" My voice pitched higher. "Send Tanner home? He's helping me with my investigation."

"You may be surprised how capable Nate is if you give him a chance."

I sank onto the edge of the bed and recalled his takedown of Shotgun Guy last night. Yes, Nate was capable. Of getting into a heap of trouble.

But if it weren't for him, I wouldn't have the half-exposed photo of the killer's legs or the piece of sea glass found at the murder scene, not to mention have been rescued so quickly after the hit-and-run. Harold leapt onto the bed beside me and nosed my hand until I scratched the back of his neck. I clutched him to my chest. "It's not like I want him to leave, Aunt Martha."

"Good. Because that's what I told him. I also told him we'd take him and Carmen into Oak Bluffs this morning and give them a tour of the campgrounds."

"The campgrounds" was Martha's Vineyard's Camp Meeting Association or Wesleyan Grove, a historic landmark, consisting of thirty-four acres of quaint gingerbread-trimmed cottages, circling the tabernacle where I was supposed to meet my eBay antiquities seller at 11:00 a.m. It could work. After all, I told him I was visiting the island for the weekend, so it would look like I was there with my boyfriend and parents. "That sounds great. What time?"

"We'll pick you up at ten thirty."

"Perfect." I released Harold, disconnected, then rang Tanner and explained what was going on. "Could you hover around the area? Pay attention to who's watching?"

"Sure, no problem. I'll watch your back. You think Ben's your eBay seller?"

"I want him to be and don't want him to be at the same time," I admitted reluctantly. His circuitous route home from Egypt heightened my suspicions. It was a trick frequently employed by smugglers to cleanse an object's provenance. Since the burden of proof lies with the government making an allegation an object isn't legal to transport, the more ports the object has already passed through, the harder to prove it was originally stolen. Not to mention that by such convoluted treks, the object often gains paperwork needed for it to enter a more restrictive country.

"You think Ben will show his face if he sees it's you?" Tanner asked.

"If he recognizes me, probably not. I'm sure Jack or my parents would've told him I'm FBI."

"Is the seller expecting a woman? You could ask your Aunt Martha and Carmen to pose as the buyers."

My insides churned at the thought of putting Aunt Martha

in the middle of a potentially dicey situation. Not that anyone was likely to try anything with a hulking figure like Carmen standing next to her.

"We'll see," I said and clicked off so I could take my shower. I stripped out of my shorts and T-shirt, then wrapping up in the bathrobe Ashley had lent me, I tugged open the door to the guest bathroom. "A-a-ahh!" I yelped, clutching the edges of the robe together under my chin.

17

I jumped at the sight of Preston on his hands and knees under my sink. "Yikes, I didn't realize this was the faucet you were fixing." My gaze dropped to the bottoms of his shoes.

"It's not." He pushed to his feet. "Sorry. Didn't mean to startle you. I was just checking to make sure none of the other taps were leaking, too, before I trekked to the hardware store." He hitched his thumb over his shoulder and backed out the second door, which led into the hall. "I'm going now. See you later."

"Yeah, see you." I locked the door behind him and noticed a dusting of red flecks on the throw rug where he'd been resting his sneakered feet moments earlier. I dampened my finger and caught up some flecks. They seemed to be bits of resin.

My thoughts flashed to the souvenir Charlie had been so protective of in the airport.

I unlocked the door and hurried after Preston. "Can I see the bottom of your shoes?" The question popped out of my mouth before I remembered that I could be talking to a murderer and my off-duty weapon was back in the guestroom with . . . my clothes.

Preston glanced at the bottom of his shoe in which more bits of resin were still embedded in the fine tread. "Sorry, did I leave a mess behind?"

"Red flecks."

"Yeah, that's resin off a crazy souvenir Charlie brought back from his trip."

"You saw him? He gave it to you?" My mind spiraled through reasons why, none of them good.

"No." Preston looked confused. "The police brought it to me. Aren't you the one who told them to search Charlie's house for smuggled antiquities?"

"Antiquities?" Ashley said with a gasp from behind me. "The agent that searched Uncle Jack's house asked if he'd mentioned anything about antiquities. Do you think—?" She clutched her throat as if she couldn't voice what she feared.

"The police have no proof the deaths are connected to each other," I said. *Or to antiquities.*

"But . . . but . . . if they're both connected to antiquities"—her eyes turned hollow—"that means Carly was right. Uncle Jack was—" Her voice broke on a sob and Preston pulled her into his arms.

And I knew her well enough to know she wasn't that good an actor. If Preston was somehow connected to the smuggling, Ashley was completely in the dark.

"I'm afraid so," I said softly and then met Preston's gaze over Ashley's shoulder. "The police brought you the statue?"

"Yes."

Huh. My discussion with Moore at the beach must've

convinced him to spread the investigation's net a little wider. Or . . . Isaak had.

"Call the police station if you don't believe me," Preston said defensively. "A cop watched me the whole time. Something about chain of custody."

"I didn't say I didn't believe you. Were any of the items antiquities?"

"No. I thought the red resin might've been masking something more valuable, so I scraped it. But it was solid resin. Either Charlie didn't keep the stuff in his house or the cops had no clue what they were looking for."

"Or Charlie was innocent."

Preston shrugged. "Innocent men don't usually get murdered."

▪▪▪

An hour later, at my request Carmen parked his rental on Oak Bluff's main shopping street. If my inquiries agitated our eBay seller, I didn't want him seeing me with Aunt Martha and Carmen. As we poured out of the car, I said to Aunt Martha, "How about we meet back at Slice of Life Cafe for lunch in an hour and a half?" I lowered my voice to a whisper. "I'd like a chance to talk to Nate alone." I knew that would win her approval without raising questions about anything else I might have up my sleeve. And if I did need to pull another trick out of said sleeve, I could reach her on her cell phone. I could always count on Aunt Martha to be game for an adventure.

She cracked a satisfied smile, no doubt assuming I wanted to be alone with Nate. "Fine idea."

I led Nate through a small alley between the gingerbread

cottages, their porches practically sitting on the sidewalk, and filled him in on my appointment and plan to surreptitiously scout the area for the seller before deciding how I should approach the meeting.

He clasped my hand. "We should look like a couple enjoying the sights."

The warmth of his touch zinged through me, flaming into my cheeks. And what was I supposed to do with that? We were minutes away from making contact with a probable criminal. To cover my befuddlement and spying, I went into tour guide mode. "In the 1830s, people traveled from far and wide to attend revival meetings in the central tabernacle," I babbled. "They erected their tents in the fields around it, and then over the years, these cottages replaced the tents."

As we reached the commons, I glimpsed Tanner taking in the sights too. Had Nate glimpsed him before me? Was that why he clasped my hand?

My head started to hurt. Maybe Tanner was right about me, and I was inept at reading guys' signals.

Nate squeezed my fingers reassuringly as if he'd read my thoughts. He positioned me in front of a pretty pink house and snapped a photo on his cell phone, then repeated the exercise in front of a yellow one and a purple one as I took the opportunity to scan the grounds surrounding the tabernacle. No one except Tanner was in sight.

Had my seller figured out it was a setup?

Nate and I strolled along the row of houses flanking the other side of the central, park-like grounds. Suddenly he clasped me around the shoulder and positioned our backs toward another colorful house. "A selfie," he said pressing his head to mine and smiling up at his cell phone camera held out at arm's length. Under his breath, he added, "Two houses down, second-story window. There's a guy with binoculars."

Laughing, I snatched his phone from him and motioned him toward the next house. "My turn to take a picture!" As I pretended to try to set it up just right, I slanted a glance at the window a nanosecond before a guy stepped back into the shadows.

"What do you think?" Nate asked without moving his smiling lips.

I snapped the picture of him, hooked my arm through his, and led him past the house. "I think you're pretty good at this stuff." I gave him back his phone and thumbed a message to Tanner on mine.

"Not good enough to leave your sidekick at his hotel though?" Nate needled, the teasing lilt not quite succeeding at masking his disappointment.

"Sorry. His badge might come in handy."

Nate patted my arm still hooked through his. "Hey, at least I get to play the date."

My heart hiccupped. Did that mean he wished we weren't pretending?

Focus! I headed for the cottage's door.

Nate caught my hand, stopping me short of the porch. "What are you doing?"

"Introducing myself." I tossed him a cheeky grin, but he didn't look as if he appreciated it.

He tightened his hold and stood his ground. "Are you sure that's a smart thing to do?"

"It's unexpected. Catching people off guard gives you the upper hand."

"Hmm, I'll have to remember that." His gaze dropped to my lips, and a tingly feeling swirled through my tummy.

The sensation was quickly eclipsed by the heat of Tanner's glare on the back of my head, and I extricated myself from Nate's grasp. He joined me at the door as I knocked.

Finally, an older guy in sweat pants, a T-shirt, and a ball cap opened the screen door. "No solicitation is allowed in this neighborhood," he barked.

At his voice, I did a double take. "Oh, you're Joe, right? The estate sales guy?" I almost didn't recognize him in the casual clothes. "We met outside the funeral home yesterday."

"Sorry, I don't remember. I go to the funeral home a lot." He had the decency to look sheepish about admitting to blatant solicitation after slamming me for it seconds earlier.

"You said you and Jack were old friends."

"Oh, right. You were with his niece. I remember now. How can I help you?"

"I'm here about the amulet."

"The amulet?"—he turned a tad peaked—"I'm sorry. I don't think I have one of those."

"The one you advertised on eBay," I pressed, hoping to trip him up. "I'm your 11:00 a.m. appointment."

"There must be some mistake."

I nixed my "you do realize it's a felony to lie to a federal agent?" line for a more amiable approach. "I know. I know. We were supposed to meet at the tabernacle, but I couldn't help but notice you watching from your second-story window. Not that I blame you. I know how it is. You can't be too careful these days when meeting a stranger."

"I wasn't watching you," he sputtered. His gaze bobbed

from Nate to me to the tabernacle grounds behind us. "Birding," he blurted. "That's what I was doing. Watching the birds. I'm a birder."

"Oh, I'm sorry." I didn't believe him, but I gave him my best I'm-so-embarrassed impression.

"It must be fascinating to watch for the rock ptarmigan migrating back to the area this time of year," Nate interjected.

Joe visibly relaxed. "Yes, that's always a spring highlight."

The corner of Nate's lip twitched. Oh, he was quick. And he knew his birds better than this supposed birder.

A phone rang from somewhere deeper in the house. "Excuse me," Joe said. "I need to get that." He shut the door in our faces before we could object.

"He's no birder," Nate said, escorting me back to the sidewalk.

I grinned. "Yeah, got that." I angled a peek down the side of the cottage, but the next one sat too close to allow a glimpse into the backyard, and it didn't look as if the street behind it would offer any better vantage point.

"It's past 11:00," Nate said. "We going to plant ourselves in front of the tabernacle just in case Joe was telling the truth about not being your scheduled appointment?"

I shifted my focus to the grounds around the tabernacle. There was no sign of anyone else besides Tanner.

"Why not?" I steered Nate toward a section less visible from Joe's windows. "I'm sure he was lying, but I want to see what he does next."

Carmen and Aunt Martha meandered up a far alleyway.

I texted her and asked her to stroll the next street and let me know if she saw Joe come out the back of the yellow and orange cottage. She texted back a smiley face and waved, before disappearing around the corner.

Five minutes passed. Ten.

Nate zeroed in on a petite Hispanic woman approaching the house. "You see that?"

"I see her." I glanced across the grassy grounds to where Tanner had parked himself on a bench with a decent view of both the house and tabernacle. His slight nod said he'd noticed the woman too.

The woman rapped her knuckles on the front door and immediately let herself in.

"There's no sign of Joe or anyone on the other street," Aunt Martha said, sashaying up to us, her arm hooked through Carmen's.

"Thanks anyway," I said.

"We walked back and forth more than half a dozen times," Carmen added. "Figured *we* were starting to look suspicious."

Aunt Martha tipped her head back and admired the tabernacle. "I hear they'll do weddings here," she gushed.

I choked on what I'd been about to say. Was that a hint for Nate? Or for Carmen?

Before any of us could offer a pithy comeback, a shriek erupted from Joe's cottage.

18

Tanner raced to Joe's cottage, with Nate and me right behind him.

The woman we'd seen enter the cottage a minute earlier burst out the door, gasping.

Tanner reached her first. "What's wrong?"

She frantically jabbed a number into her cell phone. "He's been stabbed!"

Tanner pushed through the door as Nate guided her to a chair on the porch. "Go on," he said to me. "I'll stay with her and make sure paramedics are on their way."

I nodded and raced inside.

"Over here," Tanner called from the direction of the kitchen.

Joe sat on the floor, his back propped against the counter, his legs sprawled, holding a tea towel to his neck.

"Who stabbed you?"

"No one stabbed me," Joe said, irritation bleeding through his voice.

Tanner picked up a small, half-full, blood-tipped hypodermic needle from under the edge of the oven. "Then where'd this come from?"

Joe snatched it from Tanner's hand, contaminating whatever fingerprints we might've lifted from the shaft. "I'm diabetic. Maria surprised me in the middle of preparing my insulin shot. My arm jerked. I must've fainted."

"Paramedics will be here soon," I reassured, not buying his explanation. Why on earth have the needle pointed toward his face in the first place?

"I don't need a paramedic." Joe started to push to his feet, then swaying a little, seemed to think better of the plan and plopped back on his behind. "I'll be fine. I just need to sit another minute."

The back door stood slightly ajar. I glanced out the window but didn't spot any movement. If only Aunt Martha had hung back a few moments longer. "Who else was here?" I asked.

Joe hesitated.

I pinned him with a sharp look.

"I told you. Maria, my housekeeper."

"She came in the front door. Who ran out the back?"

"No one." Joe did push to his feet this time and tossed the needle into a pail under the sink. "Thanks for checking on me. I'll be fine now."

Nate joined us. "He okay? Martha and Carmen are sitting with the woman. She's pretty shaken up."

"I'm fine," Joe reiterated, clearly losing his patience. His hand holding the tea towel dropped to his side, revealing a minor puncture that would probably be several nasty shades of purple by nightfall.

Tanner urged him to sit in a chair. "I'll feel better if you let me disinfect the wound before we go. Do you have anti-septic?"

Joe exhaled a resigned sigh. "The medicine cabinet in the bathroom at the top of the stairs."

"I'll get it," I volunteered and hurried to the stairs, pausing long enough to scan the tabletops and bookshelves of the adjoining living room for evidence of the Egyptian amulet or other antiquities. *Nothing.*

Nate trailed me up the stairs a moment later and whispered, "I told him I needed to use the facilities." He was starting to sound as eager a sleuth as Aunt Martha.

"If something's not in plain sight, we can't use it as evidence," I instructed him and opened a door that could've been the bathroom. It wasn't.

It was a long bedroom with a sloped ceiling, its decor Spartan.

Nate opened the door opposite. "Maybe this one's the bathroom."

It was a mirror image of the other bedroom, this one with a view of the tabernacle. "I would've expected a guy who sells estates for a living to have more furniture and knickknacks than he could use," I mused, scanning the room.

"Notice what else isn't here?" Nate asked.

I jerked my chin toward the stack of thrillers on the night table. "Birding books. No surprise there."

Nate stepped into the room, fished the end of his sleeve over his hand, and opened the night table drawer.

I smiled to myself at his improvisation.

"That's how they do it on TV," he said, apparently reading my thoughts. It was kind of unnerving how adept he was at doing that.

Nate glanced inside. "No binoculars either." He peeked around the open closet, under the bed. "Whoever ducked out of the back door could've been our peeping Tom."

"Maybe a partner." Maybe Ben.

"We don't need it anymore," a woman's voice drifted up the stairs. "The paramedics are here."

I hurried to the bathroom anyway and grabbed the disinfectant, accidentally on purpose leaving the medicine cabinet door open, then left the room to Nate and rushed back downstairs.

Joe's housekeeper stopped her ascent.

"You feeling better?" I asked, urging her to turn around with me and return to the kitchen.

"*Sí*, thank you for your help. You must think I'm *loco*. But I have this crazy fear of needles."

"Not a problem. I'm glad we could help."

"Your aunt and her friend told me to tell you they were heading to the restaurant," Maria went on, although somehow I suspected that wasn't *all* Aunt Martha was doing.

By the time the paramedics finished treating the wound, Nate had returned, but the slight shake of his head said he hadn't found anything useful.

Joe shuffled us toward the door along with the paramedics, muttering his thanks.

I hovered in the doorway long enough for the paramedics to move out of earshot and then said to Joe, "I'm guessing whoever did this to you already informed you that I'm a federal agent."

His Adam's apple bobbed.

"Are you confident you'll survive his next visit?"

"I told you. It was an accident."

"Hmm. You realize it'll only take a phone call to trace the source of the eBay ad."

He squirmed.

"If we discover it's you, you could be charged with obstruction of justice."

"Okay, yes, I placed the ad. It's not a crime and neither is changing my mind about wanting to sell the amulet."

"Is that what happened?"

"Yes, that is, my client did," he said tersely. "Now if you'll please excuse me, I need to recheck my blood sugar."

I stuck my foot in the doorway. "Wait. Did your client say why?"

"No."

"What's his name?" Tanner interjected.

Joe's attention snapped from my foot to Tanner. "That's privileged."

Tanner snorted. "You're not a lawyer, doctor, or priest."

"Clients expect discretion."

"We can get a court order," I said.

"You do that." Joe kicked my foot out of the way and closed the door without waiting for a response.

Tanner squinted at the door as if he had X-ray vision and could see what Joe was up to behind it. "Do you think Joe was the smuggler your uncle planned to report to the feds?"

"I think it'd be prudent to watch what he does next," I said.

"Maybe we should try asking Marianne about him," Nate suggested. "She seemed to despise Joe enough to expose all his secrets."

"The woman just lost the two most important men in her life," Tanner countered. "Do you honestly think she's going to care about filling you in on Joe's lack of business ethics?"

"If she thinks his *business* is connected to Jack's death she will," I argued.

Tanner gave me his patronizing field-training-officer look. "You can't go in there like a bull in a china shop and expect to get answers. You need to tread lightly."

"We can do that." I just wish I didn't sound so defensive saying it. It wasn't as if I wanted to intrude on Marianne's grief. I turned to Tanner. "Do you mind keeping an eye on Joe? In case he makes a move."

"I can do that," Tanner said tersely.

"Oh, and maybe question the neighbors," I added. "Find out if anyone saw someone leave by the back door, because I'm 95 percent positive Joe was lying about no one else being there."

"Already tried." Aunt Martha and Carmen sidled up from around the side of the house. "No one's home."

I suppressed a grin. I knew her restaurant comment to the housekeeper had to be a ruse. Aunt Martha's curiosity was too acute to allow her to walk away from something so suspicious.

"What now?" Aunt Martha asked.

"Nate and I need to pay Marianne a visit," I said, as Nate thumbed something into his phone. "Why don't you and Carmen have lunch at the cafe, and we'll catch up with you there?"

"You don't need me to give you a lift?" Carmen asked.

Nate showed me the map on his phone's screen. "No need. Marianne lives only a couple of blocks away. We can cut through here."

Carmen caught Aunt Martha's hand. "We'll see you later then."

Aunt Martha looked as if she'd rather tag along with us, but she didn't say so.

As we turned onto Marianne's street, a shiny black sedan crawled past. "Hey, was that Frank Dale?"

"That's his license plate, all right," Nate confirmed.

I gaped at him. "You memorized his plate?"

"Never mind that. Call Tanner. It's too coincidental that Frank would be in the neighborhood now. He could be the visitor Joe refused to ID."

I made the call, and for half a minute Tanner and I debated whether it was smarter to follow Frank or sit on Joe.

"You're going to lose him," Nate said as the sedan disappeared around the corner.

"I'll follow him," Tanner muttered from the other end of the line.

"If you get the chance, check him and his car for binoculars," I said a second before Tanner clicked off.

Nate chuckled.

"What's so funny?" If he were Tanner, I might've suspected him of fibbing about Frank's license plate. Sending Nate on a wild goose chase was just the kind of prank Tanner would pull.

Nate once again caught my hand in his. "Just appreciating getting to have you to myself for a while."

"Tanner's happier being on the hunt anyway."

Nate shook his head. "You might be a highly trained special agent, but I'm afraid you have blinders on when it comes to Tanner."

"Nah, he's like a big brother. Just likes to give me grief."

Nate's pressed lips and micro-shrug said he thought I was deluding myself.

He must've seen last night's kiss between Tanner and me—the one I'd been pointedly trying to forget.

Okay, maybe I *was* deluding myself. My big brother sure never kissed me like that.

19

Nate stopped me before we turned onto Marianne's street. "Wait here a minute." He ducked down the next street and emerged a few minutes later with a bakery box.

"What's in there?"

"Fresh-baked cookies. She probably doesn't have much of an appetite these days, but I remember appreciating our neighbors bringing my brother and me food after our parents died."

My heart crunched at his thoughtfulness and his loss and the gravity of Marianne's situation. *I can tread lightly*, I repeated to myself to block out the echo of Tanner's bull-in-the-china-shop jab.

"It'll be okay," Nate reassured, but his uncanny ability to sense what I was thinking was starting to creep me out.

What other thoughts had he *overheard*?

At the sight of a red sports car parked on the street, I slowed my pace. "Looks like Marianne's daughter is there too."

Nate squinted through the car's passenger window.

Sunlight glistened off a sun catcher, made of wire and sea glass, hanging from the rearview mirror.

Nate pointed to it. "Looks like Carly might be a sea glass collector."

"You know the sea glass won't be admissible evidence, and even if it was, any decent lawyer would argue it could've fallen out of anyone's pocket long before Jack's death. It's not a clue we can put stock in." No matter how many times we seemed to be reminded of it.

The front door of the little purple gingerbread cottage opened, and Marianne's head poked out. "May I help you?" she said—only she didn't sound as if she wanted to be helpful.

I smiled. "We were admiring the sun catcher in your daughter's car. Did she make it?"

Marianne hugged her middle with trembling arms. "That's *my* car. And I made the ornament."

"Wow. It's amazing." I crossed to her front porch, the crushed-seashell path crunching beneath my feet.

Marianne's wary look edged toward alarm. "What are you doing here?"

My heart jumped to my throat with the realization that she probably feared more bad news. It always seemed to come in threes.

Nate stepped beside me and held up the bakery box. "We wanted to extend our condolences."

Marianne's gaze dropped from his face to the box and back to his face. She blinked, looking confused. "Do I know you?"

"Oh, I'm sorry. This is my friend Nate." I reached for her hand and clasped it in both of mine, real sympathy edging out my ulterior motives as I felt its fragile trembling. "I was so sorry to hear about your son's death. No one should have to face so much loss in such a short time. If there's anything I can do . . ."

She shook her head, then tugged her hand from my grasp and covered her mouth, muffling a sob. "Everyone's being so kind."

Nate solicitously clasped her elbow and guided her back across the threshold to a nearby sofa. I sat on one of the armchairs kitty-corner to it in a cozy arrangement facing the front window and a small TV.

"What you need is a nice hot cup of tea to go with these cookies," Nate said.

Marianne pushed to her feet, but Nate smiled in that sincere way he had that no woman could oppose and gently pushed her back down. "You sit. I'll make it." He disappeared into the kitchen.

"I really don't feel up to company," Marianne said, but I could tell Nate's charm was weakening her resistance

"You'll enjoy Nate's tea," I reassured, capitalizing on his headway. "He knows how to make it right."

Marianne offered a tremulous smile.

If only Tanner could see me now. Nate and I made a pretty good team. And not a single broken china cup in sight!

Marianne leaned back a fraction on the sofa, although she still didn't look comfortable.

"While we wait," I said casually, "I was hoping you could tell me what you know about Joe."

Her face blanched. "I don't know anything. Please—" She sprang back to her feet. "I'd like you to go."

My hand lifted in inarticulate protest as my heart sank. *Oh no.* Tanner would never let me live this down. *Bull – 1, Serena – 0.*

Before I could attempt a save, Nate appeared in the kitchen doorway, holding a stack of small plates. He smiled at Marianne, and she sank back down onto the sofa with a wordless little exhalation.

Nate placed the plates beside the box of cookies on the coffee table, reengaging Marianne in comforting small talk while I glumly envisioned a stampeding bull goring the TV set, then charging through the shelf holding Marianne's Precious Moments figurines.

Just as the imaginary shards of decimated figurines hit the carpet, Nate shot me a significant look and I hastily regrouped.

Right. I was a good interrogator. My instructor at Quantico had told me as much.

I looked at Marianne's watery, bloodshot eyes, and my heart tumbled in my chest. Tanner was right. This case was uncomfortably personal for me, but that didn't mean I couldn't be a professional.

Nate spoke from the kitchen doorway. "Ashley tells me your son was a tour director like Serena's brother."

Marianne stiffened at the mention of my brother. Or maybe at the occupation he had in common with Marianne's son . . . especially if Detective Moore had shared with her his theory that Charlie exploited the occupation to smuggle drugs.

"If Charlie was anything like my brother, I'm sure he loved every minute of his job," I said. "The chance to travel to exotic places and meet lots of different people."

"Yes," she mumbled and perched on the edge of the sofa once more, her back rigid.

Nate returned with a tray of tea. "Charlie must've had

lots of suggestions for where you and Jack could go on your honeymoon."

If looks could kill, mine would've slayed him. What was he thinking bringing up memories of the honeymoon she'd never have?

But her puffy eyes got a wistful, faraway look in them. "Yes, Charlie was helping us plan a trip through South America. He and Jack spent hours poring over possibilities." Blinking rapidly, she accepted the cup of tea Nate pressed into her hands.

I clapped shut my gaping mouth. Not that I should be surprised she found comfort in the recollection. After my granddad died, I'd longed to reminisce about him with others.

"With Jack owning his own business," Nate went on, "I imagine he was happy to give himself an extra long holiday too."

A tiny smile teased up the corners of Marianne's lips. "Yes, Frank told Jack to take as long as we wanted." She dabbed at her eyes with the facial tissue crushed in her hand. "He's been so sweet."

"Has Frank been to see you?" I asked, hoping to circle around to his appearance in the neighborhood and possible visit to Joe's.

"Yes, he was just here." She sipped her tea, her posture relaxing a little. "He wanted to make sure Carly and I were okay and to let her know she could take as much time off work as she needed."

I added another drop of milk to the tea Nate had poured for me. Then in a tone that betrayed only mild curiosity, I asked, "How long did Frank visit?"

Marianne's gaze darted to the small mantel clock sitting on the bookcase. "I'm not sure. An hour or so."

Hmm. Based on how long we were at Joe's after the attack, Frank could have fled from there to Marianne's to establish an alibi for his presence in Oak Bluffs. In Marianne's state, she would likely concur with whatever time he said he got here. "Where's Carly now?" I asked.

Marianne's teacup rattled in its saucer. "I don't know!" She plunked the cup and saucer on the end table and snatched up a fresh tissue. "I told Frank I was worried about her. The police kept asking about drugs, as if that's what got Charlie killed." Marianne wrung the tissue in her hands. "Carly lost her temper. Stormed off on her bike. Without her coat. Or her phone. Frank said he'd drive around and try to find her."

"She's been gone all night?"

Marianne shook her head. "Since this morning. I wasn't in any condition to answer questions when the police came last night and gave us the horrible news." She suddenly stood up, walked over to a computer desk in the wide hallway leading from the room, and then handed me a photo of Carly and Charlie beaming at the camera, their arms slung across each other's shoulders. "That's my Charlie. He was a good man. He didn't have anything to do with drugs."

"How do you think he ended up in the water?" Nate asked gently, as I discreetly texted Tanner an update on Frank.

"He was probably fishing and had a spill," Marianne said. "Charlie loved to fish."

My mind zigzagged to Tanner's suspicions of Preston as I scrutinized the photo more closely. "Whose truck is this?" The pair stood in front of a Jeep that looked an awful lot like the one that mowed down Dad.

"Charlie's."

But Charlie wasn't on the island when Jack was killed, so why come after Dad and me? It couldn't be the same truck. It didn't fit. Not when Charlie was dead now too.

"The police still haven't found it." Marianne's bottom lip quivered as if she might start crying again. "But . . . they're hoping when they do, its location will tell them where Charlie—" Her voice cracked. She swallowed hard. "Where Charlie fell into the water."

Nate gave her arm a reassuring squeeze. "Perhaps your daughter went looking for the truck too."

Oh no. That wouldn't be good. If Charlie was part of a drug ring, as Moore suspected, and if Carly happened upon her brother's truck and saw something she shouldn't, she could be next.

Marianne shook her head. "She would've asked to borrow my car to do that."

"Carly doesn't have a vehicle of her own?" She looked to be around my age. Too old to be relying on a parent's car.

"No, she's always borrowed mine. Or Charlie's truck when he was off the island."

"Wow, nice brother. Mine would never let me touch his baby." I set the photo on the table next to the tea tray, debating how to steer the story around to Joe without causing her to give me the boot, now that I was rocking this soft interrogation thing, thank-you-very-much.

Nate touched Marianne's arm once more, and as her attention returned to him, his fingers curled around her wrist, although she didn't seem aware of it. His baby blue eyes could be very disarming.

What was he up to?

Nate's gaze shifted to some point beyond Marianne's shoulder. "Are those Bushnell binoculars?"

She startled. "Pardon me?"

Nate released her wrist and pointed to the binoculars on the bookshelf behind her. "I'm interested in getting a pair for myself. Are those ones good?"

"Oh . . . yes . . . they are."

I sent Nate a curious glance. Did he think Marianne had been at Joe's?

But she hated him. Then again . . . Joe did have a needle in his neck when we found him. Or maybe Frank brought the binoculars here from Joe's so they wouldn't be found in his car.

Marianne pressed her fingers to her temple. "I'm afraid I need to lie down. I have a headache coming on. Thank you for the visit and the cookies."

"Here"—Nate gathered the teacups onto the tray—"let me get these for you before we go." He shot me a pointed look.

Yeah, my last chance. Got it. "Marianne, did Frank mention paying that flea market vendor, Joe, a visit before he came here?"

Genuine surprise lit her eyes. "No. Why?"

"Did Jack mention to you calling the FBI?"

Concern joined surprise in her widening eyes. "No. Why?"

"At the funeral home yesterday, I sensed you knew more about Joe than you were saying. Are you aware of any illegal buying and selling he's been party to?"

She snorted. "Have you ever known a pawn broker who doesn't turn a blind eye to where something came from?"

"Hmm. But do you know of something for a fact?"

Massaging her temples, Marianne stood.

Uh oh, the bull was back.

Marianne glanced into the kitchen. "Just leave the dishes. Thank you," she said to Nate, then to me added, "I'm sorry. I do need to lie down."

Nate joined me in the hall. "You take care."

We stepped onto the front porch, and after the door closed behind us, I whispered, "What was with the wrist holding in there?"

"I saw it on a *Mentalist* episode." He winked. "Who needs Quantico when you can learn it all from TV?"

"And what, pray tell, did you learn?"

Nate started down the street. "Her pulse jumped when I asked about the binoculars."

I matched his strides. "Which made you deduce what?"

"That she was afraid I'd make the connection to Joe."

"Wait. You think *she* was the one at Joe's?"

"No, I suspect it was Frank, but I'm not sure why she'd cover for him."

I mulled that over for a moment. "She must not suspect him of having anything to do with Jack's or Charlie's deaths."

"Doesn't mean he didn't."

"True. Jack could've confronted him about a new addition to his antiquities collection. Maybe Frank offered to buy him out to buy his silence, but Jack wouldn't go for it."

"And Joe could've been his middleman, but Frank recognized you, sensed a setup, and told Joe to play dumb about the amulet. They could've quarreled over it afterward. Would explain the needle jab and why Joe pretended it was self-inflicted."

"Seems like a plausible motive, but what we need is solid

evidence." I thumbed a text message to Tanner to find out if his tail had materialized into anything yet.

"Don't forget about Ben," Nate said as we headed toward the restaurant where we'd agreed to meet Aunt Martha. "He's got to fit into this somehow."

"Yeah, maybe it's time to confront Lisa again. She must know more about his whereabouts than she's admitted."

My phone rang. "It's Tanner." I clicked CONNECT.

"Did you cut yourself?"

"What?"

"On the broken china."

"What?"

"Bull in china shop." Tanner chortled.

"Ha-ha. Did you get anything on Frank?"

"Yeah, you're going to want to get over here."

20

I jotted down the address Tanner gave me for Charlie's house, then Nate and I sprinted to the Slice of Life Cafe.

Aunt Martha and Carmen were sitting on the covered front porch sipping tea. "Ah, good, you're here. We were beginning to think you forgot about us," Aunt Martha said as we rushed inside. "We already finished eating."

"That's great, because we have to go."

Carmen and Aunt Martha sprang to their feet, and Carmen tossed more than enough money on the table to cover their lunch bill. "Where to?"

Nate glanced at his smartphone. "Seaview Avenue toward Edgartown."

"Ooh, isn't this exciting?" Aunt Martha cooed, scurrying toward Carmen's rental parked on a side street by Union Chapel.

Nate flashed me a grin. He always got a kick out of Aunt Martha's enthusiasm for a good mystery.

Hello? Two dead bodies and Joe with a needle in his neck, I telepathed.

Carmen careened right onto Ocean Avenue and picked up speed on the incline to Seaview.

"Watch that car," Aunt Martha cautioned as he turned onto Seaview without stopping at the intersection.

"Get us there alive," Nate quipped.

Carmen shot a panicked look to the rearview mirror, and my heart plunged. "What's wrong?"

He threw the car into neutral and pumped the brakes. "We've lost the brakes."

The incline steepened.

"Drive into the field." Aunt Martha pointed to the park opposite Inkwell Beach, empty except for a lone jogger and his dog. Thank goodness kids were still in school!

Carmen swerved, just missing the fence, and plowed over the little white painted boulders with a skull-rattling thunk. Airbags exploded from the front dash. Unfortunately, Nate and I had no such cushioning and banged our heads on the backs of Carmen's and Aunt Martha's seats.

Aunt Martha batted the deflating airbag out of her face. "Look out for the dog!"

Carmen swerved blindly and inadvertently kicked the gas in his reflexive impulse to brake.

I braced my arm on the back of the seat as we bumped over a hunk of wood, heading straight at the cars parked along the other side of the field. "Crank it right. Right."

He did and within another twenty yards, the car ran out of momentum and came to a stop.

I tumbled out of the backseat with an unladylike groan as approaching sirens blared. I massaged my aching neck. "Are you two okay?"

"Right as rain," Aunt Martha said, sounding as exhilarated

as if she'd just climbed off a horse at the Flying Horses carousel down the road. "Those airbags really work!"

Carmen dropped onto his back and shimmied under the car. Nate did the same from the passenger side.

I hit Tanner's number on my speed dial. "Can you pick us up?"

"Uh, no, we've got a situation here. What's going on?"

"Car trouble."

"Well, get here as fast as you can," Tanner said.

A squad car screeched to a stop at the curb, and the officer jogged across the field toward us. "What do you think you're doing?"

"Our car lost its brakes," I explained. "We drove into the park to slow it down."

"The brake line's been cut," Carmen barked from beneath the car. He crawled out and wiped his grease-covered hands on the tissue Aunt Martha handed him.

"Both lines," Nate confirmed, rising from the other side of the car.

My heart rioted as my mind zigzagged through who knew I was here. Joe. Frank. But neither would have known what car I came in.

The officer whipped out a notepad and pen. "Who are you? Why would someone cut your brakes?"

"To try to kill us. Why do you think?" Carmen groused.

Nausea roiled through my stomach. Preston had been in the adjoining bathroom when I made plans with Aunt Martha this morning. He could've easily overheard us. I didn't want to believe he could've done this. But he'd also been out in his truck the night Dad was hit. And he could've easily identified Carmen's rental.

"And you are?" the officer asked Carmen.

"Carmen Malgucci."

The officer's pen slid off his notepad. "Of the Malgucci crime family?"

"We're here from St. Louis," I interjected, identifying myself as a fed. "I've been investigating an art crime that may be connected to the recent homicides on the island. I assume that's why we've been targeted."

The muscle in Carmen's cheek noticeably flinched.

"What?" I said.

Carmen shrugged. "Some of my relatives have crossed a few people."

The officer's gaze darted past the gathering crowd of gawkers to one end of the road, then the other. "Are we talking organized crime?"

Oh, great. Martha's Vineyard was a popular playground for the rich. Why not vacationing mobsters? Yes, why not? Better them than my prime suspects.

"I'm sorry, dear," Aunt Martha said to me, pressing her phone to her ear.

"Who are you calling?" I asked as Carmen told the cop where the car had been parked and suggested pulling footage from any security cameras in the area that might've filmed whoever did this.

"Winston." Aunt Martha turned her focus to the ground and spoke into the phone. "Yes, it's me. Seems a bird-watcher has clipped our wings."

I smiled at her colorful description. Her friend probably didn't have a clue what she was talking about.

"Could you pick us up at the park across from Inkwell Beach?" she went on. "My niece has somewhere she needs to be." She clicked off and returned her attention to me. "He'll be here in five minutes."

"Wow, thank you. He lives that close?"

She thrust her chin in the direction we'd come. "Beside that anti-virus software magnate's mansion on Ocean Avenue."

I whistled. "Nice."

"Carmen and I can handle the incident report," Aunt Martha said.

"Thanks." I gave the officer my business card. "I need to go. If you have any more questions for me, you can reach me at the cell number."

He didn't look like he was agreeable to the idea of my leaving, but I headed toward the street before he could argue.

Behind me a car door slammed, then the slap of shoes closed in on me. "Wait," Nate said. "You forgot something."

I glanced over my shoulder. "You?"

"And your purse." He held up my bag, which he must've grabbed from the backseat of the car. I glanced at my watch, wondering what Tanner had uncovered at Charlie's and if our saboteur had taken off after him after disabling our ride.

Thirty seconds later a shiny new Land Rover pulled to the curb behind the police car. Winston jumped out and tossed the keys to Nate. "Take good care of her."

"You're leaving it with us?" I guess I didn't do a good job of keeping the surprise from my voice, because he laughed.

"I live on an island. It's not as if you could get far if you decided to steal it. And don't worry about your aunt and her friend. I'll make sure they're set up with a new pair of wheels too."

"I appreciate it. Thanks."

He glanced past us and shook his head at the scene in

the field. "Looks like a page right out of the playbook of Madame X."

"You've heard of Madame X?" I turned to Nate and explained, "Madame X is legendary in federal law enforcement circles. Pulling off stunts no one thought possible. Think female James Bond." I grinned at Winston. "Were you CIA? FBI?"

"Secret Service."

"Wow, I knew Aunt Martha had a lot of well-connected friends back in the day, but I had no idea how well connected. So, you actually met Madame X? What was she like?"

"We'd better get going," Nate interjected. "Tanner's waiting."

I ducked my head, suddenly realizing how fan-girl I must've sounded. "Right." I shook Winston's hand and climbed into the car beside Nate. "Do you think we should've stuck around? Aunt Martha is going to have the cops bothering Joe with her bird-watcher allegations, but even if he had an accomplice, I—"

"I don't think that's who Martha meant by a bird-watcher." Nate pulled into traffic.

"What do you mean?"

"*Birdwatcher* is British slang for spy."

"It is? How do you know that?"

Nate chuckled. "I used to watch those mysteries she loves so much with her."

"Ahh. Because I can't see how Frank would've known what car I came to town in. Carmen parked blocks away from the tabernacle."

"Assuming *you* were the target."

"You think it could've been Carmen?"

Nate quirked the same noncommittal shrug as Carmen had. "The rental is registered in his name."

"Sure, but it doesn't take any advance planning to decide to cut a brake line. Anyone could've seen me arrive in Oak Bluffs. And then waited for his chance." *Anyone*.

"You think it was Ben?"

It was my turn to offer the noncommittal shrug. I didn't like the idea of it being Ben any better than Preston. But it made more sense.

"Ashley know anything about cars?" Nate asked.

"Seriously?"

"Hey, the day I arrived, she was convinced you were here to steal her fiancé. Jealousy can make a person do crazy things."

"Well, now that you *and* Tanner are here, I'm sure she can see that I have my hands full."

He grinned. "So, who is winning?"

Oh man, my mouth needed brakes worse than Carmen's car.

Nate turned the corner onto Charlie's street.

A squad car with flashing lights was parked in front of it, and a cop was patting down a suspect taking the position—his hands on the squad car's trunk, his feet spread apart.

"Whoa, is that Tanner?"

21

Nate pulled to the curb two car lengths behind the cruiser, grinning from ear to ear at the sight of Tanner being frisked. "Isn't that the cop who was investigating Charlie?" Nate pointed to the plain-clothed Wahlberg look-alike standing on the sidewalk, watching the pat down, a phone to his ear, and scrutinizing what looked like Tanner's FBI badge.

I opened the car door. "You'd better wait here." I strode toward the detective, my hands out where the other edgy-looking uniformed cop dealing with Tanner could see them. "Detective Moore, that agent's working with me."

He pocketed his phone, having finished the phone call that had probably confirmed the badge was legit, and nodded to the cop. "Give him back his gun." Detective Moore handed Tanner his badge. "Sorry about that, but you can see how it looked."

"What happened?" I asked.

Tanner's gaze strayed to the windshield of the Land Rover we'd pulled up in, and he grimaced.

Yeah, Nate was going to love reminding him of this one.

"When I heard the dispatcher report a prowler at his address," Moore explained, "I thought I might catch one of Charlie's drug contacts."

"He saw me peering in the side window," Tanner continued. "I followed Frank here and after he went inside, I circled the house to see what he was up to. That's when I realized he wasn't alone and called you. The detective here pulled up in an unmarked car as I was testing the window lock."

I rolled my lips to keep from smiling. From the grass stains on Tanner's knees, it looked as if the detective had caught him by surprise.

"And of course," Tanner went on, "he didn't believe I was a fed any more than I believed he was a cop, so I resisted."

I nodded. "Who else is in the house with Frank?"

"Carly. The victim's sister," Detective Moore said. "Another uniform is babysitting them. I'm heading in to talk to them now. Care to join me?"

"Lead the way." As we fell into step beside each other, I asked, "So you still think Charlie is part of a drug ring?"

"We didn't find any antiquities in his place, if that's what you were hoping. But his truck had traces of cocaine in it."

"Where'd you find his truck?"

"The east shore of Tisbury Great Pond. You know it?"

"Yes, my parents are staying at a friend's place a few hundred yards inland from the west shore."

"The location's consistent with where the tide carried his body. According to the coast guard, the undercurrent in the channel between the pond and the ocean is treacherous."

I nodded. "My uncle always warned us not to play around it. Find any other evidence in the truck?"

"No sign of foul play." Detective Moore opened the front

door and motioned me to precede him inside, then squinted back at Tanner, who'd started up the walk. "Your partner looked more peeved about you showing up with that other guy than about being patted down," Moore observed.

I chuckled. "That's because he knows Nate's going to have too much fun teasing him about it."

"Nah, I don't think that's it." Moore shot me a wink as he followed me inside.

I choked on my next question as I glanced at Tanner, not sure I wanted to know how Moore had jumped to that conclusion. Nope, definitely sure I didn't want to know. "How about the truck's body? Any man-sized dents in the front fender?"

Moore paused in the entranceway. "The trauma on Charlie's body was consistent with being battered against the rocks. You think he was run over by his own truck then thrown in?"

I lowered my voice. "A truck like Charlie's ran my dad down outside Jack Hill's house Wednesday night."

Moore's brow furrowed. "And you think Charlie was the driver? Why?"

"We'd just exited Jack's house, so I figured the driver was worried we'd happened upon something he didn't want found. But if there's no evidence he was smuggling antiquities then he's probably not our man."

"Your perp could've just been distracted by his cell phone or from having too much to drink at the beach."

"Was there a dent in the fender?" Tanner irritably repeated my question as he joined us in the hall.

"It had a few dings. Seems to be an epidemic with vehicles on the island. But you're welcome to stop by the police compound and take a look at it." Moore led the way into the living room and dismissed the female officer who'd been sitting with Frank and Carly.

They both sprang to their feet. "What are you doing here?"

"Assisting Detective Moore with his investigation."

"You're a cop?" Carly asked, shock lifting her voice.

"A federal agent." I guess I shouldn't have assumed Jack or Ashley would've mentioned my job to her. "I specialize in art crime investigations."

Carly's eyes dilated with an emotion I wasn't sure how to interpret. Her gaze abruptly shifted to Frank.

He fisted his hands. "We don't know anything about any art crime. Why are we being detained?"

"You were trespassing," Detective Moore said firmly.

Carly turned away. Given her theatrics the day we arrived at Jack's, I expected her to get in Moore's face, tell him she had every right to be here. Instead she picked up an old framed family photograph from the end table and traced the faces. "Charlie left the house to me," she whispered, her bottom lip quivering, her watery gaze fixed on the image.

"And I was looking for Carly," Frank interjected. "Her mother was worried about her."

"Was the house unlocked when you arrived?" Moore asked before I had a chance to suggest separating the pair—an action that should've been taken from the start.

"Yes," Frank said. "I saw a bike—which turned out to be Carly's—lying in the driveway and found her inside."

Carly returned the photograph to the table, then sank onto the sofa and hugged her legs. Her sleeves rode up her arms, revealing bright red marks the size of thumbs and fingers.

She tugged the sleeves back to her wrists and slanted a wary glance at Moore before ducking her head.

"I'd scarcely gotten past 'hello' when your men arrived," Frank went on.

"Did Frank threaten you?" I asked Carly.

Her gaze snapped up. "What?" She darted another glance at Moore. "No." Her gaze skittered to the hall beyond—a hall with three closed doors, likely two bedrooms and a closet I trusted the pair of cops now waiting outside had cleared, as well as an open bathroom door.

"We should question them separately," Tanner said and reached for the first door handle as if it would open to a room to suit our purposes.

Carly's gaze abruptly dropped, and Tanner took that as a cue to draw his weapon and step to the side before pushing open the door. The room was empty, except for a desk and chair.

Frank's face reddened. "What is going on here?"

"That's what we're here to find out." Detective Moore clasped Frank's elbow and motioned toward the hall. "Would you mind stepping with me into the other room so we can talk in private?"

Frank jerked his arm from Moore's grasp. "Yes, I mind. I know my rights. Unless you're arresting me, I don't need to stay here and talk to you."

"We're trying to determine who may've wanted Charlie dead," Moore said. "Why wouldn't you want to help us?"

Frank shook his head and pointed a finger at me. "She said she's an art crime investigator. This isn't about Charlie."

Moore cocked his head. "I investigate drug crimes. Are we getting warmer?"

Carly's fingers dug into the couch. "I already told your people last night that Charlie didn't do drugs! Not ever." She swiped at a tear that leaked onto her cheek but didn't meet our gazes.

Frank joined Carly on the sofa and pulled her into an embrace. "Of course he didn't, dear. You mustn't let their questions disturb you."

From the way she stiffened and looked at him, she seemed as disturbed by her boss's sudden hug as Moore's innuendo.

Seeming not to notice, Frank patted her back and looked up at Moore. "Are we through now?"

I sensed we'd get more out of Carly if we cut Frank loose, so I signaled to Moore to let him go.

Frank stood and when Carly didn't rise too, he stretched his hand toward her. "Aren't you coming?"

She shook her head. "I . . . I want to go through more of Charlie's stuff. Can you let Mom know I'm okay?"

"Of course. You take care now." Frank graced the rest of us with a terse nod, and Moore escorted him out.

Tanner motioned down the hall. I'm going to use the facilities—code for I'm going to look around.

I tugged a chair kitty-corner to Carly's spot and then hunching forward, gently nudged up one of her sleeves. "Did Frank do that to you?"

Her eyelids all but bounced off her eyebrows. "No."

"Then who was it, Carly? The marks don't look as if they could've been made long before Tanner got here."

"I . . . I . . ." She gripped her wrists with the opposite hands, her fingers turning white. "I do it to myself sometimes."

"What's down the hall?" I asked, catching her sneak another glance that way.

Her attention cut to me. "Nothing. Just rooms. And that other agent."

The room shuddered, as if an outside door had been opened and let in a gust of air. I lurched up and glanced around the corner—not the front door. Tanner had closed the bathroom door. Could that have done it?

Carly's face was white. On impulse, I pushed open the second bedroom door just as someone jumped out the window. "He's getting away," I shouted to Tanner and raced out the front door. "Stop him!" I shouted to the cops I expected to find outside, but the police cruiser was gone and Frank's car was just pulling away from the curb.

Moore must've thought I'd meant Frank and lurched after the car, managing to slap the rear fender before Frank sped off, ignoring him. I sprinted for the corner of the house just as the male Caucasian raced past and veered right with Tanner in hot pursuit.

Nate jerked open his driver's door, slamming it bull's-eye into the young man's gut. Sent him flying on his rear. As Nate scrambled out, the rest of us pulled our guns on our runner.

The guy's hands shot in the air. "I didn't do anything. I didn't do anything," he shouted in a whiny, defensive tone I'd recognize anywhere. Ben's.

22

"Ben?" My voice choked up with a rush of emotion. Oh, wow, I hadn't realized until that moment how worried I'd been about him. I'm not sure I would've recognized him if he hadn't spoken, though.

His former blond crew cut had grown out into a mousey brown shag, and he had the kind of beard donned by terrorists in the video clips they were so fond of airing. I shuddered.

"Benjamin Hill, you have a lot of explaining to do."

"This is the nephew?" Tanner braced his hands on his knees and sucked in air.

"You okay?" I asked.

"Yeah. I caught him in the backyard, but the kid's slippery."

Moore patted Ben down and then pulled a pair of handcuffs from his utility belt.

"Those won't be necessary," I said. "Will they, Ben?"

"No," Ben said between huffs of his own. "I'm on your side."

I bristled at the claim I'd heard far too many times from worse slime than Ben. Although if he'd been smuggling antiquities for the slimeball who killed Uncle Jack, I might have to rethink the rating. "Why'd you tell Ashley you missed your flight?" I asked, hoping to lower his guard a little further before asking about Charlie's and Jack's deaths.

"I hated to not be there for her. I swear. But I had to figure out what was going on."

"Okay, so explain it to us."

"Don't you have to read him his rights first?" Nate asked.

Ben's eyes practically popped out of his head. "What's he talking about? I didn't kill Charlie!"

"His is the least of the suspicious deaths you look good for," Nate said.

I glared at him. We were just talking. Ben wasn't under arrest.

Nate splayed his fingers, palms out, and backed out of my way. Moore impatiently slapped the handcuffs he was still holding against the side of his leg.

Okay, clearly as far as Moore was concerned, Ben was under arrest. I recited his Miranda rights.

Ben vigorously shook his head. "Serena, you know I'd never kill Uncle Jack."

"We know you were already on the island that night, and your lies to Ashley about your whereabouts are pretty incriminating," I said.

"Yes, I arrived earlier than planned and hitchhiked to Uncle Jack's. But when I got to his house, he wasn't there. I saw a woman through the window. I assumed it was Ashley. I dropped my backpack behind the porch chair and called to her. Whoever was inside doused the lights, and the next thing I knew I was waking up on the porch with a sore head."

"What time was that?"

"I don't know. Late. After dark. At first I thought Ashley must've figured I was a prowler and bonked me, but then that didn't make sense. Once I was out, she would've recognized me." He scratched his beard. "Even with this. That's when I realized I must've surprised a prowler. I let myself in the house, but it didn't look as if it'd been trashed or anything. I searched the fridge for ice for my head, and when I couldn't find any, I headed across the compound to Ashley's. But she wasn't home either, so I started walking to Preston's, figuring I'd find her there."

"Why didn't you just call her cell phone?"

"I wanted to surprise her."

"Okay, so then what happened?"

"Lisa was driving out of the beach area as I came up on Preston's place. I must've looked out of it, swaying and stuff, because she ordered me into her car. I told her she could just leave me at Preston's, but there were no lights on at his place."

I exchanged a glance with Nate. Preston had said he was home the night Jack died.

"We tried calling Uncle Jack a few times over the next couple of hours, and finally Lisa suggested I just sleep on her couch until morning. I ended up sleeping until early afternoon." He rubbed his head, as if remembering the goose egg he'd incurred. "By then Lisa had gone out, so I walked down to Jack's. I saw Marianne's red sports car whip into the driveway, then saw the cop a nanosecond before Carly accused me and Ashley of murdering Uncle Jack."

Ben clutched his head. "I dropped to my knees, stunned. Then self-preservation kicked in and I ducked into the woods."

"Why?"

"I figured I knew why Uncle Jack had been killed. And that I'd be next."

My heart dropped a beat as my mind flashed to the hit-and-run that could've taken out Dad and me. "Why's that?"

He slanted an edgy glance from Tanner to Moore.

Moore narrowed his eyes. "We know about the drug ring. You give us names and we'll make sure you have protection."

Ben looked at Moore as if the policeman were smoking way too much of the drugs he was all but accusing Ben of smuggling.

"Ben?" I pressed when he didn't respond.

Ben's gaze snapped back to mine. "I don't know anything about drugs."

Moore emitted an impatient grunt. "This is getting us nowhere." He ratcheted the handcuff and slapped it onto Ben's wrist. "We'll finish this at the station."

Ben struggled against his hold. "What are you arresting me for? I didn't—"

"Breaking and entering for a start." Moore clamped the second bracelet around Ben's other wrist.

"Wait." I clasped Moore's arm as he repeated Ben's Miranda warning, which I was sure was only meant to intimidate Ben further since Moore didn't intend to question him until they got to the station, where the warning would have to be repeated yet again.

I waited for Moore to finish, then asked Ben again, "Why was Jack killed?"

Ben's shoulders slumped, the fight draining out of him. "Because we were going to report an antiquity smuggling scheme to the feds," he said softly.

It was the assumption I'd been investigating under, but

hearing him voice it aloud still kicked up my heart rate. "If you believed that, why didn't you go straight to the police?"

"Because . . . I was afraid that's what got Uncle Jack killed."

"We'd better continue this interview inside," Tanner said and directed a pointed look past Nate's car to a woman and her poodle, walking at a snail's pace on the other side of Charlie's street.

A neighbor or two peered from their front windows at us as well. None looked particularly worrisome, but given what happened at Joe's and the excitement with the brakes, the fewer people who knew who I was interrogating the better.

I shot Detective Moore a firm look. "Agreed?"

He emitted a huff but muscled Ben toward the house, where Carly now stood behind the screen door, her arms wrapped around her middle.

Trailing behind them, I sent Isaak a quick text to alert him we'd found Ben at Charlie's and he had information about the antiquity smuggling.

He texted back: *On my way*.

"I guess you still want me to wait in the car," Nate called after us.

He'd been instrumental in Charlie's capture, so it seemed cruel to cut him out of the action now.

"Good plan," Tanner said, falling into step beside me.

"Actually, maybe you should take over lookout duties," I said to Tanner, "in case there are any grounds to Ben's fears that the police can't be trusted."

"As you wish."

I did a double take. Wait a minute. Was that a *Princess Bride* reference?

He gave me an innocent-looking grin.

Nate eyed the exchange. "Thanks, Farm Boy," he said drily, taking Tanner's place at my side.

Carly stepped onto the porch and held open the screen door for Moore and Ben.

Nate motioned me inside as he introduced himself to Carly and relieved her of door duty. "You must be Carly. I'm so sorry for your loss."

A truck slowed in front of the house, and Nate ushered Carly inside before she became the subject of gawkers too.

We joined Moore and Ben in the living room. Moore hadn't removed Ben's handcuffs but had at least made the concession of switching them to the front so Ben could sit comfortably. He smirked at Nate, then whispered in my ear, "Switch-hitting the sidekicks?"

I rolled my eyes at the joke.

Grinning more broadly, he moved behind Ben and casually leaned against the wall, his attention shifting to Carly.

I took the chair opposite Ben. "So how'd you find out about this antiquity smuggling scheme?"

"He's lying!" Carly clutched the back of the chair she'd been about to sit in. "My brother wasn't a smuggler." She glared at Ben. "Isn't it bad enough my brother's dead without you ruining his character?"

"I take it you knew Ben was hiding in the bedroom?" I said. "And . . . chose not to tell us?"

Carly darted a wary glance Moore's way, then folded shaky arms over her chest. "He was here when I got here. Told me this ridiculous story about my brother. Then Frank showed up and Ben grabbed my arms, told me to stay quiet about his being here."

Okay, that explained the marks on her arms.

"He said Frank may be connected to Charlie's death," Carly went on, shooting Ben another sour look. "Which is crazy. Frank wasn't here to snoop. Not like Ben. Then the police showed up and I didn't know what to do. Those first two cops searched the rooms and didn't find Ben, so I figured he'd gotten away while Frank and I were talking." She snuck another glance at Moore, whose face had reddened at the revelation of his colleagues' incompetence.

I returned my attention to Ben. "Do you have proof Charlie was smuggling antiquities?"

"He mailed them to the island. I didn't see the name on the package, but it was a PO box in Edgartown."

"How big was the package?"

Ben mimed a box double the size of a shoe box.

I glanced at Moore. "The police find anything like that when they searched the place?"

"Nope."

"Can you call the Edgartown Post Office and ask if a parcel has come in from South America?"

"I can't believe this," Carly shouted. "Ben breaks into Charlie's house the day after my brother is killed and you're going to believe what he says. How do we know he didn't send whatever he claims Charlie mailed?"

"What was mailed?" I asked Ben.

"A polychrome Maya pot. I've been researching subsistence diggers for an article and then I spotted Charlie buying this pot from one of them."

Yeah, probably for less than fifty dollars when Maya pots sold for upward of ten thousand dollars to final buyers in the United States.

"I figured Charlie wasn't up on the law and warned him if the government caught him leaving the country with antiquities, he could be in big trouble."

"How did he respond?"

"He said it was just a souvenir for a friend. Not to worry about it. We laughed about the chances of meeting up in a small Guatemalan town, had lunch together, then parted ways."

"But you saw him mail the pot?"

"Yeah, I followed him to the post office."

Moore pocketed his phone and narrowed his gaze on Carly. He was no doubt gauging what she knew about her brother's alleged side business.

"What does it matter if Charlie did or didn't mail it?" Carly shrieked. "He's dead. You should be looking for his murderer, not dragging his name through the mud when he can't defend himself. How do we know you're not blaming Charlie just to get yourself off the hook for whatever you're caught up in? Is it drugs?" She waved her hand at Moore. "That's what those cops were trying to pin on Charlie this morning. And for all I know"—she pointed at Ben—"you killed him."

23

"You're talking crazy," Ben shouted at Carly.

An uncomfortable tension cinched my chest. There could be something to Carly's accusations against Ben. Charlie's frequent trips abroad certainly set him up nicely to take the fall. Had I been too quick to give Ben the benefit of the doubt?

Moore, on the other hand, appeared bemused by Carly's accusations.

"I didn't kill Charlie," Ben reiterated.

I shot him my lie-detector squint to see if he'd crack, the way he used to as a preteen.

"Who's the buyer?" Detective Moore asked, getting to the crux of the matter, and to who, if Ben could be believed, was likely behind the deaths and attacks on me.

"I don't know," Ben said. "Uncle Jack and I were going to press Charlie for details when I got home. Jack figured the feds would offer Charlie a deal in exchange for information and the return of the antiquities."

"That's ridiculous," Carly snapped. "Jack was about to marry our mother. He wouldn't turn in his future stepson!"

"No, that's the reason he'd want to help him," Ben countered.

"How is it that *you're* such an expert on antiquities?" Moore pressed.

"I told you. I'm writing an article on subsistence diggers. If he'd bought from a street vendor, I'm not sure I would've been able to tell if it was real or fake any better than he would."

"Would you recognize *drugs* if you saw them?" Detective Moore shot me a look that said I was being played.

"Jack called the feds to report an antiquity smuggling ring and cited Ben as the source," I informed Moore. "Has the post office seen the parcel come in?"

"They're looking into it."

"It could've been held up at Customs."

Moore gave a terse nod, then glanced at Carly, who looked ready to tear Ben limb from limb. Not that I could blame her.

Nate snagged my attention and mouthed *casserole lady*. I frowned.

"Marianne's fight with Jack the night he died," he whispered close to my ear.

Right, the fight Diana told us about when she dropped off the casserole. A fight about turning Marianne's son over to the authorities? I turned to Carly. "Your mother and Jack fought before Jack headed to Menemsha Hills the night he died. Do you know what that was about?"

"No."

"She didn't mention it?"

"No."

I found that hard to believe given Marianne had lamented about it with Diana, but maybe Carly and her mother didn't have that kind of relationship.

I returned my attention to Ben. "Outside you said you didn't go to the police because you were afraid that's why Uncle Jack was killed. How do you figure?"

"I had no idea who Charlie was working for. For all I knew, he could've been a cop or in cahoots with them, or someone who was rich enough to ensure our allegations never went anywhere . . . one way or another."

"But Jack wasn't killed," Carly blurted, albeit a tad less adamantly than when she'd accused Ben and Ashley of killing him mere days ago. "That officer said I was wrong." She swiped at the tears that spilled onto her cheeks.

An attempt to protect her mother? The fact Marianne found Jack's body had put her on my suspect list the day I arrived, coupled with the fact I didn't really know her. Finding her rummaging around in Jack's house the next day, purportedly in search of more photos for a slide show for the funeral had also niggled my latent suspicions. And this revelation meant she had motive—to save her son from jail.

But it didn't explain Charlie's death. Unless . . .

"When did you learn Jack planned to turn Charlie over to the authorities?" I asked her.

Carly froze like a deer caught in the headlights. Several seconds passed. "Just now," she whispered.

I shook my head. "You cut Ben off before he'd even accused Charlie."

She squirmed. "Ben told me earlier."

Ben affirmed her statement with a nod.

"Then what did you and Charlie talk about when you met in Edgartown the other day?" I asked.

The pulse point on her neck visibly bounced. "You've been following me?"

"Now why would I do that?" I baited, not quite believing the torment etched in her face was solely grief.

Her crossed arms tightened across her chest. "I have no idea."

I paused to see if she'd spill whatever she was clearly hiding.

She didn't.

"I went to Edgartown to speak to Jack's partner, and I noticed you talking to Charlie on the street," I said.

Her tense posture softened and she took another swipe at the tears rolling down her cheeks.

Nate pressed a tissue into her hand.

"Thank you," she murmured, then to me said, "We talked about Mom. She fell apart after her last husband died. Ended up in the hospital. We were worried how she'd be." Carly gulped down a sob. "Now . . . now . . . with Charlie gone . . ."

Nate squeezed her shoulder comfortingly and Carly fell silent, pressing the tissue to her eyes.

I steeled myself against the sobs welling up in my own chest and forced myself to focus. If the fight between Jack and Marianne had been about Charlie, would Marianne have told her son? The same night? After he got home and learned of Jack's death? It would've given Charlie motive to drive by Jack's house and see what incriminating evidence he might find. Only to find Dad and me coming out of the house.

An inspection of Charlie's front bumper should answer that question.

But it wouldn't identify the person responsible for his death—his partner, I suspected. Because as far as the partner was concerned, Charlie was the only one who could ID him and therefore the only loose end.

"Can you go now please?" Carly pleaded. "I just want to be left alone."

My heart went out to her. Getting to the bottom of who murdered Jack was how I dealt with my grief. Or maybe how I avoided dealing with it.

"I don't think leaving her here alone is a good idea," Moore said. "Whether she wants to believe it or not, her brother was seen in the company of known drug dealers. They see her here, they could decide to silence her too."

"Why are you doing this to me?" Carly sobbed.

"For your own protection," Moore said coolly.

The *Murder She Wrote* ringtone chimed from my phone, and my heart jumped to my throat. "Excuse me," I said, "I need to take this." Normally, I wouldn't interrupt an interview to take a call from Aunt Martha, but what if she'd been hurt by that airbag after all? Or what if whoever cut the brakes had tried something else?

I clicked on the phone. "Aunt Martha, what's wrong?"

"This is Officer Baxter of the Tisbury police department. Whom am I speaking with?"

"Tisbury? What happened?" I exchanged a worried glance with Nate and then lowering my voice, withdrew to the hallway. "Where's my aunt? Is she okay?"

"Yes, and you are?"

"Special Agent Serena Jones, FBI. What's going on? Why do you have my aunt's phone?"

Nate stepped into view at the edge of the living room, concern etched in his face.

"A mischief complaint has been filed against her by the local car rental agency," the officer said.

"Mischief?" The spike in my voice could've cracked an

eardrum. I hauled my voice down a few decibels. "What kind of mischief?"

Amusement twinkled in Nate's eyes. He was all too well acquainted with how often Aunt Martha got into mischief.

"Hacking into the local car rental agency's computer system."

"What?"

"Let me talk to her," Aunt Martha insisted in the background and then came on the line. "Tell this young man his department investigated your father's hit-and-run. He won't listen to me."

"It wasn't the *Tisbury* department, Aunt Martha. It was *West* Tisbury."

"West. East." She emitted a frustrated huff. "A simple search should've still confirmed my story. He thinks I'm barmy just because my hair is gray."

"Where are you?"

"The rental agency. The manager is shielding the identity of the hit-and-run driver who mowed down your father."

"What?"

"You heard right. The tow truck driver who came and hauled Carmen's rental away said this was the fourth problem this week for the rental company. And number three came in Thursday morning. A customer returned an SUV with a dent in the front fender. Claimed he hit a deer."

The same night as the hit-and-run. "Did you get a look at the vehicle?"

"No, it'd already gone to the auto body shop for repairs. And the manager wouldn't give me the customer's name, so while he was inspecting the new rental with Carmen, I took a looksee myself. The manager had a conniption and called the police. But he won't give the officer the name either."

"Okay, let me talk to the officer." When he came back on the line, I asked him to contact Officer Lennox with the West Tisbury department and explained why the person whose name Aunt Martha wanted to retrieve should be questioned, along with the technician who fixed the car. If the suspect really hit a deer, the technician would've seen traces of fur.

The officer assured me he would do so and let Aunt Martha go with a warning to leave the investigating to police. I wouldn't hold my breath on the second part. Not even a couple of thugs duct-taping her hands to her steering wheel and threatening to shoot her had dampened her thirst for a good, real-life mystery for more than twelve days and seven hours. And the fact the creep had cut Carmen's brakes made it personal.

Not to mention I was 99 percent sure Aunt Martha thought she was invincible.

She came on the line again and asked me what Tanner found.

"Ben. I'll explain when I get back to the house." First I needed to grill him on how he was getting around the island. His taxi driver friend had corroborated his hitchhiking claim for the night he came in, but Ben could've rented a car the next day. "Are you and Carmen heading back to Preston's now?"

Aunt Martha let out an annoyed snort. "No. After the manager caught me on the computer, he didn't want to rent us another car."

I couldn't blame him. "One of us can pick you up."

"Don't worry, Winston won't mind coming back for us."

"If you're sure. Please be careful and maybe don't mention the cut brakes to Mom."

"Wouldn't dream of it. She has enough to fret over with helping your dad plan tonight's memorial service."

Right. I glanced at my watch. Still had three hours. I wished Special Agent Jackson would hurry up and get here.

As I stepped back into the living room, Moore said, "I think it's time to take this interrogation to the police station. I'll see the young woman gets home safely."

Carly rose abruptly. "I need to use the bathroom."

I motioned her to go ahead and watched down the hall until she closed the bathroom door behind her.

Moore moved to my side and spoke in a low voice. "I hope your trust in Ben is an act because from where I sit, he looks good for the whole shebang."

"Carly is hiding something. Anyone with two eyes can see that." But I turned to Ben and, hoping to catch him off guard, asked him point-blank, "Why'd you switch out your rental vehicle?"

24

Ben sat on the sofa in Charlie's living room and stared at me dumbfounded. "Huh?" He leaned forward, a move that might've been contrived to encourage me to believe him, but I already believed the confusion on his face. "I've never rented a vehicle in my life. I'm not even twenty-five."

That didn't make it impossible, just more expensive. "How have you been getting around the island since Lisa took you in?"

Ben raked his fingers through his hair. "After I walked down to Jack's Wednesday afternoon and overheard Carly's accusation, I was whirling. I didn't know what to do. I didn't know if he'd gotten hold of the feds or had talked to the local cops. I figured I needed to lay low until I could read some reports and find out what the cops were saying, so I headed back to Lisa's, staying in the woods so I wouldn't be spotted.

"I trolled the news sites for hours. When I saw the text from Ashley asking if I missed my plane, I realized saying yes could be my ticket to being invisible. I figured Charlie was bound to hear and I'd be able to watch his movements with no one the wiser."

Moore folded his arms and locked a cold hard stare on Ben.

"It wasn't how that sounded," Ben backtracked. "I figured he had a partner in this smuggling scheme he was working. I thought I might spot them meeting."

"How'd you *watch* his movements without wheels?" I pressed.

"I borrowed a pickup from a friend of mine who's off the island."

"Borrowed or stolen?"

"Borrowed," Ben said firmly. "I had a standing offer to use it. He's an island guy. The keys were under the mat. I didn't steal anything."

"When was that?"

"Wednesday night."

I glanced down the hall to check up on Carly, but the bathroom door was still closed. "What time?" I asked Ben.

"Not long after sunset. I'd been waiting for dark to go back to Jack's to grab my backpack. I figured I couldn't pull off the *I missed a plane* angle if you guys found my backpack."

Nate pinned Ben with a laser-like glare. "Where's the truck now?"

Ben swallowed, his gaze bouncing from Nate to me.

Because he was guilty of running my dad down? Or because Nate looked primed to tear him limb from limb? I squelched a chuckle at how cute Nate looked going all protective over me, even if 'pickup' didn't fit the description of the vehicle that had clipped Dad. I nodded to Ben. "Answer the question."

"Around the corner. The black Ford."

Nate rose. "Excuse me."

Detective Moore started after him, probably worried Nate would contaminate possible evidence.

I grabbed Moore's arm. "Let him go. Tanner's out there," I reminded him, then returned my attention to Ben. "You never got the backpack. What happened?"

"The road was crawling with cops when I tried to go back later that night. By the time I finally got my chance with no one around, the backpack was gone."

"So why didn't you go see Ashley then and there?" I said to Ben. "Didn't it occur to you if we'd found your abandoned backpack, we'd be worried you'd been killed too?"

His eyes widened. "No, I never . . ." He scrubbed his hand over his face and, hunching over, sunk his elbows into his thighs. "I didn't mean to scare Ashley. I was trying to keep her safe."

"And how did you think you'd accomplish that?" Moore spoke up.

"By figuring out who Charlie was working for. Jack told me Charlie would be getting back from a trip to South America the same day I was supposed to get in, so I followed him. I figured he'd set up a meeting with his buyer to get paid for whatever he'd mailed."

"Did he?"

"Not that I saw. He dropped by Jack's office, but Frank wasn't there." Ben glanced toward the hallway and lowered his voice. "That's probably when you saw Carly talking to him like you said before."

I nodded encouragingly, although I had to wonder if he was weaving a story around the tidbits I'd fed him. I snagged Detective Moore's gaze. "You notice a black pickup tailing Charlie?"

Moore shook his head and that worried look returned to Ben's eyes.

Outside, gunshots erupted.

I dove for Ben and pushed him to the floor, shielding his body with mine.

"Shots fired. Shots fired," Moore shouted into his radio and relayed the address. He dove to the side of the window and peeked out the bottom corner.

"Can you see Tanner and Nate? Are they okay?" My heart galloped a hundred miles a minute.

"No, no I can't see—" He gasped.

My blood chilled. "What?" I scrambled to the window.

"Duck!" Moore screamed above the squeal of tires.

Something crashed through the window, and the room ignited in flames.

"We need firefighters," Moore shouted into his radio.

"Go, go, go," I shouted to Ben, scrambling out of the way of the spreading fire. "Out the back. We'll be right behind you." I bobbed my head just high enough to scan the scene outside. No sign of our gunman. Or Tanner and Nate. By the time I turned back to the room, the flames had licked up the sofa.

"We've got to get out of here," Moore said.

Staying hunched low, we ran for the hallway, the intensity of the heat doubling by the second.

Smoke clawed my throat as I looked for Ben and Carly. "The back door's open," I said, racing past the kitchen doorway to the still closed bathroom door. "Ben must've gotten out." I pounded on the bathroom door. "Carly, fire! We have to go!"

No answer.

I tried the knob. "It's locked." I pounded harder. "Carly, open up!"

Moore kicked the door in, scanned the room, ripped the shower curtain from the rod to look in the tub. The window over the tub was open. "She went out the window."

Moore pushed me toward the back door. "Go! But be careful. The shooter could've circled around."

We dashed out, still hunched low. "Ben? Carly?" I hissed, loud enough for them to hear me but hopefully not loud enough to attract the attention of our gunman. The yard was small and empty. I glanced through a slat of the cedar fence separating Charlie's yard from the yard behind. "No sign of them this way."

"Here either," Moore called from the right.

"Surely they wouldn't have run to the front," I said.

"Unless they had a death wish," Moore agreed grimly.

"Find them. I've got to check on Tanner and Nate." I vaulted the side fence and skirted between it and the neighboring house for cover.

Sirens wailed in the distance. My gaze swept the street and my breath stalled.

Ben's truck was in flames. No sign of a gunman. I dashed to the street. "Nate! Tanner!" *Oh, Lord, please let them be okay.*

A large man sprayed a fire extinguisher at the flaming truck. A dark-haired woman appeared behind him and waved me over, pointing me to the yard on the other side of the truck. "They're here!"

I raced toward her.

Tanner stood, his eyes meeting mine, looking unharmed, and relief rushed through me like a tsunami.

Until my gaze dropped and I saw Nate's still form sprawled on the grass at Tanner's feet.

I took in his blackened face and promptly lost my breakfast.

Nate pushed to his feet. "Never seen her do that before," he said, his tone punchy.

"I've seen her come close a time or two," Tanner countered.

"I would've tried to get myself killed before, if I'd known how much you cared," Nate said with a loopy grin.

Tanner rolled his eyes while I covered my mouth, blinking back tears. I took a swig from the water bottle the dear woman who'd flagged me over offered and got my emotions back in control. Then I swiped the moisture from my lips and faced the pair. "Can you identify who did this?" My gaze dropped to Nate's chin, because I wasn't ready to let him see what might be in my eyes.

"A guy in a dark blue Jeep," Nate said.

"It was a black Tahoe," Tanner corrected.

Nate shook his head. "It was a Jeep Cherokee. No front license plate."

Tanner mimicked the head shake but didn't repeat his opinion.

"What was the target?" I interjected, oddly comforted to see them back to disagreeing with each other.

"Looked as if Nate was the guy they wanted," Tanner said. "He strode out of the house and told me he was inspecting Ben's truck. I was in the middle of answering a text from headquarters, so it was a good ten seconds before I turned to follow him. When I did, I saw the *Tahoe* turn onto the street and a flaming bottle fly out the rear window toward Nate."

251

"I didn't see it coming," Nate said. "I dove for the dirt at the gunshots and rolled under the truck for cover, but got winged by a hunk of glass."

"Did you see the shooter?" I asked Tanner.

"I was the shooter," he grumbled. "I was trying to stop them. They whipped the second bottle toward the house, then sped off."

"He got burnt trying to help the other one out from under the truck," my water bottle lady added.

A fire truck pulled up and two firefighters made short work of ensuring the flames were smothered as firefighters from a second truck went to work on Charlie's house.

I introduced myself to the pair manning the truck fire. "Is an ambulance coming? We have a cut and a second-degree burn that need treating."

"Should be here any minute."

Moore stalked across the street. "Your old family friend saw his chance to escape and took it. I called in a BOLO. Carly's bike is gone. She shouldn't be difficult to spot. I'm going to start looking."

"Do you think one of them orchestrated the hit so they could get away?" Nate asked.

"Frank could have, after he left," Tanner said. "Where's your agent who was supposed to be here?"

"I don't know what's keeping him," I said, the myriad of potential connections between our suspects swirling through my mind.

The arriving ambulance bleeped its siren and parked a safe distance from the fire.

"At least the paramedics are here," I said to Tanner and Nate.

252

"This"—Moore motioned to the charred truck—"looks like the work of drug dealers to me. Face it, Serena. Whatever Charlie was into, Ben was too."

An image of Ben running in his tight-fitting jeans flashed through my mind, and my chest tightened. He'd spun a believable yarn that put him on the good-guy side. But what if instead of him going to Jack, Jack found out about Ben's little side business and threatened to turn him in if he didn't turn himself in first? After all, Ben toured the world just as often as Charlie. Could Ben have killed Jack in cold blood?

My stomach roiled at the thought.

"You're sure they both got out of the house?" Nate asked as a paramedic steered him toward the ambulance.

"Yes." I folded my arms against a shiver. "Carly slipped out the bathroom window, maybe even before the commotion. And the back door was open, so we know Ben ran out ahead of us."

Tanner grimaced. "I may've left the back door open when I ran after him the first time."

I shot a panicked glance at the now fully engulfed house and then raced toward the fire chief to alert him.

"Serena!" Ashley, far down the street, on the other side of the fire truck, sprinted up the sidewalk toward me. Her voice pitched higher as her gaze bounced from face to face. "Where's Ben?"

25

Preston followed Ashley at a more sedate pace, his grim expression shifting from the burning house to me.

"Your aunt Martha said Ben was here," Ashley shrieked as police officers intercepted her.

"Ma'am, you need to stay back."

"My brother. Where's Ben?" she wailed.

I shot a pleading look to Preston, who seemed to guess we couldn't produce Ben. He clasped Ashley firmly about the shoulders and whispering in her ear, coaxed her back.

Ashley's gaze fixated on the burning house, her face white, and my heart went out to her.

The minutes dragged. Tanner pulled me aside, his arm covered in goop. A pace behind him, a paramedic impatiently looked on. "Did Ben have a phone on him?"

I squinted at Tanner, taking a moment to deduce what he was really asking. "He didn't arrange this stunt, Tanner. Why would he?" I slanted a glance back at Ashley. "Taking off now only makes him look guilty."

"Good point," Tanner conceded, "but maybe he needed

to destroy evidence. That, or someone tipped off Charlie's buyer."

"You think?" I snapped, not proud of myself for it, but Ashley's sobbing pleas for her brother—the only family she had left—had me mentally kicking myself for the way I'd handled the whole interview.

"It could have been Carly." Tanner waved off the paramedic attempting to finish his job on Tanner's arm. "She seemed to think Ben killed her brother. Revenge is a powerful motive."

"I don't buy that. If she believed Ben killed him, she would've given him up to the police the instant they arrived on scene."

"Well, there is one more possibility we've overlooked."

"What's that?"

"Your pal Nate has enemies of his own."

I snorted and turned to face the music with Ashley. If Ben didn't turn up, she'd never forgive me for not calling her the second I found him.

"Hey." Tanner grabbed my arm, looking totally serious. "Don't dismiss the idea. Nate told me about your *car trouble*."

"Yeah? Did he mention the car was in Malgucci's name? Not Nate's."

"You're forgetting about his plane getting shot down over Yugoslavia."

"Tanner, let the paramedic finish tending your arm. I don't have time for the games right now."

"You should just kiss the guy. Get him out of your system."

I'm pretty sure that my eyeballs popped out of my head and bounced back like in those crazy cartoon characters. "I can't believe we are having this conversation." I crossed my arms. "No, we aren't having this conversation, because a conversation takes two people. Two *sane* people. And you've clearly knocked a screw loose."

"Oh, c'mon, Serena, you were staring at his lips back there. You think I wouldn't notice?"

Oh, great, so I save myself from Nate reading what's in my eyes, only to make Tanner think . . . "Maybe I was wondering if he kissed as good as you," I needled, then felt heat suffuse my face as my words replayed in my head.

Tanner's smirk told me my botched comeback hadn't gone unnoticed.

Perfect. He'd milk that one for the rest of my career.

A celebratory shout rose from the crowd as a firefighter escorted a limping Ben from around the back of the house. Ashley broke away from Preston, dashed past the officer managing the crowd, and leapt into Ben's arms.

Tears burst from my eyes at the touching reunion.

"Where'd you find him?" I asked the firefighter since Ben was still too busy with Ashley.

"He jumped out a bedroom window. The closed door saved him from getting smoked, but he sprained his ankle getting out." The firefighter handed me a framed photograph of a man and two kids digging in the sand at the beach. "He says he had to save this for Carly."

I studied the picture, wondering if Charlie and Carly were the children. I could sort of see the resemblance. I flipped it over to see if there was writing on the back.

Scrawled in black magic marker across the frame's backing read: *Charlie, Carly, and Dad treasure hunting on Chappy.*

Moore crowded in behind me and reached for the photo. "Can I see that?"

Ben glanced up from hugging his sister for the dozenth time. "The instant I realized the fire was going to destroy every last physical connection Carly had to Charlie, I knew I had to save something for her. And remembered the picture I'd seen beside Charlie's bed. We lost all the pictures of Ashley and me and our parents in the fire that took their lives." His voice cracked. "I had to save that for Carly."

My eyes teared up a second time. To think I'd been thinking he'd run away when he'd been risking his life in such a selfless, noble act.

Preston stepped up behind me. "That's Ben. Always looking for a new angle to score with the women."

Huh. Sounded as if Preston didn't think too highly of his future brother-in-law.

Moore handed back the picture. "I'll drive around and see if I can locate Carly."

Special Agent Isaak Jackson joined me and apologized for the delay. "Your colleague caught me up on what happened."

As the paramedics checked Ben for burns and smoke inhalation, I filled Isaak in on Ben's story about Charlie and the parcel. "I think it'd be better if you finish the interview," I said.

"Agreed."

I introduced him to Ben, then returned to Ben's charred, borrowed truck and fixated on the cracked front headlight.

Nate leaned over my shoulder, his breath whispering through my hair. "It's missing a few pieces."

I straightened slowly, our breaths mingling as I turned. "Hey," I said softly.

He tucked a stray hair behind my cheek, his gaze dipping to my lips.

From somewhere behind me, I heard the distinctive sound of Tanner clearing his throat and took an abrupt step back. "Uh, how's the arm?"

"Fine. Four butterfly bandages and a dose of antiseptic took care of it. The grilling by the investigating officer was more painful." Nate paused and glanced at his phone, thumbed in OK, then returned it to his pocket and his attention to me. "I think the officer thought I was a drug dealer. He wasn't buying my innocent bystander line until Tanner vouched for me."

I couldn't help the surprised look that must've crossed my face.

Nate chuckled. "Yeah, surprised me too." He squatted and took a closer look at the damaged headlight. "Did the police find evidence of a shattered headlight after your dad's hit-and-run?"

"Not that they mentioned or I saw." My gaze strayed to Ashley hovering over Ben.

"I guess you're hoping it wouldn't be a match if there was?" Nate said.

I let out a sigh. "Yeah, I want to believe him." If he'd save that picture of Carly's father for her, how could he murder the man who'd lovingly raised him since he was twelve? "As you no doubt overheard, Aunt Martha thinks the culprit used a rental that was returned the next day."

Nate nodded. "We still have Charlie's Jeep to check out, too, right?"

"You sure you want to be within a hundred yards of me? Let alone in the same vehicle? Being the occasional target kind of goes with my job description. But it's not what you signed on for."

258

He searched my eyes and after an eternal soul-stirring moment seemed to find what he was looking for. "Yes, it is." The corners of his eyes crinkled. "Or have you forgotten why I flew here in the first place?"

An indescribable warmth spread through my chest at the intensity of his voice.

Tanner joined us and snagged my gaze.

His earlier kiss-him comment echoed through my mind and my face heated. "The guy throwing the flaming bottle must've mistaken Nate for Ben," I said, like I should've when he needled me half an hour ago.

Tanner scrutinized Nate then Ben. "Same average height. Same average build. Same average shade of brown hair. Yeah, could be if you ignore the fact Nate doesn't have a beard or shoulder-length hair."

I resisted the compulsion to punch his so-not-average muscled arm. If I let his goading irk me, it would only encourage him. "That's a new look for Ben. He's been in the jungle awhile."

"I see you let the other agent take over Ben's interrogation," Tanner said.

"Yeah." Someone with more emotional distance than I had needed to. My head was spinning from the dozen different directions this case was pulling me.

26

Thirty minutes later, as Nate and I prepared to head to the police compound, Tanner tapped the windshield of the Land Rover Winston had lent us. "Is this bulletproof glass? I think this is bulletproof glass."

"Could be. Winston is former Secret Service."

Tanner cocked his head and scrutinized the corner of the windshield, then shoved Nate aside and stuck his head inside to look at whatever had caught his eye from another angle. "He's got a surveillance camera on this thing. And it looks like it's still running." He sank into the driver's seat and surveyed the knobs, dials, and buttons on the dash. "Give me the keys." He flapped his fingers at Nate.

Nate handed them over and Tanner scrolled through options on the mid-dash screen. "Try auxiliary under A/V," Nate suggested.

Tanner gritted his teeth but did as Nate suggested. The camera's view appeared on the screen.

I lunged into the seat beside him. "How do we rewind?"

Tanner tapped the screen in three different places but nothing happened.

Nate leaned in and over him and two taps later, we were watching the events of the past couple of hours rewind at ten times the speed.

"We're getting close," I said as I appeared in view running toward the burning pickup. "Slow it down."

Tanner tapped it to two times the speed, then hit PAUSE as the gunman's truck backed up to the corner.

"No, keep rewinding," I said. "I want to know how long it was sitting there watching us."

He hit rewind until the truck disappeared from the corner, then he hit PLAY.

"2:46," I read from the screen as the car parked at the corner. "A minute or two after Carly went to the bathroom."

Tanner's walk toward Nate blocked the camera's view of the driver as he turned the corner. Then, even though I knew what was coming, I jumped as a bottle flew from the back window, and Ben's pickup burst into flames. Tanner opened fire. Nate dove. The suspect's vehicle kept rolling toward ours. A second bottle flew from the back window on the other side of the truck—the one that hit Charlie's house.

"Freeze it there." I squinted at the screen. "It's definitely a Cherokee, like Nate said." And it looked uncomfortably similar to the truck that hit Dad. The black-and-white image prohibited us from confirming the color.

"Is there a way to upload the video to a computer so we can enhance the image? See if we can make out the faces as the Jeep got closer?"

"Yeah." Nate thumbed something into his phone. "We

need Winston's password, then we can upload via Bluetooth. I'm sending Martha a text now."

"The driver's wearing a ball cap with a half-circle logo on it." Tanner freeze-framed the image. "See that? Recognize it?"

"No."

"Okay." Tanner jotted notes in a notepad and climbed out of the driver's seat. "I'll get the general description to the officer in charge and meet you at the police compound. Hopefully by the time we're done there, you'll have heard back from your aunt." He looked at Nate. "Be careful."

"How'd you know so much about the camera system in this thing?" I asked as Nate consulted a text on his phone and then keyed something into the vehicle's console.

He shrugged. "Had a lot of time to kill when we first arrived and you asked me to wait out here." He spread his finger on his phone's screen and looked in satisfaction at the image—a grainy side profile of the truck's driver. "Got it."

My heart flip-flopped as I watched how intently he worked. "I'm glad you're okay," I said softly.

He glanced up and with a tender smile tucked a stray strand of hair behind my ear. "I'm glad you're glad," he murmured. He leaned forward slightly, and my breath caught.

He was going to kiss me. Was he going to kiss me?

Heat flashed over me faster than the flames from that stupid Molotov cocktail.

He grazed his knuckles down the curve of my cheek, his face close enough that a hint of spearmint wafted to me on his soft breath.

I loved spearmint.

Nate smiled and I suddenly heard Tanner's mocking *just kiss him and get it over with* sing-songing through my mind.

Tanner needed to get out of my head. The thought of Tanner's *kiss* especially needed to get out of my head.

Nate's thumb brushed across my lips, but a little of the light seemed to slip from his eyes.

He pressed his lips together and straightened, his hand dropping to the steering wheel.

Huh?

What just happened?

"We better get going. We have a killer to track down."

Ohh-kay then.

Men. No wonder I usually stuck to chasing down criminals. At least they were predictable.

Besides, emotions clouded judgment. An FBI agent couldn't let emotions get the better of her. "I never should've involved you."

"You didn't. I volunteered."

"I could've got you killed."

"No, an idiot in a baseball cap could have. You had nothing to do with it."

"You'd be at home safe and sound right now if it wasn't for me."

Nate studied me for an uncomfortably long time. "Playing it safe is overrated." His head tilted, his gaze momentarily slipping to my lips.

The hint of regret that flickered in his eyes sent a crazy jolt to my heart. Was he playing it safe when he didn't kiss me?

His gaze shifted back to the windshield.

"I'm paid to put my life on the line," I said, glibly.

"And riding shotgun for you is a risk I'm willing to take."

I crossed my arms, pressing them against the ridiculous rat-a-tat in my chest. "Well, I'm not."

"Good thing I'm driving then." He turned the key in the ignition.

"It's not smart to partner with someone you care about. It could affect your judgment."

The rat-a-tat came again. Only it wasn't in my chest. Tanner tapped his knuckles on my passenger window. Heat climbed to my cheeks as I rolled it down, wondering just how long he'd been standing there.

The rigid slant of his jaw suggested it'd been long enough. "One of the firefighters said the ball cap is from a pub in Oak Bluffs that sponsors a baseball team." He relayed the address. "Want to go there first? Or the police compound?"

"How about you head straight there, and we'll do a quick stop at the compound to inspect the front of Charlie's truck, then meet you there?"

He gave a curt nod and strode to his car.

"You telling me you don't care about Tanner?" Nate said.

"What?"

"You said it's not smart to partner with someone you care about. You telling me you don't care about Tanner?"

"No. I mean, yes. Of course, I care about him, but not . . . in *that* way." My cheeks felt as if they were on fire. I bit my lip, remembering the kiss Tanner laid on me last night. *Oh, man, I was a mess.* Maybe Mom was right. If I dated more . . . a kiss wouldn't have been such a big deal. *Right?*

Nate reached across the console and squeezed my hand. "I don't scare away that easy."

Electricity zinged up my arm at his warm touch. I was in big trouble. Uncle Jack was dead. I needed to focus and all I could think about . . . I tore my gaze away from Nate's mouth. "Okay, then." I cleared the rattle from my throat. "Let's roll."

Nate backed away from the fire trucks blocking the street and pulled a U-turn.

My cell phone rang and Preston's home number appeared on the screen. I sucked in a big breath and prayed Mom hadn't heard about the excitement as I clicked CONNECT.

"Serena, are Preston and Ashley with you?"

"Uh"—I glanced out the window as we passed where they'd been parked—"not anymore. I imagine he and Ashley followed the uh." I caught myself before saying ambulance, not wanting to have to explain why Ben was on his way to the hospital for smoke inhalation. "Uh, are with Ben. Why?"

"Are they coming back here before the memorial service?" Anxiety rippled through her voice. "We don't have a car to get there. You heard that Carmen's rental had a mechanical problem?"

"Yeah, I heard that." She didn't know the half of it. *Thank goodness*. She'd be in a full-blown panic.

"And he's having trouble getting a replacement car. Can you believe that? It isn't even summer yet. Winston dropped Aunt Martha here and then went off with Carmen to see what they could drum up. But what if they don't get back in time? We don't want to miss the service. And Preston's not answering his phone."

"Hold on a minute, Mom." I covered the phone and asked Nate where he parked his rental since we drove to Oak Bluffs with Carmen and Aunt Martha.

"In Preston's driveway."

"And the keys?"

He reached into his pants pocket and came up empty-handed.

He checked the backseat. "They're in my jacket pocket, but I must've left it in Carmen's car."

I uncovered the phone's mic. "Did Aunt Martha bring Nate's jacket home with her?"

Aunt Martha must've overheard the question because a second later I heard "found them" in the background.

"If we or Carmen or Preston and Ashley don't get back by five thirty, then you can drive Nate's rental to the church, okay?" I said.

"Oh dear, are you sure we're allowed to do that?"

No, but . . . "Mom, it'll be fine." I hoped.

Nate found the police compound in record time, and it took even less time to ascertain that the front of Charlie's truck was dent free and devoid of any other discernible forensics evidence.

"I'm glad it's clean," I admitted. "Marianne has enough on her plate with losing her fiancé and her son, on top of her son being investigated for drug and/or antiquity smuggling. I didn't want to add a hit-and-run to the list."

"I heard the victim's fishing rod was caught on some debris around the mouth of Tisbury Great Pond," the tech who showed us the truck said. "Looks as if he could've simply lost his footing while fishing."

"Yeah, I'm sure that's what his killer wants us to think," I muttered as Nate and I returned to the Land Rover.

He headed for the pub. "You sure you're not just seeing what you expect to see? Accidents do happen."

"You honestly think Charlie's death was an accident?"

"Not if Ben's telling the truth. But we're chasing ghosts. Apart from Ben's statement, we have no evidence antiquities have even been smuggled into the country."

266

"We will when that package arrives. Trust me, Ben's not that good a liar."

"For Ashley's sake and your family's, I hope you're right." Nate parked behind Tanner's rental, in front of a pub sporting the same logo as the one on the driver's ball cap.

"You wait here," I said, climbing out of the car.

He met me at the curb and reached for the pub door.

"Did that explosion wreck your hearing?"

He flashed a silly grin. "You're forgetting who has a picture of the suspect on his phone." He motioned me in ahead of him.

"What can I get you?" the Irishman behind the bar drawled as the tinkle of bells overhead quieted.

I glanced around the room, but Tanner was nowhere in sight. I flashed my badge at the barkeep. "We're looking for a guy who drives a dark Cherokee and wears one of your ball caps."

"Lass, like I told the other officer, we've sponsored baseball teams on the island for years. Every fella and their granny have one of our caps. And if you haven't noticed, Jeeps are popular too."

Nate showed him the image he'd downloaded to his phone from the car's surveillance tape. "You recognize this guy?"

Irish glanced at the phone and said "No." Only, he said it too fast. "Why you lookin' for him?"

"He dropped something," Nate said without missing a beat, "and we want to get it back to him."

I scarcely stopped the laugh that burst from my chest at Nate's glib comeback. Ball Cap Guy had *dropped* something, all right.

Irish motioned toward a bulletin board on the back wall

between the restroom sign and a dartboard. "You can pin up a notice if you like."

I scanned the women's restroom for signs of anyone hiding out. Nate scanned the men's. Both were clear.

"What do you think?" I asked Nate.

"I think we should come back after the memorial service and check out the evening clientele."

"Catching him here would be a long shot," I said.

"At this point, it's the only lead we've got."

A text came in from Tanner: *Come around the back of the pub.*

The pub backed onto a narrow alleyway. Tanner was leaning against the building's graying cedar-shaked wall, his arms folded over his chest, his expression grim. "Okay, so I was wrong about the make. The truck was a Cherokee, not a Tahoe," he groused.

"I thought we'd already established that from the surveillance tape?"

Tanner pushed himself off the wall and pointed across the alleyway.

Well, he got the color right. A black Jeep Cherokee was parked in a small loading dock area carved between two buildings. My mind flashed back to the hit-and-run. Were we looking at the same culprit?

I hurried over to the vehicle. The front bumper showed no evidence of colliding with my father, but the pair of bullet holes in the fender, inches from the tire, and a third through the hubcap confirmed it belonged to our drive-by culprit. "Slick shooting," I said to Tanner.

Tanner's somber expression morphed into a grin. "Found the package you were after too. It's on the front seat."

"Are you serious?" I peered through the window. Sure enough, a package wrapped in brown paper, bearing stamps from Guatemala, lay unopened on the passenger seat.

"The customs label says *home décor item*," Tanner said. "A clever ruse if it turns out to be an antiquity."

I tried the door, but it was locked. Not that I could legally help myself to the package without a warrant, let alone open it. "It's addressed to Hill and Dale Architects."

"Yeah, didn't you say that's where Charlie's sister worked?"

"Yes. But if she was helping her brother, he sure wasn't paying her well. She still lives with her mother and rides the bus."

"I don't know," Nate interjected. "She carries a three-hundred-dollar purse and wears designer clothes."

My expression must've given away my dismay I hadn't picked up on that, because Tanner chuckled. "I don't even want to know how he knows women's purses."

Nate shrugged. "Former girlfriend who cared about her fashion statement a little too much."

Tanner's eyebrow arched as he turned his attention to me.

What did he expect? Nate was probably the sweetest guy I knew. Of course he'd had other girlfriends. Not . . . that I was putting myself in that category. *Oh, man.* My cheeks were definitely heating up again. I pulled out my phone and looked up the number of the local police station.

"I already called in the license plate," Tanner said. "Belongs to a Devin Fields. He lives in a house at the edge of town. I figure he's probably around town somewhere, but I didn't want to lose sight of his truck and miss him."

"Okay, Nate and I will search the area. I'll update Moore." The call went to voice mail, so I let him know we'd found the package and asked if he'd located Carly. With the addressee being Hill and Dale Architects, her flight looked more suspicious than ever, and I'd have a lot more questions for her once we confirmed the package's contents. I texted Special Agent Jackson next and suggested he work on getting us a warrant as soon as he finished with Ben, then pocketed my phone. "Call if you spot our guy," I said to Tanner.

Nate and I walked up the street, slipping into each shop to scout for Devin. As we stepped into a coffee shop and the rich aroma of coffee and mouthwatering smell of baking bread teased my senses, my stomach grumbled.

"What do you say we grab a sandwich and coffee here?" Nate said. "We missed lunch and at this rate, we won't have time to grab dinner before the memorial service."

"Good plan. Can you order me a clubhouse while I check in with Special Agent Jackson?" I sat at a table in a quiet corner of the shop, my back to the wall, so I could watch passersby.

A text had come in from Moore: *Now I see why you keep the sidekicks around. Good work. Still no sign of Carly. Keep me posted on the parcel status.*

Chuckling at what Tanner and Nate were bound to think of the sidekick moniker, I texted back a *Will do*, then phoned Isaak.

He answered on the first ring. "I got your message."

"If it turns out to be an antiquity, we're going to want search warrants for Devin's place, the architect firm, and Carly's and Frank's. You may want to let the post office know we located the package already too."

"About that. When I called the Edgartown police station earlier, they said no one contacted them about a package."

"Not surprising. Detective Moore likely called the post office directly."

"What time was that?"

"I don't know. Early afternoon."

"The post office closes at one on Saturdays. Doesn't reopen until Monday morning."

Huh. "Well, once he realized the post office was closed, he must've figured we could deal with it later. We were eyeball deep in interrogating Ben and Carly at the time. You finished questioning Ben?"

"Yes, at the hospital. I didn't want to keep him from his uncle's memorial service."

I glanced at my watch. *Still had an hour to make it*. "How credible do you think Ben's story is? I mean, we located the package. But unless we manage to lift Charlie's prints from it, we'll only have Ben's word that Charlie mailed it."

"I don't know what to tell you, Serena," Isaak said. "Ben was cooperative, but his alibi for the time of Jack's death is holier than Swiss cheese. It sounds like he's trying to cover his butt."

Yeah. I really wanted to believe Ben didn't have anything to do with Jack's or Charlie's deaths or the hit-and-run, but I was having a difficult time believing an innocent man would leave his sister to grieve alone for the uncle who'd been like a father to them for so many years.

"What about the truck he's been borrowing? Get anything off it?"

"I called the owner and Ben's story checked out. Given what happened to it, I doubt the guy will be so easygoing about lending out his next truck."

"Right."

Nate joined me at the table and set a sandwich and coffee in front of my place.

Thank you, I mouthed.

"I'm working on the search warrant," Isaak went on. "I want to question Marianne about Charlie and the argument you mentioned she had with Jack too. But that can wait until after the service."

"I'm sure she'd appreciate the reprieve."

"I've got to tell you, Serena, that at this point, even if there are antiquities in that parcel, the police haven't found anything to suggest Jack's or Charlie's deaths were murder."

"Excuse me?" I said indignantly, drawing curious looks from other customers. I lowered my voice. "Ben's truck and Charlie's house were firebombed. Clearly, someone doesn't want us to find something."

"I hear you. And I know you don't want to hear this, but Moore could be right that this is about drugs, not antiquities."

"Then how do you explain the parcel? Ben wouldn't have convinced Jack to call the feds if he'd made up the smuggling scheme."

"Are you sure? Jack was about to change his will, presumably to cut Ben out of a significant portion of the inheritance he'd been expecting—a portion that would then go to Jack's new wife and possibly her children, Charlie included. Accusing him of being a smuggler, and subtly implicating his sister by shipping the package to Jack's business, was an ingenious way to convince Jack to put the will change on hold."

I sighed. I wasn't sure of anything anymore.

"I'll admit Ben did seem genuinely worried about endangering his sister by being near her."

"Uh, *yeah*. He should be. Did you offer him protection?"

"An officer followed them home. There will be a few at the memorial service tonight and then I'm assuming we can count on you to watch for trouble when you all return to his sister's house for the night?"

"Of course. I'll see you later." I clicked off and Nate frowned at me.

"Who's going to watch your back?"

"My Glock," I said glibly, downplaying the obvious—that after three near misses, I was as likely a target as Ben.

The stubborn look he'd worn when he informed me he didn't scare away easily reappeared on his face. But I was too tired to counter whatever protection plan he was cooking up in that brain of his and took a big bite of my sandwich instead.

We made short work of polishing off our late lunch, then hiked up and down the streets, looking in all the shops. There was no sign of Devin anywhere.

Nate and I returned to the alley.

"No luck, huh?" Tanner said. "You may as well head over to the memorial service. I can keep watch here."

"You want backup?" Nate asked.

"I'd rather you watch Serena's back," Tanner said, although he looked pained to say it.

"We'll check Devin's house first," I said. "Maybe he walked home or got a lift."

"It can wait. You don't want to miss the memorial service."

"But I should—"

"Serene—uh," Tanner determinedly interjected. "Some things are more important than catching the bad guy."

I shut my mouth on the rest of my protest. "Who are you and what have you done with my friend?" I joked, but Tanner's gaze remained steady.

"It's because I'm your friend I'm telling you where you need to go. Now go."

27

Mom hustled over to us the moment Nate and I stepped into the church. "I was getting worried you wouldn't make it."

Nate shook Dad's hand and asked how his leg was feeling, then chatted with Aunt Martha. She rummaged in her purse and then handed him something. Nate glanced my way but quickly returned his attention to Aunt Martha, who was still chattering on.

"It was so nice of Nate to bring you," Mom enthused. "Carmen didn't bother coming. Where's Tanner?"

"He had something else he needed to do." I spotted Frank loitering outside the restrooms and excused myself to go talk to him. I forced myself to make small talk to lower his defenses, then hit him with a nonchalant, "Who handles the mail for your firm?"

"Carly picks it up from the post office and deals with as much as she can, then passes the rest on to me or Jack." The muscle in his cheek flinched. "Well, I guess just me now. Why?"

"Are you expecting a package, containing home décor items, from South America?"

Frank frowned. "Not me. Why? Oh, wait, Jack may've been. He was designing a place with a Mayan theme. Even had Carly print some pictures off the internet for him."

Okay, that might explain where the picture in Jack's pocket came from. "We believe the contents of the package may shed some light on whether Jack's death was truly an accident. Do we have your permission to inspect it?"

"Of course. I'll ask Carly to—"

Marianne emerged from the nearby ladies' room.

"Excuse me," Frank said and beckoned Marianne to join us. He slipped his hand around her waist and dipped his head to hers. "How are you holding up?" he asked tenderly.

She gave him a small, shaky smile. "Okay."

I offered my condolences to her once more.

"Can we finish this discussion later?" Frank asked, returning his attention to me. "I promised Marianne I'd escort her into the sanctuary."

"Yes, that's fine. But we do have your permission to open the package?"

"Yes, I'll let you know as soon as it comes in."

I squinted at him, trying to decide if he was being cooperative because he was innocent or because he naively assumed we wouldn't get our hands on the package before he did. I debated for half a second, then dropped the bomb that should elicit the answer. "Actually, the parcel was found, along with some of your firm's other mail, in a vehicle licensed to a Devin Fields."

"What?" he growled.

"Do you know who he is?"

"No, and I haven't a clue how he got his hands on our mail."

Marianne clasped his arm placatingly. "I think I may. Devin is Carly's boyfriend. His mom works at the post office."

Whoa, this was looking worse for Carly by the second. My gaze slid down Frank's bulky figure—definitely not the physique of the person caught on Jack's camera.

"She likely gave the mail to Devin to save Carly a trip," Marianne went on. "The mail's probably been piling up at the post office since Wednesday."

"You think so?" Frank asked, relief leaching from his voice.

"I'm sure that's all it is," Marianne assured.

"Okay, thank you," I said, and turned away before Frank had a chance to recant his permission.

"Wait," Marianne called after me. "You made it sound as if you found Devin's truck, but not Devin? Did he have car trouble?"

"No, his truck fit the description of a vehicle seen around Charlie's house at the time of the firebomb."

"Of course it would. He went there to see Carly. He stopped by our house with flowers and to drop off that mail, I suppose. Frank had just called to tell me he'd found her at Charlie's, so I urged Devin to go see her, to keep her company."

Frank's call to Marianne must've omitted who else had been there with Carly. I staunched the impulse to ask if Devin was the jealous type. Marianne didn't need more stress, minutes before Jack's memorial service. Instead, I thanked her again and slipped into a quiet corner to call Tanner.

"He's still a no-show," Tanner said.

"I talked to Frank about the package addressed to his firm, and he didn't know anything about it."

"You believe him?"

"He didn't so much as twitch when I brought it up. It's looking more and more like Carly acted as the receiver for her brother. She handles all the firm's mail and Devin is her boyfriend."

"Ahh. So she likely called or texted him when Ben first ran, or you said later she went to the bathroom? Asked him to create a diversion so she could get away," Tanner theorized.

"Maybe, but Marianne said she sent him to the house."

"Given the family's loss, we may want to wait until we confirm there are antiquities in the package before we confront Carly."

"Frank's given us permission to open the parcel."

"That's great, but first I need Devin to open his truck. Anyway, don't worry about any of that now. You need to be there with your family—in body, mind, and spirit."

My chest tightened at the thought of the gaping hole Jack's death left in so many people's lives. The years away had insulated me from fully feeling its impact. But Tanner was right—I owed Jack and my family my full presence.

Nate sidled up to me, straightened my shirt collar. "The family's heading in. Everything okay?"

I pocketed my phone with a silent nod and let him escort me in behind my family. Marianne, Frank, Ben, Ashley, and Preston sat in the first pew, and we filed into the one behind them. The remaining pews were already packed, and throngs of others stood along the walls. My heart lifted to see how dearly Jack was loved, that so many would come to bid him farewell and support his family. "Where's Carly?" I whispered to Nate.

"Her mother said she wasn't feeling well."

I glanced around the sanctuary and spotted a couple of other officer types doing the same, Special Agent Jackson among them. Maybe the state police hadn't completely dismissed the possibility of foul play. I didn't see Moore.

I dug my phone out of my purse so I could text him that Carly had apparently been in touch with her mother and that Carly's boyfriend had been behind the attack at Charlie's.

He phoned straight back, earning me a glare from my mother. "So a jealous boyfriend was behind the attack, huh?"

"Is that gloating I hear in your tone? Tell me you didn't think the attack had to do with whatever Charlie was involved with."

"Sure I did. Tossing firebombs at houses is exactly the kind of tactic I'd expect from a drug lord. From an antiquities dealer . . . I'd expect something subtler. Like poison in the pâté, maybe."

"Hmmm. You have any leads on who took out Charlie?"

"No, no one's talking." Translation: his informants had nothing.

Mom sliced me another scolding look.

I told Moore to keep me posted and then turned the phone to silent.

The service started with Jack's favorite hymn, "Amazing Grace," then person after person streamed forward to share how Jack had touched their lives. One family was the recipient of a Habitat for Humanity home he'd spearheaded and designed. Several were from organizations working in the developing world that Jack had partnered with on various humanitarian construction projects. Some had had Jack as a baseball coach in bygone years. Others had had him as a

Boys Club leader and got the crowd laughing with tales of the pranks Jack loved to play on them.

Still others had been helped by Jack's mentoring on various personal matters. All remarked how he'd always been quick to lend a helping hand or offer a listening ear or a word of counsel when sought. His greatest desire was to honor God and help others with the time, skills, and wealth he'd been given.

I sighed with the uncomfortable realization that my own life was pretty self-centered by comparison. I practically lived and breathed my job. Didn't spend nearly as much time with friends as they'd like. Sure, I helped out at the drop-in center once a week teaching art, and yeah, deep down I longed to ignite in them the creative spirit my granddad had nurtured in me, but I didn't want to overcommit, not when I still had Granddad's murderer to track down.

"Where were you?" Nate's quiet question jerked me out of my thoughts.

I looked at him blankly. "Pardon me?" That's when I clued in that people were already meandering out. "Oh." I shrugged. "Just thinking about what people may say about me when I die. 'She was a dedicated agent.'"

"You're so much more than that."

I shook my head. "Not really. Granddad used to urge me to follow my dreams. But after his murder, dreams of changing the world with my art morphed into dreams of becoming an FBI agent and tracking down his killer. Not exactly the kind of world changing I'd once envisioned myself doing, but the world needs people willing to stand in the gap for justice too, right?"

"Yes. But that's work. Where do you live?"

My heart thumped. I knew he was quoting a line from one of my all-time favorite romances—*Sabrina*, with Harrison Ford. But he was totally serious.

"We'd better join the family," I all but blurted, "or I'll earn another scolding from my mother." I winked, hoping he wouldn't notice how much his question had rattled me. Sure, I knew I was a workaholic, but my reasons were noble. Tanner at least understood that much.

28

Showtime.

Tanner's one-word text mobilized me into action.

Once Mom understood what was at stake she'd forgive me for ducking out of the post-service reception. By the time they all got back to Preston's she was bound to have heard about the excitement at Charlie's this afternoon. Still, I avoided her line of sight as I signaled Isaak to meet me at the exit.

Nate was still glued to my side, which was a good thing because he was also my ride.

"What's up?" Isaak asked.

"Tanner has eyes on Devin Fields. Entered the pub fifteen minutes ago. Was swaying like he'd already gotten a head start drinking. Tanner's already alerted local PD."

"I didn't manage to get the search warrant," Isaak said.

"Doesn't matter. The package is addressed to Hill and Dale Architects, and Frank Dale gave me permission to open it."

"Then what are we waiting for? Let's go talk to this guy and get that package."

Nate and I jumped into the Land Rover and Isaak tailed us in the personal SUV he'd ferried onto the island.

"There's Tanner," I exclaimed, pointing.

Tanner loitered on the sidewalk with a clear view into the pub.

Cars lined the street, so we circled the block and parked farther up the hill. A van pulled in behind us. The cheery passengers spilled out, appearing eager to begin their Saturday night festivities. We waited for them to saunter inside before approaching Tanner.

"We need to inspect the package first," Isaak said. "If we're looking at antiquities, then he'll be our collar. If the firebombing is all we have on him, then it'll be the local cops' turf."

"Forget that," Tanner said. "He targeted two federal officers. That makes it our turf."

"Besides," I added, "we don't have authority to break into his truck to retrieve the parcel. We're going to have to convince him to hand it over."

"There's a cruiser idling around the corner," Nate said.

"I asked them to be ready to pull Devin over if he made a run for it," Tanner explained.

"Okay, give Serena and me two minutes to get into position by his truck," Isaak said. "And then you two can flush him out."

"Be careful," I said to Nate. "If he tosses Molotov cocktails, chances are he also carries a weapon."

"That makes us even." Nate winked.

But the reminder he was packing heat left me feeling more unsettled. I kind of liked the litter-pan-scoop-wielding Nate who could joke about the gun pointed at his chest. I smiled at the memory of the time I'd mistakenly pulled a gun on him. Then again, if it were anyone but me with a finger on the trigger, I guess I'd be happy he traded his scoop for a gun.

The back alley was dark, with random patches dimly lit from light seeping out the odd window on the buildings along it. I pointed. "The truck's there."

"You stand by the driver's door, and I'll flank the rear door of the pub," Isaak ordered.

I glanced through the truck's window. The parcel still sat in the same place on the seat. Excitement welled up my chest. In a few minutes, I'd finally have some answers.

Standing there in the dark, waiting for Tanner to deliver our man, seconds felt like minutes and Dali's melting pocket watches painting took on a surreal meaning for me. Then . . .

Shouts erupted. A siren bleeped. Footsteps pounded down the alley.

"Grab him," Tanner shouted.

Devin sprinted through a patch of light, and I raced to intercept him. I tackled him to the pavement, dug my knee into his back, and waited for the fight to drain out of him, then wrenched his arms behind him and cuffed him under the glare of the headlights of the cruiser that followed Tanner and the suspect down the alley. "You're under arrest." I rose and hauled Devin to his feet, reciting his Miranda rights on the spot because there was no way I was waiting until we got back to the station to question this jerk. I wanted to get a look at what was inside that parcel.

"Good work, Jones," Tanner said, sounding out of breath. Nate and two uniformed police officers gathered around us as well.

"I can't believe you let him get away from you."

284

"That was my fault," Nate admitted. "We joined him at his table and I said, 'Remember me?'"

I grinned. "I'm guessing he did?"

"Yup, bolted faster than you can say *expeditiously*."

"Ha, Mr. Sutton would be proud." Sutton lived in our apartment building. He was a retired English professor and every morning he shared a new word with the residents and urged us to use it. *Expeditiously* was the one he'd passed along as I was leaving for this trip.

"This is your fault," Devin said to Nate, his speech slurred.

"How do you figure?"

"Carly loved me. Then *you* came along and messed with her brain."

Whoa, Nate was his target? Not Ben?

"I never even met Carly before this afternoon," Nate said defensively.

Devin shook his head in wide, exaggerated wags. "You're lying. Her boss said you came around asking about her."

"Frank?" I exchanged a glance with Nate. Frank told us he didn't know if Carly was dating anyone. But if Devin asked him about Carly seeing anyone else, they were clearly acquainted.

"Yeah, Frank."

Okay, maybe this was more convoluted than it seemed. Maybe Frank used Devin's jealousy to his advantage. Only . . . if Frank was our antiquities buyer, why give me the go-ahead to open the parcel?

Unless it was a plant. He could've wrapped something else in the same packaging, something that wasn't illegal, and given it to Devin for us to find. "Where did you get the parcel from?" I demanded.

Devin shot me a confused look.

"The parcel in your truck."

"Oh. My mom gave it to me to bring to Carly. She works at the post office."

Just as Marianne had supposed. It would be easy enough to verify. "When did Frank tell you about Nate's interest in Carly?"

"I'm not interested in Carly!" Nate interjected.

"Sorry. *Supposed* interest," I corrected.

"At the office yesterday afternoon. I stopped by to give her a lift home, only to find out she took the day off and didn't tell me. That's why I asked Frank if he'd seen her with another guy. She's been kind of distant for a few days."

"Uh, dimwit," Tanner interjected, "her mother's fiancé just died and they found the body. A little understanding instead of suspicion would've saved you from the bracelets."

He shook his head. "No, there's a guy. I heard her on the phone when I showed up last night and then she tells me she wants to cool it."

"She'd just found out her brother was dead," Tanner snapped back. "Did it occur to you that she didn't have the energy to deal with your insecurities on top of her own pain?"

Devin shrugged. "I guess that could've been it."

"How'd you know where Nate would be?" I jerked my chin toward Nate.

"I didn't. I took flowers to the house. You know, on account of her brother. Her mother told me she was at Charlie's place."

I nodded since Marianne's statement had already corroborated that much.

"So I brought the flowers there. Only she wasn't by herself." Devin's gaze shot daggers at Nate. If he hadn't been handcuffed, I had no doubt he would've gone for his throat.

I glanced at Special Agent Jackson, who was standing off to the side recording the conversation in his notebook. "And that made you mad," I said to Devin, stating the obvious for the record.

"I went crazy! I sped off and picked up my buddy and got the bottles ready and then we waited in my truck around the corner for the bozo to come out." He ducked his head. "I just wanted to scare him. You know?" His head snapped up once more. "But then he goes and shoots at me. That's when my friend saw Carly in the house with another guy."

"That was me and Detective Moore he saw. Not Carly."

Devin blinked, his eyes a tad blank, as if he couldn't quite register his mistake.

"She wasn't there?"

"No," I said, which was more or less true since I didn't know when exactly she'd escaped out the bathroom window.

Like a light had switched on in Devin's brain, he suddenly grew animated. "So . . . she doesn't know what I did? I could still have a chance with her."

Tanner shoved him toward the waiting police car. "When you get out of jail."

"Wait," I said. "Devin, I need you to open your truck so I can retrieve the mail belonging to Hill and Dale."

"Key's in my pocket."

Tanner did the honors and handed me the fob. I blipped it unlocked and returned the key.

Isaak snapped on latex gloves, photographed the stack of mail on the seat, then lifted out the lot and took a cursory glance around the cab.

I reached past him, activated the lock, and closed the door. "Inspect the parcel at the station?"

"Yes."

Tanner handed Devin to the cops for transport.

"You and Nate may as well take the rest of the night off," I said. "Get some dinner. I could be hours yet."

"That's okay. I've got nothing better to do," Tanner said.

"Me neither," Nate concurred. "Besides, I'm your ride."

"I could drive you back to Preston's to pick up your rental," Tanner offered. "Leave the Rover for Serena."

"The rental." How could that lead have slipped my mind? "I never heard back from Officer Lennox about who returned the damaged rental car Thursday morning."

"I got the report on that," Isaak said. "Dead end. It was one of the state troopers who came to the island to investigate Jack's death."

"And that automatically makes him innocent?" Nate asked. "Haven't you ever heard of corrupt cops?"

"What was his name?" I asked Isaak.

"Alan Moore."

"Really? Interesting."

"Sounds dodgy," Nate said, adopting one of my aunt's expressions. "Moore had to have overheard Martha's call. I did. Why not fess up on the spot?"

"He may not have heard. He was focused on Carly and Ben at the time. And at the Boston airport he watched Charlie like a suspect, not a partner."

"And he didn't arrive on the island until the day after Jack died," Isaak added.

"All that tells us is he didn't kill Jack," Nate said.

"Well, if he didn't, it's doubtful he'd be worried my

snooping would uncover evidence to incriminate him," I reasoned.

"Maybe not in Jack's death, but what about the smuggling ring?"

I yanked open the car door. "Let's see what's in the parcel before we go there, because if Charlie was smuggling antiquities and Moore was in on it, risking exposure by investigating his partner for drug running seems pretty insane. Don't you think?"

"Maybe he didn't know. Didn't you once tell me antiquity smuggling operations typically run a lot like terrorist cells? With members of the various parts of the operation not knowing those involved further along—or back—in the time line?"

Yeah, okay. It sounds like something I said. It was one of the reasons we were usually careful about not making arrests too soon. Arresting a minor—easily replaced—underling in the food chain only served to tip off the people running the show that we were on to them before we had enough intel to shut them down.

Charlie was likely such a cog. But one who knew too much.

The question was, who or what had tipped off the ring's mastermind?

29

I followed Special Agent Jackson and the police cruiser transporting Devin to Oak Bluff's police department in the Land Rover while Tanner drove Nate to Preston's to retrieve his rental. Devin would spend the rest of the weekend in Dukes County Jail in Edgartown, which was no country club for convicts despite the gorgeous Main Street facade. But first I had a lot more questions I wanted to ask him.

Unfortunately, I wasn't the only one with questions.

Mom phoned, having just heard about the afternoon's attack. "Do you think it's safe for Ben to stay at the house with you and Ashley?" Mom asked in a hushed tone. "Can't the police put him in protective custody or something?"

What was I, chopped liver? "You don't have to worry, Mom. The attacker was after Nate, not Ben."

"What?" she shrieked.

I pulled the phone from my ear to soften the blow. Okay, I could've phrased that better. I nodded to the officers escorting Devin to an interrogation room to await the officer who'd been investigating this afternoon's fires.

"Mom, I need to go. Nate will explain when he gets there." I clicked off before she could grill me further. I bypassed the interrogation room and followed Isaak to a back room. The rest of my questions for Devin could wait until after I looked inside the package.

Isaak dusted the parcel and lifted more than two dozen prints. He then removed the outer layer of brown wrapping paper and repeated the process on the interior layer, managing to lift a half dozen more prints.

I handed them off to the expert who'd compare them to the prints taken from Charlie's body and then I scooped up the PD's camera to take pictures of what was inside the box.

"Ready?" Isaak asked me, grinning.

"Get on with it!"

He slit the tape sealing the cardboard box and gingerly plucked at the packing paper inside.

At the sight of an ancient vase, I gasped and lowered the camera for a closer look. "It looks almost identical to the Fenton Vase in the picture Jack had been carrying." I studied the images on the side of the vase of a Mayan ruler sitting cross-legged on a bench, wearing an enormous headdress, pointing to a basket full of corn. *Such a crime.* "To think if an archeological team had excavated this vase, it may've significantly deepened our knowledge of the Mayan culture. Instead, thanks to some looter, the context of the find—the key to our understanding—has been lost forever."

"I suspect the looter would've been more concerned about putting food on his table," Isaak said.

"True enough. And it doesn't help when indigenous people can make more money digging for terra cotta than farming.

What irks me is the entitled attitude of the collectors who fuel the market."

"Is it genuine?" Isaak asked as I picked it up to examine the bottom then the interior.

"We're going to need an expert to make that judgment call." Estimates pegged the number of fake Mayan pots on the market these days at 85 percent. Even U.S. museums were suspected by some of unwittingly displaying the odd forgery.

I phoned Preston and explained the situation. "Can you give us your opinion on its authenticity?"

"Tonight?" He didn't sound as if he liked the idea of venturing out again.

I guess I should've expected the reaction. Professors kept different hours than law enforcement.

"Tomorrow is fine," Isaak said.

I relayed the message to Preston and told him I'd touch base with him again in the morning.

Isaak took over the camera and snapped more photos of the vase, then inserted the memory card into a printer in the corner of the room and printed copies.

A knock sounded at the door and our fingerprint expert let himself in. "We have a positive match. Several in fact."

"To Charlie Anderson's prints?" I clarified.

The man consulted the paperwork in his hand. "That's right. Three thumbprints. Two index finger prints and a pinky." He handed over the paperwork.

"Great, thank you." Oddly, I didn't feel the elation I'd expected. Pinning a smuggling charge on Marianne's son, on top of what she'd already been through this week, gave me little satisfaction. I shook my head. "I really wanted to believe Carly's adamant defense of her brother this afternoon wasn't an act."

"I suppose there's a remote chance that she honestly didn't know what her brother was into. At least not until she heard Ben's story."

My heart hitched. "If that's true, then Carly could be our killer's next target." Then again, it was more palatable than the alternative. I texted Moore, but recalling Nate's suspicions of him, I hesitated clicking SEND. Then again . . . his response could be telling.

Still no sign of her, he texted back.

I expected him to hand off the search now that we'd confirmed Charlie was dealing in antiquities, but he wasn't ready to dismiss his intel on a drug connection. A reasonable enough explanation.

Isaak gathered up the printouts and tapped them into a neat stack. "Let's talk to Devin."

We carefully wrapped the vase, labeled it for evidence, and checked it into the PD's evidence room until we could arrange for its transport to the FBI's Boston headquarters. By the time we reached the interrogation room where Devin had been deposited, the room was empty. We stopped a passing officer. "Where's the suspect who was being held in this room?"

"Transported to lockup. Too drunk to question, the detective said."

I thanked him for the update but inwardly fumed. I didn't disagree Devin might've been too sloshed, but the detective should've at least consulted us first. I believed Devin's story that he acted out of jealousy, but if he'd dated Carly for any length of time, he might know a thing or two about Charlie's apparent sideline business.

Isaak glanced at his watch. "We're going to need search warrants for the architect firm, for Frank's and Carly's homes, and for whatever else they own or rent—car, boat, storage locker. But I'll have an easier time convincing the judge once your expert confirms the vase's authenticity."

"Two people are already dead and Carly is missing or gone to ground. Take your pick. From where I'm standing, whether it's genuine or not, someone didn't want us connecting it and who knows how many more pieces to him."

"Or her."

"Exactly."

"Well, we could stop by Marianne Delmar's and see what she has to say about her son's alleged activities and her daughter's possible involvement. If she grants us permission to search the house, it'll save us the red tape."

I exhaled a reluctant sigh. The poor woman had already had a brutal enough day.

As we reached the lobby, Tanner strode in carrying a bag of Chinese takeout. "Finished already? I figured you could use some supper."

The food smelled fantastic.

"I ate before the memorial service," Isaak said.

"We're heading to Marianne's to question her about Charlie," I added even though I was salivating like a Pavlov dog.

"I can help Serena with that," Tanner said to Isaak. "You're supposed to be on vacation here, aren't you? I'm sure your family would appreciate having you back."

"Yeah, I'm sure they would. But if you two want to question Marianne, I'll pay Frank Dale a visit."

"Sounds like a good plan," I concurred, practically tasting the moo goo gai pan already. "I'll update you on what we learn."

Isaak gave a casual salute and strode out.

Tanner handed me the take-out bag. "Leave the Land Rover here and you can eat while I drive."

I was too famished to argue. As he wound through Oak Bluffs' residential streets, I gobbled the food, mmm-ing over the yummy taste, between telling him about the vase and Charlie's fingerprints on the package.

"So I guess I was wrong about the Fenton Vase picture found in Jack's pocket being a plant to misdirect investigators."

"Frank mentioned that Carly printed some Mayan pictures for him. Frank had assumed they were for a design he was working on, but maybe it was to show the feds what Charlie had allegedly mailed. Or maybe to show Marianne."

"And if Carly knew what her brother mailed to the office, she could've been the one who set off the alarm bells."

"For Marianne's sake, I hope not."

Tanner parked at the curb opposite Marianne's house and I gobbled faster. The living room light was on and the shadow of an occupant was visible behind the drapes. "No hurry," Tanner said. "She's not going anywhere."

I shoveled the last few forkfuls into my mouth, then stuffed the carton back in the bag. "That was good. Thank you."

"Hey, don't forget the fortune cookie. It's in the bag."

"I'm good."

"Ah, c'mon. Don't you want to know what your fortune is?"

"You don't actually believe in them?"

He grinned. "They're fun."

I pulled the plastic-wrapped cookie out of the bag and pressed it into his hand. "The fun's all yours."

"If you insist. *I'm* not afraid to embrace my future." He ripped the plastic, cracked open the cookie, and silently read the little slip of paper inside, then popped the cookie into his mouth.

"What did it say?"

"I thought you didn't believe in them."

I plucked the slip of paper from his fingers, not trusting the laughter in his eyes.

Romance will soon blossom.

30

"We'd better get started on the interview," I blurted, climbing out of Tanner's rental. Back in St. Louis, I'd have immediately tossed a teasing comeback about his cookie's fortune. I mean, the man was married to the FBI. We'd been like-minded in that regard. But something about the way his eyes had softened as he watched me read the fortune made me think maybe he hoped it would come true. With me.

And I didn't know what to do with that.

The flutter in my heart was an uncomfortable cross between excited anticipation and full-out panic. How could I be equally intrigued by the idea of a romance with Tanner and of one with Nate? In the middle of an investigation, no less!

"Hey, isn't that Moore?" Tanner pointed to a dark sedan parked two houses down on the other side of the street.

I squinted at the windshield. "I think you're right."

Moore lowered his window as we approached.

"Switch-hitting again, I see," he said to me and chuckled, then turned his attention to Tanner. "How's the arm?"

"Not bad. I guess Serena forgot to loop you in that this has shaped up to be an antiquity smuggling case after all?"

"Sure, but we still have a reliable source that puts Charlie at a known drug lord's house, and I want to talk to Carly about what she knows."

Tanner nodded. "Fair enough. We're headed in to question her mother."

"Hey," I said to Moore as Tanner started back across the street. "I heard you had a run-in with a deer the other night."

"Yeah, I grazed her hind end. But she ran off into the woods, so hopefully she survived. How'd you hear about that?"

"A friend had mechanical trouble on his rental from the same dealer."

"Ah."

As I rejoined Tanner on the other side of the street, he said, "You believe him?"

"Yeah. He didn't hesitate a second and held my gaze through the entire explanation. I don't think he's dirty."

"And the fact he looks like a movie star doesn't have anything to do with your conclusions?"

"Right, because actors are sooo innocent." I glanced over my shoulder at Moore's car pulling away from the curb and waved.

"Just checking." Tanner knocked on Marianne's door. After the third knock she finally answered.

"I'm sorry to bother you at this hour," I said, "but I'm sure Carly's told you about Ben's allegations."

"No. What are you talking about?" Marianne's brow furrowed, although from the way she shrunk back an instant later, I suspected she'd guessed what the allegations were.

"May we come in? We think you might be able to help us pinpoint the person responsible for Charlie's death." That was the big question mark in my mind, because as good as Carly looked for Charlie's accomplice, I hoped for her mother's sake she didn't kill him to save her own hide.

Marianne hesitated.

"You may be surprised what clues you've picked up that you aren't even aware of," Tanner said, maneuvering us inside before she could object.

We declined her offer of coffee and joined her in the front room. Flower arrangements decked every spare table and shelf. But the colorful blossoms and cloying fragrance only seemed to deepen the oppressive sense of gloom in the house. I shook off the thought and focused on the task at hand.

"Marianne, did Jack express concerns about Charlie smuggling antiquities into the country?"

Her face paled and she slumped into a chair. "It's not true."

I perched on an upholstered armchair opposite her. "Which part? That he spoke to you? Or that Charlie was involved in something illegal?"

She bowed her head. "Jack talked to me. I was horrified he could believe such lies about my son. He wouldn't tell me who told him." Marianne twisted the facial tissue she held in her hand as tears leaked from the corners of her eyes. "Charlie was a good boy."

"I know you want to believe that, but we have fingerprint evidence corroborating the allegations."

Marianne vigorously shook her head.

"We suspect whoever Charlie was working with silenced both him *and* Jack," Tanner interjected.

"No! The police said Jack fell down the steps. That it was an accident."

I steeled myself against the squeeze in my chest. Because my agent side was clanging all kinds of alarm bells. She sounded as if she had a much more personal reason for not wanting to believe he was the victim of foul play. Did Marianne honestly find it more comforting to believe Jack's death was an accident?

I couldn't. It was too senseless. Not that his death at the hand of a criminal he was trying to bring to justice wasn't senseless too, but at least it was heroic.

"Can you tell us who Charlie spent time with when he was home?" Tanner asked.

"I don't know. He's lived on his own for years."

"Were you surprised Charlie could afford to buy his own place?"

Her eyes widened. Clearly she hadn't questioned her son's financial status. "He doesn't waste his money. He hasn't had a girlfriend that I know of in a while."

Still, a place like Charlie's on Martha's Vineyard, even with low interest rates, would've been a stretch. My brother couldn't have managed it, and he did the same kind of work as Charlie. "How about old friends from school?" I asked. "From the neighborhood? Did he keep in touch with any of them?"

"He used to hang out with the boy next door. Carly would know better than me who he spent time with back then. The kids didn't usually bring their friends home."

"Did Charlie know Frank?"

"Jack's partner? Sure. After Jack and I started dating, Charlie would sometimes pick his sister up from work and bring her out to Quansoo Beach."

I nodded. This time of year anyone could use the beach, but come summer, access was restricted to residents and their friends—a perk of knowing the right people.

"Charlie and Carly were close then."

Marianne inhaled sharply.

"I'm not implying Carly was involved in whatever Char—"

"It's Joe," Marianne blurted.

"Pardon me?" I exchanged a glance with Tanner, who seemed equally thrown.

"Charlie was working for Joe."

"The estate sale guy?"

"Yes."

We pushed her for details but Marianne pressed her fisted hand to her mouth and muffled a sob. "Talk to Joe."

31

Joe didn't seem surprised to see us back at his gingerbread cottage. He invited us to sit in the front room.

"Was Charlie working for you?" I asked Joe as soon as everyone had taken a seat.

"Marianne tell you that?"

"Yes."

He contemplated that a moment. "Like I told you earlier, all my purchases and sales are above board."

"Was Charlie working for you?" I repeated more insistently.

"No. Never. And despite what Carly claimed, she wasn't either when they arrested her."

What? I refrained from blurting the thought aloud, but he must've noticed my surprise. "What was she arrested for?" And how on earth had I missed an arrest in her background check? The charges must've been dropped. Expunged.

"Antiquities smuggling."

My breath hitched.

"Marianne neglected to tell you that? That's what she

came to see me about this afternoon. Pleaded with me not to speak of it."

This afternoon? I looked at Tanner. *Was Joe saying what it sounded like he was saying?*

"What changed your mind?" Tanner asked.

I leaned forward, remembering the needle in Joe's throat. If it'd been Marianne's doing, he would've exposed her then and there. Wouldn't he?

"I figure if she sent you here," Joe said, "she's decided punishing Charlie's killer is more important than protecting Carly."

My heart pounded. Carly killed Jack? Was that what Joe was saying? "What do you mean by protecting Carly?"

"When Carly was in college, customs caught her smuggling a Mayan statue out of Mexico after spring break. She'd worked the previous summer for me and claimed I'd asked her to smuggle it into the country.

"She was lying, of course. And the police figured that out quick enough. They never found anything illegal in my entire stock. Not that that stopped Marianne from blaming me for corrupting her daughter." He shook his head. "The truth is, she probably blamed herself more than anything. She fell apart after her second husband died. Didn't give Carly the parenting she needed when it mattered most."

I exchanged a glance with Tanner, trying to decide if I bought Joe's story. Marianne didn't act as if she thought Joe killed Charlie, but she'd seemed to think Joe should know who did.

"In a way, the arrest was the wake-up call that turned Marianne's life around. She managed to get the charges dismissed and cautioned Carly and her brother to never mention them to a soul. Since detectives from the mainland investigated the allegations against me, no one here heard about them, and I was as happy as Marianne to keep it that way. Allegations like that don't exactly build customer confidence."

"So when Jack confided in Marianne about his suspicions of Charlie, Marianne feared Carly had gone back to her old ways?" I surmised.

"Not at all. She figured I'd recruited Charlie. Didn't believe my denials."

"Then why didn't she report you?"

"Like I said, she didn't want to risk Carly's history being dredged up."

"So stabbing you with the needle was her revenge?"

He stroked the back of his fingers over the puncture site. "It truly was an accident. She lashed out at me, but she didn't know what she was doing."

Even so . . . awfully big of him to not press charges. Then again, I suppose that would only open his business up to the wrong kind of publicity.

"Marianne thinks you know who killed Charlie," Tanner interjected. "Do you?"

"Haven't a clue. There are plenty of folks on the island rich enough to hire a personal antiquities shopper. The kid had a great cover for the job."

"Anyone in particular come to mind? Someone who collects Mayan antiquities?" I asked.

He picked up a notepad from his end table and jotted a name and number on it. "He's the biggest art dealer on the island. He may be able to point you in the right direction."

I glanced at the name—a dead end Isaak had already tried to milk. Dealers were notoriously protective of their clients' identities. Then again, the dealer could be the mastermind behind the whole operation. Hopefully, the search warrants would turn up a connection.

"What about Carly?" Tanner asked. "You think she could've been working with her brother?"

Joe shrugged. "We haven't exactly been on speaking terms since she hung me out to dry."

We thanked Joe for his time and retreated to Tanner's rental, where I put in a call to Isaak and put it on speakerphone.

"I don't know what to think about Frank," Isaak said. "He admitted to asking Joe to place the ad on eBay for the Egyptian amulet."

"He was Joe's client?"

"Yup. Claimed it was the first time he'd ever done anything like that, but said he changed his mind when he saw you and Nate waiting at the tabernacle. Figured it was a sting."

"Huh, so Nate had called that one right."

"Frank insisted, though, that as far as he was concerned his collection was legit. Even showed me his grandfather's will with an itemized list of every piece."

"But you didn't believe him?"

"No, I did. He gave me a tour of the house, told me about each piece, but I also counted at least six pictures of Marianne in the house."

"What kind of pictures?" Tanner asked.

"Innocent-enough looking ones in isolation. One of Marianne and Carly at a customer appreciation event. One of her and Jack on his boat. One of her serving Frank cake at a surprise birthday party Jack threw for him. One of her at the beach, turning back to the camera and laughing with Jack walking ahead in the distance."

"Okay, we get the idea. He's obsessed with her."

"Yeah, but his alibi for the night Jack was killed checks out."

"He's not obsessed. He's in love," I corrected. "You can see it in how he looks at her."

Tanner choked on a laugh. "Oh, you can, can you?"

I shot him an irritated look. "Yes. You *can*," I insisted.

Tanner raised his hands in surrender, still with an annoying half grin on his face. "I'm not arguing with you. Sometimes it's easier to see those kinds of things in others than for ourselves."

"Exactly—he may not have realized how much he cared for her until it was too late. It explains why Frank wanted to buy Jack out. It was the noble thing to do."

A raised brow replaced Tanner's amusement. "So what you're saying is if a guy loves a girl who is being pursued by another guy, pulling himself from the race proves his love is pure?"

"Yes."

"I'll let you two finish the debate on your own," Isaak interjected. "I have a family to get home to. The team will meet at the Oak Bluffs station at 9:00 a.m. to execute the search warrants. See you then."

I clicked off my phone and finished my argument. "If a guy truly loves a woman, he'll want what's best for her. He wouldn't want to jeopardize her happiness by sabotaging her wedding plans."

"Even if he's ready to propose their own happily ever after?" Tanner's voice spiked with a tone of disbelief. "He is in love with her after all, right?"

"But he obviously didn't make that known soon enough,

before her emotions were entangled elsewhere, and not wanting to cause her any distress, he'd do the noble thing and bow out."

He looked at me speculatively. "You really think that's noble?"

"Yes!"

Tanner started the car and pulled away from the curb. "Killing him would be more expedient."

32

Tanner was unusually quiet as he drove me back to the police station. Maybe feeling self-conscious about the "expedient" quip. We were talking about my family friend after all. He stopped in front of my borrowed Land Rover. "Get some sleep, Jones. Tomorrow you'll get your answers."

"I hope so. Thanks for your help today."

A smile flitted across his face. "Any time."

He waited while I climbed into the vehicle, trailed me as far as his B&B, then flicked his headlights and turned off. A couple of minutes later my phone rang.

"It's Moore. Learn anything I should know about?" He sounded as if he was driving too.

"We're executing search warrants in the morning. Turns out Carly was arrested for smuggling as a coed."

"Who told you that?" Irritation laced his voice.

"Don't beat yourself up. Our background check didn't turn up the report either. The guy she accused of putting her up to it told us."

"Oh yeah?"

308

Realizing I'd passed Ashley's road, I pulled a U-turn.

"Joe got any idea where she may be holed up now?"

Spotting the road this time, I turned into the woods. "No."

"You got a plan to flush her out?"

"No, heading back to my friend's for a good night's sleep."

"Ditched the sidekicks, did you?" He chuckled.

Slowing down for the driveway, I chuckled too. No denying it must've seemed comical the way I'd show up at one scene with Nate and at the next with Tanner. "They've gone home. Goodnight."

My headlights swept across Jack's porch as I pulled into the driveway. Someone was on the porch steps. I parked in front of Ashley's cottage and could see her and Ben's silhouette, through the curtain, sitting in front of the TV. I squinted at Jack's porch. I wouldn't put it past Aunt Martha to wait out here for an update on the investigation, but she'd stand up and yoo-hoo me. I reached for my phone to use the flashlight app.

The visitor rose from the step, triggering the motion detector light. Carly.

No way. I thumbed a quick text message to Tanner: *You won't believe who's waiting for me on Jack's porch—Carly.*

She was hugging the same thin sweater around her middle as she'd been wearing earlier.

I couldn't see her hands, so I slid out from the passenger side of the vehicle to give myself cover.

"Al killed Charlie," she wailed across the distance between us, "and he's going to kill me."

"Okay, take it easy. Can I see your hands?"

They flew into the air. "Please, you have to listen to me."

"I will. I just need to know you're not going to pull a gun

on me." I beamed the cell phone's flashlight over her hands, pockets, waistband.

"I don't have a gun."

I swept the light beam over the rest of the porch, then stepped out from behind the cover of my vehicle. "You fled from the scene of a crime, Carly. This is standard precaution, okay? Please turn and place your hands against the wall so I can check you for myself."

Her story spilled out as I patted her down. "He's been blackmailing me for years. Threatened to turn us in if we didn't pay. So we did. We always paid. But then when he heard about Jack—" Her voice cracked.

"Okay, you can put down your hands and turn around."

"He must've gotten scared we'd turn on him to cut a deal. That's why he killed Charlie. I'm sure of it." She swallowed hard and, finally seeming to register my instructions, lowered her hands and started to turn toward me.

"Who?" I asked.

Her gaze shot past my shoulder.

Instinctively, I dove.

But not quickly enough. Probes caught me in the shoulder and a gazillion watts of electricity jolted through my body. Dropped me to the ground. My limbs shook uncontrollably. A fist clipped me in the jaw. Then everything went black.

33

I drifted into consciousness, feeling as if I was falling. I landed with a bone-jarring thud.

"We're going for a little ride," a familiar voice whispered in my ear, followed by a knockout blow to the head.

I awoke to the low whirr of a motor

My eyes flew open. But blackness still enveloped me.

And the suffocating smell of gasoline.

A trunk. I was in a trunk! I tried to scream but tasted cloth. I instinctively reached for it. Only . . . my arm wouldn't move. This couldn't be happening. This couldn't be happening. This *so* could *not* be happening.

I writhed against the binds holding my arms wrenched behind my back. Tiny pebbles dug into my cheek. Pins and needles prickled my legs, which were also bound.

I strained to finger the knot securing my wrists, but could scarcely graze the rope.

Panic set in with a vengeance. My breath came in short desperate gulps. Well, as much as I could gulp with a gag between my lips. And yeah, my brain knew that was a bad thing. That it'd use up the oxygen faster. But I couldn't stop. I could barely endure confined spaces at the best of times. *Oh, Lord, please, let this be a dream.*

Breathe. Tanner's calm voice came to me, as audibly as if he were right beside me. My mind flashed to how he got me through a panicked elevator ride. Except . . .

A trunk was twenty times smaller. Carbon monoxide could be seeping in through the holes. If there were holes. And if there weren't holes, I could run out of oxygen in . . .

Breathe, Tanner's order whispered through my mind once more.

I squeezed my eyes closed and forced my breathing to slow—long inhalations through my nose; relaxing exhalations through my mouth.

Other realities began to set in. The gentle roll of the floor beneath me. The quietness of the motor. It couldn't belong to the car I was in . . . if I was even right about being in a trunk. A boat maybe? A ferry?

Yes, that had to be it. The ferry to the mainland was forty-five minutes. It gave me time. But how much? I had no idea how long I'd been out.

I worked my jaw to try and edge the cloth out of my mouth, but it was no use.

I drew my knees to my chest and wriggled my hips through the circle of my arms, followed by my legs.

Whew. My muscles relaxed a fraction at the reduced strain. I yanked the gag from my mouth, but still couldn't maneuver my fingers enough to loosen the ropes around my wrists. I made short work of untying my ankles. Then, ignoring the screaming numbness that gripped my legs with the returning circulation, I maneuvered the best I could, feeling around for the trunk's release latch. Where was it? I felt my pockets for my cell phone. It was gone. So was my off-duty weapon.

My breaths were coming too fast again. Remembering Tanner's calming voice, I drew a long, slow breath and scrutinized the blackness, hoping for a glow-in-the-dark trunk release. No such luck. I felt up and down the rear panel, praying my abductor hadn't been smart enough to dismantle the latch.

Who was he? Someone strong enough to hoist me into his trunk. And where had the vehicle come from? Ashley's had been the only other car in the driveway. I'd seen lights behind me on the road at one point, but I didn't hear anyone drive up after I parked. He must've already been parked farther up the road, watching and waiting. A setup, like I'd feared.

Had to be or Carly would be here too.

He's going to kill me. Carly's voice echoed through my brain—the terrified tone that had neatly drawn me into the Taser's range.

My finger caught on a sheared-off bolt. "Ow!" My heart sank. He'd cut the latch. I strained to recall what I'd thought sounded so familiar about his voice when he said we were going for a ride.

A loud thump vibrated through the floor beneath me. What was going on?

The car's engine roared to life.

No! I quelled the impulse to kick and scream. This could be my last best chance for someone to hear or see me, but if no one did, my abductor would know I'd come to and do something about it the first chance he got.

Another engine came on and a thin beam of light seeped into my prison.

There was a car behind us! With one great heave, I kicked the corner of the trunk, aiming, I hoped, for the taillight.

The car lurched forward, sending me tumbling. My face slammed into metal. Pain exploded from my nose. I cradled it with my bound hands and kicked again.

A hoarse curse cut through the engine noise and the car braked abruptly.

I stilled, holding my throbbing nose and my breath.

A horn beeped.

The car lurched forward once more and I breathed again. Except from the change in noise of the tires, he was off the ferry too soon for it to be the one to the mainland. It must be the little ferry that crossed the channel to Chappaquidick. How long did I have before he found a secluded spot to pull off and check on me?

The rough cords binding my wrists chafed my lips. Releasing my nose, I realized I could tug at the ropes with my teeth. Why didn't I think of that sooner? The cords felt like binder twine—thin and prickly. I ground them back and forth between my front teeth until I isolated one, then pulled.

The ropes tightened against my wrists.

I isolated a second cord and tried again, prayed whoever tied me up couldn't tie knots as well as Ben. *Ben?* Could he have done this?

He'd been in the house with Ashley. I'd seen his silhouette. Or was it Preston I saw?

I isolated a third cord and tugged. It slackened and my hopes surged. Ashley must've heard me scream. Called the police. And Tanner . . . Tanner would've hightailed it over to Jack's the second he saw my text. He'd be looking for me. He'd have every cop on the island looking for me!

I tugged faster, switching between cords until the ropes were loose enough for me to wriggle my hands free.

I patted my hands along the floor, searching for something I could use as a weapon. *A tire iron would be good, Lord.*

The trunk was stripped clean.

Straining to move as quietly as possible, I searched again for the latch. Not finding it, I reoriented myself and yanked back the fabric lining the wall of the trunk on the driver's side. Most cars had a trunk release cable you could activate from the front of the car, and if I could find it . . .

The car started to slow then suddenly swerved, throwing me to the other end of the trunk and back again.

A string of curse words punctuated by a loud smack split the air. "Do that again and you can join her in the trunk," a deep male voice bellowed from the front of the vehicle. "You leave over Maya dead body. Got it?"

"You won't get away with—" a female shrieked and then suddenly clammed up.

Carly. And she didn't sound copacetic with her partner's plan.

But if that were true, why didn't the guy put her in the trunk earlier? He had to have overheard what Carly told me. And if Carly were so scared of him, why didn't she run when he zapped me? Scream for Ashley? Something?

She must've been going along with him. He couldn't have managed to subdue both of us. Unless he'd reloaded a second after knocking me out and then Tasered her too.

Carly's first words outside Jack's came back to me then. "Al killed Charlie." I'd been so hyper focused on ensuring her being there wasn't a setup that the allegation hadn't registered.

Who was Al? Albert. Alvin. Alan.

My breath caught. *Alan Moore?*

As I scrambled once more to feel for the cable that would release the trunk, my thoughts flipped back to the interrogation at Charlie's. To Carly's wary glances at Moore. To her cry of *why are you doing this to me?*

What had she said before that Taser scrambled my brain? He'd been blackmailing her.

Of course. In my last conversation with Moore, when I told him Carly was arrested, he'd asked if *Joe* knew where she was. But I never mentioned Joe's name. I'd been so distracted at missing my turn, it hadn't registered. Moore must've been part of the investigation, kept his eye on Carly and Charlie after that, and when he caught them smuggling again, blackmailed them for his silence.

Snippets of Carly's frantic explanation came back to me then. He'd been afraid she'd cut a deal, she'd said. That's why he'd been so desperate to find Carly after her escape from Charlie's house. That's why he'd only pretended to contact the post office about the parcel. That's why he kept trying to make the investigation about drugs. He'd probably fabricated the intel on Charlie's meet with a drug dealer to explain the murder Moore had been planning. Only, Carly gave him the slip before he could take care of her too.

My fingers curled over a wire, and I gave it a hard tug. Nothing happened. I tried again. Still nothing. Willing my pounding heart to slow, I felt around for another.

Once I learned of Carly's former arrest, Moore must've known it was only a matter of time before I connected his name to the investigation. That's why he asked if I'd ditched Nate and Tanner. How could I have fallen for his I-hit-a-deer story? He must've been watching me since that first night, staged the accident to put an end to my snooping.

To think I'd trusted him. Checked in with him countless times on the status of the investigation.

The car jerked to a stop, and my head bounced off the carpeted back of the rear seat. A car door slammed.

This was my chance! I kicked in the backseat and scrambled through. "Drive," I shouted to Carly, slapping the door lock.

"I can't. He took the keys!"

Moore appeared at my window with a gun and up popped the door lock.

"Run," I screamed and hurtled out the opposite door.

34

Carly and I jumped out of the car and dashed straight into the woods. The underbrush was sparse, which made for easier running but not hiding. And the sound of branches slapping past us was too easy to track.

A flashlight beam cut through the darkness and bounced off the trees.

"Duck behind there," I whispered to Carly, pointing to an uprooted tree. "I'll draw him away." I scooped up a club-sized branch.

Carly clutched my arm. "No, don't leave me!"

"Down," I hissed and pushed her to the ground a nano-second before the light beam swept past where we'd been standing. I clamped my hand over her mouth and bodily forced her to remain still.

Moore's footsteps trekked away from our position. Did he really not hear her cry out? Or just mistake the direction of the sound in the darkness?

A third possibility snaked through my thoughts—she'd deliberately alerted him. I had no illusions Carly wouldn't sell me out if she thought it would save her hide. "Why didn't Moore tie you up?" I whispered in her ear, then eased the pressure of my hand over her mouth just enough to allow her to answer.

"Charlie hid evidence and I'm Moore's only hope of finding it."

"What evidence? Where?"

"Charlie secretly recorded my last conversation with Moore about his next payment. For insurance, Charlie said. Only . . ." A hot tear spilled onto my hand hovering over her mouth. "Threatening Moore with it didn't convince him to spare Charlie's life."

"Where's the evidence?"

"I don't know. Charlie never told me. But Moore was convinced Charlie hid it somewhere on Chappy. Asked me where we used to go treasure hunting with our dad."

Because of the photo Ben saved.

"I couldn't remember where Dad used to take us, but I figured the longer I pretended I did, the better my chances of getting away."

"Shh." I concentrated on the sounds around us. I thought I'd heard the hum of an engine, but now there was no sound beyond the wind whispering through the treetops. I edged up a fraction to see around the upturned tree root. There was no sign of Moore, but no way would he give up the search with what he had at stake. There was only one main road through Chappaquidick. If I ran toward the ferry dock, it shouldn't be long before I intercepted a car, maybe even Tanner's. I ducked back down. "You wait here. I'm going to go for help."

"No, please, take me with you."

"I can run faster on my own. Does Moore have a partner?"

The last thing I wanted to do was flag down any reinforcements he might've called in to help him with his manhunt.

Hand over her mouth to cover her whimpers, Carly shook her head.

"Okay, don't move." I scrutinized the surrounding forest once more, then took off toward the road. Even with as lightly as I tried to tread, my footfalls sounded like the stomp, stomp of a giant piece of machinery.

I hadn't put more than twenty yards between us when Carly's cry pierced the darkness, followed by Moore's voice. "I've got her, Jones."

I froze.

"I've got your gun pointed at her head." Carly's sobs punctuated his words.

I didn't move. Didn't speak.

"I guess you'd just as soon I shoot her?" Moore taunted. "She told you she silenced Jack, then?"

My breath caught. Was it true? Or was he fishing for a reaction? Something to give away my position? My mind rewound through everything Carly said from the moment I got to Jack's. Her voice had cracked on *then when he found out about Jack.*

I'd assumed she meant that when Moore found out Jack had called the FBI, Moore killed him. But . . . he'd arrived on the island the same day as me. I gave my head a mental shake. Not necessarily—he could've been here the night before and taken the ferry out in the morning.

"I didn't. I didn't," Carly cried out. "You have to beli—"

Whatever Moore did to her cut off her explanation.

Carly must've interpreted my silence as abandonment. And I can't say I wasn't tempted. But steeling myself against the urge to play judge and jury and leave her to her punishment, I skirted around the trees, branch club still in hand, to try to get the pair in my line of sight.

Movement to their left caught my attention, and I prayed it was Tanner, not a sidekick of Moore's.

He swung his weapon that way and squeezed off a shot.

Okay, he definitely wasn't expecting a partner. I dashed out and slammed my club across his shooting arm. The gun—my gun he'd pinched from my waistband—tumbled to the dirt.

As I took another swing at him, Carly broke free of his grip and ran.

Moore caught the other end of my club midair and in a blur had me in a chokehold.

"Let her go," a steely male voice ordered from the darkness.

My heart dropped. *Nate? How did he find me?*

Holding me as a shield, Moore jerked down and scooped up the dropped gun.

I rammed my heel into the arch of his foot, jabbed my elbow into his gut, and then reared, driving him into a tree behind us, but his chokehold on my throat tightened. Cut off my airway.

Stars danced in front of my eyes.

Then cold hard steel dug into my temple. "Drop your weapon or she's a dead woman," he growled in the shadowy direction Nate's voice had come from.

"She dies, you die," Nate said way too coolly for my comfort.

This was not poker. You don't bluff about expert marksmanship. Not when your opponent is a twitch away from blowing the brains out of the pot.

Moore's laugh sent an arctic chill down my spine.

"It's over, Moore." The steely declaration sliced through my oxygen-deprived brain and Moore's hold around my neck instantly slackened.

The pistol lifted from my temple and someone behind us grabbed it from his hand.

Sucking in air, I pulled away and turned to see my rescuer. "Tanner! I knew you'd find me."

His gun still trained on Moore, Tanner spared me only a second's glance as he passed me the recovered weapon. "Grab Carly," he said, then ordered Moore to the ground.

"I'll get her," Nate volunteered as Moore dropped to his hands and knees.

One hand slipped inside his jacket.

"Gun!" I shouted at the same instant he rolled to his back and opened fire.

35

Moore's shots went wide as he swept Tanner's feet out from under him.

My gun jammed. I flung it down and lunged at Moore to buy Tanner time to regain his feet.

Moore tossed me off.

My back slammed against a tree, knocking the breath out of me.

Moore leveled his gun at my chest.

I dove to the dirt and the bullet bit bark.

Another shot rang out, this one from farther away.

My gaze snapped to Moore's empty bleeding hand and then to Nate. His feet were squarely planted, his gun double-gripped in steady hands and trained on our suspect.

With a primal roar, Tanner tackled Moore.

The next few minutes passed in a blur. Tanner subdued Moore. Then uniformed officers stormed through the trees and restrained both Moore and Carly.

As one of the officers hauled Moore off the ground,

Moore smirked at me. "Now I see why you keep the side-kicks around."

"Did you kill Jack?" I blurted, the adrenaline running amok through my veins. I turned on Carly. "Or did you?"

"Wait," Tanner ordered and recited their Miranda rights.

I glared, even though I knew he was doing the right thing. We didn't want a confession ruled inadmissible because we'd failed to inform them of their rights.

"Okay," Tanner said after he'd finished, "now you can answer her question."

Carly shrank back.

"I was in Boston Tuesday night at a Red Sox game with friends," Moore said and named three guys who'd vouch for him. "I'll wait for my lawyer before answering any more questions."

My heart hammered my ribs as I returned my attention to Carly. Carly, who'd shown up at Jack's house accusing Ben and Ashley of murdering him.

"I didn't kill him. I swear," Carly vowed.

"Were you there? At Menemsha Hills?" I pressed.

"Just to talk to him. To beg him not to turn Charlie in. He was alive when I left him."

"Lying at the bottom of the stairs with his head cracked open on a rock?" I spat.

"He must've tripped. I didn't kill him! I wouldn't. Please, you have to believe me."

Oh, but I didn't. My hands fisted.

Tanner placed a firm hand on my shoulder. "Let's leave the rest of the questioning to the state police and Special Agent Jackson, okay?"

Everything in me rebelled at the suggestion. Without a

confession, the state police wouldn't have enough to prosecute her for Jack's murder.

"Serena?" Tanner said gently. "They'll get to the truth."

I forced my fingers to unclench and nodded.

As officers collected evidence, we trekked back to the road where a paramedic checked my vitals and another officer questioned me. When I got to the part about Nate shooting the gun out of Moore's hand, I paused and looked at him. "How did you learn to shoot like that?" I asked Nate.

"Don't be too impressed. I was aiming for his head."

I chuckled, but I didn't believe him. He'd looked calmer and steadier with that gun than any agent I'd ever seen.

"How did you find me?"

"Yeah," Tanner interjected, "how *did* you find her?"

Confused, I slanted a look at Tanner. "You didn't come together?"

"No, I raced to Jack's as soon as I got your text about Carly. By the time I got there, you were long gone. I found your phone on the porch and your purse still in the car and got a bad feeling."

"Ashley and Ben didn't hear anything?"

"No, not even me, until I pounded on her door and burst in. The TV was playing full blast."

The image of Tanner barging into Ashley's cottage, demanding to know where I was, tugged at the corners of my lips and reminded me of his warrior cry when he'd charged Moore. The FBI side of me knew I should be miffed he didn't think I could hold my own, but that didn't stop my heart from going warm and gooey at Tanner's seemingly primal need to protect me.

"I called dispatch," Tanner went on, "requested an island-wide BOLO, and asked if any cars had been reported stolen. I figured Carly couldn't have abducted you with her bike."

Almost reflexively, my breathing quickened. "Moore zapped me, then tied me up and threw me in the car's trunk," I whispered.

Tanner groaned. The ordeal would've been terrifying for anyone, but Tanner understood how much worse the confined space would've made it for me.

I smiled at him. "I could hear you ordering me to breathe in that bossy voice of yours." My heart fluttered at the little white lie, and I wondered why I'd felt compelled to tease him.

He searched my gaze, his own looking conflicted. "I'm glad you listened to me, Jones."

There he went with using my last name again. What was with that?

Drawing a line in the sand I shouldn't cross?

Because I had a bad feeling I'd been tiptoeing around it ever since that fake kiss in the car that felt a little too real.

Tanner cleared his throat. "Anyway, sure enough there'd been a car reported stolen, so I took a gamble and went after it. The owner had left his iPhone in the console, and he was helping the police track the car when I called. But the signal was so intermittent, I was afraid you'd been dumped in the state park."

The heart flutters escalated at the thought of Tanner being afraid for me.

"Meanwhile, Ashley had called Preston, prompting your aunt to call Nate, who somehow knew you were on the Chappaquidick ferry."

I squinted at Nate. "How did you know that?"

Tanner mimicked my stance. "Yeah, how did you know?"

Nate reached across the distance between us and stroked his thumb down my cheek, his lips pressed in a grim line. His fingers fiddled with my shirt collar and a moment later, he held out his hand. A tiny GPS locator sat on his palm.

"You planted a locator on me?" My voice spiked. "Why? When? How did you get it?" I gasped, remembering the when. "You straightened my collar at the memorial service."

He nodded. "Winston supplied the toys. Between everything that had happened, I was worried about what this unknown attacker might try next, so I asked your aunt if Winston had any surveillance equipment we could use."

"Winston?" Tanner sounded confused. "Isn't he a real estate agent?"

"Former Secret Service," I explained.

Tanner narrowed his eyes at Nate. "So that's why you didn't argue when I suggested taking you back to Preston's. You figured you'd watch her electronically instead."

I didn't know how to react. On the one hand, his scheme saved my life. On the other hand . . . "Why were you so secretive about it?" A fistful of righteous indignation surged through me at the thought of being spied on behind my back.

He gave me a pained look. "If you knew the chip was on your collar, you might've inadvertently alerted the suspect to the surveillance."

"How would you know that?" I scrutinized him, recalling other times he'd seemed to know things most civilians wouldn't. "And don't tell me you saw it on television."

36

Despite the late hour, everyone was waiting at Ashley's to see me after the kidnapping. Even Harold was happy to see me. He jumped into my lap the second I sat down and nuzzled my chin. "Ooh, it's nice to know I'm loved."

My gaze skittered to Tanner's and my heart thumped at the intense look in his eyes.

After hugs all around and assurances that I was unharmed, I summarized the short version of the night's events.

"So Jack's death was an accident?" Ashley asked.

"We may never know for sure," Tanner said.

I winced. *Just like Granddad's murder.*

"Well," Aunt Martha said, "at least Carly will do time for antiquities smuggling."

Yes, we'd brought her to justice of a sort, but it was small consolation. Yet . . . more than I'd managed for Granddad. Ever since learning the painting his murderer stole wasn't even the original, I'd lost hope it would one day turn up in an auction or gallery and somehow help me identify the thief.

The old familiar guilt churned in my stomach, despite the absolution Nana had given me last fall when I confessed I'd been hiding in the secret passage behind Granddad's office the night of the murder. Only ten or not, if I'd come forward then, what I saw and heard might've helped solve the case.

Nate watched me intently from the other side of the room as if he knew exactly what I was thinking. His *where do you live?* question from earlier in the evening flitted through my thoughts.

I shoved it from my mind. I lived plenty.

"We should probably let you rest." Mom's voice broke through my thoughts.

"Yes, thank you. I am tired."

Nate rose as if to leave, but Tanner intercepted him with a whispered, "Not so fast. You still owe us an explanation."

Preston drove Mom and Dad back to his house, but Aunt Martha said she'd have Nate give her a lift. Ashley and Ben retired to their rooms.

"Let's talk outside," Tanner said.

Aunt Martha concurred that was a good idea, and I suddenly felt like the only one not in the know.

Aunt Martha meandered over to Uncle Jack's front porch, and the rest of us fell into step behind her. She sat in one of the rockers, and the men leaned casually against the porch rail facing her. Tanner seemed a tad nervous. Nate had that cornered look Harold got when he knew I was about to scoop him up and banish him from my room.

"Let me guess," I said to Nate, trying to break the tension, "you used to be a cop and for some reason you didn't want me to know. You'd confided in Aunt Martha, who agreed to keep your secret until Tanner somehow found out and threatened to out you if you didn't come clean."

It wasn't until the words came out of my mouth that the pieces seemed to suddenly fall into place in my mind. Nate helping Aunt Martha secure a gun permit. All the little police details he'd claimed to have seen on TV. How calmly he'd reacted to my pulling a gun on him as he scooped cat litter. How confidently he handled his gun while facing down Moore. His joke about the CIA telling him not to tell anyone when he . . .

I gasped. "Don't tell me you're CIA?"

His heavy sigh felt like a punch to the gut.

"No way! So you and Aunt Martha would have a giggle behind my back every time I teased you about the secret agent classes?"

Aunt Martha chuckled. "That was funny."

I shot her a scowl.

"I'm sorry, dear." She ducked her head.

"When were you planning to tell me? Were you ever? I can't believe you almost kissed me when you were keeping this whopping big secret from—"

"You almost kissed!" Aunt Martha squealed. "I knew you two would be perfect for each other. Just give him a—"

This time Tanner pinned her with a scowl. "Don't you think she deserves to know what she may be getting herself into before her heart's entangled?"

I glared at him. "Why didn't *you* tell me?"

"Would you have believed me?"

I thought about that for a minute and realized he'd tried to warn me in a dozen different ways. When Nate was helping investigate the art forgery, how many times had Tanner said he didn't trust the guy? Then he told me about Nate flying planes in Yugoslavia and asked me if I did background checks on the guys I date.

Nate hunkered down in front of me. "I'd planned to tell you this week. I'd been waiting to see . . ." He shook his head. "It doesn't matter. Yes, I used to work for the CIA. I didn't tell you because it's in the past, and it is supposed to be a secret."

"But you told Aunt Martha."

"No, he didn't," Aunt Martha interjected. "I recruited him."

I gaped at her. "You? *Recruited?*"

How she knew former Secret Service agent Winston suddenly made sense. Everything did. She'd spent her entire life flying from one country to another . . . as a businessman's assistant, she'd told us.

"Of course. You're a spy," I said.

Wow. How could I have been so utterly and completely blind?

I tried to rally, mustering up a game smile. "Next you'll be telling me you're Madame X."

Nate and Aunt Martha exchanged guilty looks.

Nate straightened. "Um, yeah . . ." he began, but I brushed away his explanation, even as my jaw dropped. Madame X was only a legend in the CIA—the spy who'd infiltrated more corrupt regimes than any other. Naturally, I'd suspect my harmlessly eccentric great-aunt.

Or not. "How could . . . ?" Question after question whirled through my mind, but my mouth and brain seemed to have stopped communicating. "Do Mom and Dad know?" I finally blurted.

Aunt Martha shook her head. "No, and I'd prefer to keep it that way."

"Why?"

"Just because I've retired doesn't mean my enemies have. In fact, when our brakes blew this afternoon, I called Winston because I half-suspected a past associate had recognized Nate or me."

Nate shifted and raked his hand through his hair.

"Bad guys are looking for you?" I asked.

"No." Nate silenced whatever Aunt Martha had been about to add with a glare. "I've been out for five years without an incident."

"Why did you leave?"

"After my parents died, my brother's life ran off the rails. His reaction to the plane crash in Yugoslavia made me realize how far off. And I wasn't ready to sacrifice another family member."

Another family member? I gasped. "Your parents were operatives?"

He nodded.

My heart pummeled my ribs. Was he telling me all this because he was hoping Aunt Martha's dreams for us would come true? I glanced at Tanner, who was watching me quietly, and something shifted inside of me. I admired Nate so much. He'd sacrificed his career for his family. He knew how to embrace life. He shared my love of art and old movies and tea. And . . . he totally understood my career. But . . .

When I thought I was going to die in that car trunk, it was Tanner's voice that calmed my fears. When Nate came to my rescue in the woods, my heart had dipped just a little that Tanner wasn't there instead. Then when Tanner appeared, my heart had leapt and I was pretty sure it wasn't just gratitude.

Maybe I was crazy to think there could ever be anything more between us. We worked together. He was ten years older than me. Half the time he treated me more like a kid sister than anything else.

Except for that kiss. There was nothing sibling-like about that kiss.

Yes, the closest he'd ever come to asking me on a date was as an undercover op or maybe as a backhanded way to thwart Nate. And maybe I'd totally misread his interest.

And Nate was a spy, for crying out loud. I was totally confused. I buried my face in my hands.

Tanner squeezed my shoulder, his clasp warm and firm. "You should get some rest." He hunkered down where Nate had been only moments earlier and tugged my hands from my face. The tender look in his chocolate brown eyes made my heart somersault.

"Thank you," I said. "For everything."

His lips curved in a gentle smile that stole my breath. "I thought it'd be more noble to ensure you knew all the facts," he said softly.

Noble? My mind zigzagged back to our discussion about Frank and Marianne—how noble Frank had been to walk away. What was Tanner saying? That he wouldn't walk away without a fight?

"Do I know *all* the facts now?" I asked unevenly.

Tanner shrugged ever so slightly. "Not that I think it'd matter all that much to you, but Nate is a multimillionaire too. Old money, on his mother's side."

I blinked, not sure what stunned me more—that my

apartment superintendent was rich or that Tanner was still talking about Nate instead of himself.

Tanner stroked his thumb across my cheek and smiled. "You did good today. I've never been more proud. I'll see you tomorrow, okay?"

I nodded, still too flabbergasted to form a coherent sentence, and then he walked away.

Walked away.

Aunt Martha pushed to her feet. "We should go too. It's been a long day."

I looked from Aunt Martha to Nate and was overwhelmed by the oddest disappointment and the realization that I wished Nate and Aunt Martha had left.

And Tanner had stayed.

"Thank you for telling me," I mumbled. "I won't betray your secret."

"I know you won't," Nate said, but his smile didn't reach his eyes. "I'll be leaving in the morning."

"What? Why?"

"I think you know why. I'll pick up Harold before I go."

I stared at him mutely. I hadn't even known my own heart until sixty seconds ago. How could he?

He chuckled. "Trust me, Serena, if you looked at me the way you just looked at Tanner, I would not be walking away. Catching people off guard doesn't always give one the upper hand. But take my advice as someone who's been where you are. Life is a journey, not a destination."

"I believe Emerson said that first," Aunt Martha chimed in.

We both shot her a look.

She held up her hands in surrender. "Not that it's important who said it. I'll wait in the car."

Nate turned back to me. "You understand what I mean, right? Don't make the mistake of thinking some future state, such as your grandfather's killer behind bars, is somehow more real or important than the present."

"I hear what you're saying."

"Tanner is a good guy."

I sighed.

Nate chuckled. "I'll take good care of Harold until you get home."

"I know you will." I hugged him hard. "Thank you for being here."

37

I showed up at the Oak Bluffs police station the next morning to the news they'd executed the search warrants within twenty minutes of receiving the report that I'd been kidnapped the night before. The pile of antiquities at Frank's had understandably raised the officers' hopes they'd found the ringleader, but his documentation for each and every piece had proved impeccable.

Carly, on the other hand, had no antiquities in her possession, but a little black book police recovered from her desk at Hill and Dale Architects looked promising for helping Isaak track down her buyers. Not that Carly was being uncooperative. She'd told Isaak everything we wanted to know about the art smuggling operation. It was Jack's death she refused to comment on.

"I think you'll want to hear this." The police chief ushered me into a small room where Tanner was waiting, staring at the two-way mirror, his arm braced against the wall, his forehead pressed to his clenched fist. He looked like he'd just lost his best friend.

My heart thundered. I'd had all night to process what he'd said, and not said, and had maybe implied, and I still wasn't ready to face him. I'd been held at gunpoint, run off the road, even kidnapped, but none of those situations had scared me as much as the feelings that rushed through me at the sight of Tanner.

Straightening, he glanced my way, his professional FBI facade slipping into place and masking whatever had been going through his mind. He searched my gaze for only a second before returning his attention to the two-way mirror. "They're interrogating Carly."

My heart tripped. That was it? He wasn't curious how my talk with Nate went? Did he force Nate's confession for no other reason than I should have all the facts before going gaga over Nate?

Was my notion Tanner had a romantic interest in me nothing more than a silly dream?

The detective interrogating Carly held up a pair of jeans he said they'd found in her laundry hamper. "Were you wearing these when you went to Menemsha Hills Tuesday night?"

Holding my breath, I narrowed my attention to Carly.

"I don't know. I have lots of pairs of jeans," she said.

The detective pointed to a mark on the front of the jeans. "These have a tiny bleach stain and your mother said you used bleach before you left that night. Is that correct?"

"Yes."

"So are these the jeans you wore that night? They were the only pair in your laundry hamper."

"Then yes, probably."

The detective placed a photograph on the table. "This is the last photograph on Jack's camera."

The one Nate developed? My gaze shot to the chief, who'd joined us at the window.

"We can't use it in court because there was no chain of custody," he said, acknowledging my unspoken question, "but she doesn't know that. If she thinks we have her, then she may confess in hopes of a reduced sentence."

"Those are your jeans in the picture, aren't they?" the detective pressed.

Carly glanced at the picture and visibly swallowed. "I already told you I was there."

"We believe Jack snapped this picture as he fell down the stairs."

Her face paled. "But you can't prove that."

"It's the only wasted shot on the film. In fact, we've reviewed dozens of his negatives. No others show him accidentally snapping a picture of someone's legs or the ground or even a thumb. I think the jury will believe our theory."

"I didn't push him," she said. "He stumbled."

My breath rushed from my lungs at what her admission meant—she'd seen him fall.

"And then tumbled down the stairs to the rocky shore?" the detective clarified.

"There was nothing I could do." Carly burst into tears.

"So you ran away?"

"No, I ran down after him, but he was hurt bad, real bad. I buried my face against his chest and told him how sorry I was." Carly swiped at her eyes with her sleeve, and I felt my own eyes tearing at the pure anguish on her face. "He said, 'I love you, Carly. I will always love you.'"

I gulped a sob. That sounded just like Uncle Jack.

"I wanted to do the right thing," Carly went on, "for Jack.

He was always talking to me about how much God loves me. And I never believed him, not when God took my dad and Mom ended up in the psych ward. But I started thinking if Jack could still love me after . . . after . . . everything, maybe God could too."

"So why didn't you call an ambulance?"

"I tried, but my phone had no reception. I ran out to my car and a call came in from Charlie. I told him what happened and he told me to get out of there before anyone spotted me." She sobbed into her hands. "And now he's dead too. It's all my fault."

"Well," the chief said to Tanner and me, "it's not the confession we were hoping for, but at least she'll do time for the smuggling charges."

I let out a pent-up breath. "I think I believe her." And somehow I was pretty sure Jack would be okay with the lesser charge. He'd probably echo Nate's advice to me too. Tell me to take time to enjoy today. "Thanks for letting me watch the interview," I said to the chief.

"It was the least I could do after all you two went through to bring her into custody."

My gaze met Tanner's and the events of the night before cascaded through my mind once more.

"Can we talk?" he asked softly.

My heart did a triple somersault. "Where?"

He walked me out to the Land Rover I was still borrowing from Winston. "Follow me."

He drove to State Road and then headed toward West Tisbury.

The scenery went by in a blur as I tried to guess where he was headed and what he intended to say when we got there.

Every few seconds, he glanced at his rearview mirror as if he was afraid he'd lose me.

My heart did another somersault at that thought.

We reached Quansoo Road and he headed toward Jack's, only he didn't pull in. He parked at the Quansoo Farm trail-head just past the house and was out of the car and ready to open my door by the time I joined him.

"Let's walk." He steered me across the long open field that stretched to the sandy shoreline.

The wind wasn't too strong, but the waves still seemed to thunder. Or maybe that was my heart. Overhead, the sky was pure blue. "It is an idyllic place to vacation," I said inanely.

"Hmm." He stopped and faced me, looking serious.

I glanced back at our cars that were now mere dots in the distance. "You worried I'll want to make a run for it?" I said, but my joke fell flat when Tanner grimaced instead of laughed.

"That's not what I'm worried about," he muttered.

Oh.

The nervous flapping he was doing with his fingers against his palm was starting to make me nervous.

More nervous. Um . . .

"Nate flew home with Harold this morning," I said in a rush, not sure whether this was going to make things more awkward or less.

Tanner went still, closing his eyes for a brief moment before looking at me steadily. "That's good. Because I called headquarters this morning and requested a transfer from the major theft squad."

"What? Why?" My heart rioted. Tanner loved working major thefts. "I know that kiss was just part of our cover.

You don't have to do this. We work well together. I don't want you to feel—"

He pressed two fingers to my lips. "Serene-uh," he said, a smile finally breaking through as he shook his head at me. His mock-scolding look morphed into something . . . different. "Please don't apologize for the way you make me feel."

"I'm sorry, I—"

"Serena, agents in the same squad can't date," he said, drowning out my apology.

I blinked stupidly. "Date?"

"That's right. It's against the rules. Because when you're crazy about someone, it's too difficult to think straight. You may beat the bad guy to a pulp for laying his hands on the woman you—"

"Wait. You're crazy about me?"

The corners of his eyes crinkled once more. "You finally noticed."

"I didn't . . . I thought . . . I . . ." Too flustered to utter a coherent thought, I wagged my hands. "I don't know what to say."

Tanner caught my arms by the wrists. "Say you'll spend the day with me."

"The day? You mean . . . like a date?"

Laughing softly, he tenderly kissed the inside of my wrist and, wow, I was starting to understand what the word *swoon* really meant. "Dating. Courting," he said. "Whichever you want to call it."

My arm was still tingling from his feather-light touch. "You requested the transfer so you could go out with me?" I couldn't quite keep the disbelief from my voice, never mind how many times I'd let myself imagine the possibility he cared for me that way.

His eyes twinkled and he kissed my other wrist. "Is that so hard to believe?"

Definitely swooning. I bit my lip, suddenly feeling shy, and dropped my gaze to my hand cradled in Tanner's.

An image of another hand flashed through my mind. A memory.

My pulse jumped. "He had a birthmark on his wrist!"

Tanner frowned. "What are you talking about?"

"Granddad's killer. Remember, I told you how just before the burglar came in Granddad hustled me into the secret passage behind his bookshelves? Well, after their scuffle, I saw the intruder's hand return a book to the shelf." I squeezed my eyes shut and willed the memory to return. "He had a splotchy purple mark on his wrist."

Tanner's clasp on my hands tightened, drawing my gaze to his. The amused glint had disappeared, supplanted by a whirlwind of questions.

Nate's advice echoed through my mind. Was putting Granddad's killer behind bars more important to me than the here and now? Than Tanner?

I shook my head. "I'm sorry."

The muscle in his jaw flexed and his chocolate brown eyes grew impossibly darker.

"No, I mean, I'm sorry about getting sidetracked. The memory was just so surprising and vivid."

"I understand how important finding your grandfather's killer is to you," Tanner said softly. "You know I will always support your efforts to find him."

"Yes. But look at Jack. We'll never know if Carly pushed

him or not. What if it's the same with Granddad's killer? What if I never find him?"

"No one will love you any less."

I didn't respond. Deep down I sensed it should be enough that God knew who killed Granddad, since He must have His reasons for leaving the rest of us in the dark.

"You know I'm the last person who should give advice on having a life outside of work. But do you think your grandfather would want you to put the rest of your life on hold in pursuit of his killer?"

I thought about Tanner's question for a long time. "No, he wouldn't. Granddad loved art, but he loved his family more. He'd want me to . . ." *have a family too.* I swallowed hard.

"Okay, don't get used to this, but I'm going to get mushy here."

My heart hiccupped.

"I have to admit I never thought I'd want to settle down," Tanner said, "but from the moment you walked into my life, you've turned my world around."

"Really?" I squeaked.

His eyes danced. "Yes, really," he said, his thumb skimming the back of my hand still held in his. "The hours I spend with you are my favorite of the day. I wanted more but was afraid of jeopardizing our working relationship."

"I—"

He pressed a finger to my lips once more. "Let me finish, okay? I love your contagious smile and quick wit. I love how you challenge me and I feel honored when you seek out my advice. I don't love that sometimes you stir protective feelings in me so fierce I can't think straight."

Tears sprang to my eyes.

Tanner gently whisked a teardrop from my cheek. "Come to think of it, I guess I do kind of love that feeling too. And I love how your dedication and faith keep me centered."

My breath piled up in my chest as Tanner's expression turned rueful.

"And yes, seeing you with Nate made me ache in a way I never could've imagined." Tanner tenderly cupped my jaw. "It also made me realize that spending time with you is a gift I don't want to waste. I love our work but I love you more."

"You love me?" I said breathlessly.

"Well . . ." The mischievous grin I'd always secretly adored made an appearance, complete with dimples. "It's either that or I have a wicked case of heartburn."

"Tanner!" I swatted at him, but he caught my hand and intertwined our fingers instead.

"So what do you say? Will you spend the day with me?"

Ignoring the way our joined hands made my heart swell to bursting, I gave him a mischievous grin of my own. "Well . . ." I echoed, complete with dramatic pause, "if things don't work out between us, there's always Jeffrey Dean Morgan."

Tanner's expression turned puzzled. "Who?"

I laughed. Tanner'd been hounding me to reveal the name of his movie-star look-alike as long as we'd known each other. And now that I finally had he didn't even catch on. "Don't worry. You'll have a lifetime to figure it out."

EPILOGUE

Don't tell my mother. But she was right all along.

Tanner transferred from Major Theft to Counterintelligence and our first date spiraled into a whirlwind romantic courtship. And by autumn, Mom's fondest wish came true—Tanner and I married.

Tanner, looking unbelievably handsome in his black tux, happily obliged our glass-tinkling guests and swept me into another breathtaking kiss. "Have I told you how beautiful you are?"

I laughed. "Only a couple dozen times. How about telling me where you're taking me for our honeymoon?"

Zoe, my best friend and nine-months-pregnant matron-of-honor sitting beside us at the head table, tapped me on the shoulder. "Uh, Houston, we have a problem."

We instantly sprang to our feet. "The baby's coming?"

Her husband, Jax, rushed forward.

"I'm so sorry," Zoe said.

"Are you kidding me? This is awesome!" I squealed.

"We'll name her after you," Zoe called over Jax's shoulder as he whisked her out to their car.

Chuckling, Nate sidled up to me. "Glad to see your life is still as full of surprises as ever." He gave me a hug. "Congratulations."

"Thank you, Nate." I glanced at his date, Lisa. The same Lisa Tanner and I had interrogated about Ben on Martha's Vineyard. It turned out that as Nate was heading off island, he happened upon a traffic accident at the same time as Lisa did, and they worked together to take care of the victims until paramedics arrived. They'd been in communication ever since. "The two of you getting serious?" I asked.

Nate's eyes twinkled. "I've always wanted to live near the ocean." He extended his hand to Tanner. "Take good care of her."

"I will."

The guests seemed to take Zoe's departure as a cue for calling it a night, so Aunt Martha and Mom urged us to scoot off too.

Tanner was once again most willing to oblige and grinned from ear to ear as he carried me over the threshold of our honeymoon suite in downtown St. Louis.

"Are you going to tell me where we're going now?" I asked.

"You'll need to use your FBI detective skills." He set me down on the sofa and lifted an exquisitely wrapped gift from behind it. "Here is your first clue."

It was a large box, heavier than the bathing suit I'd need for a Caribbean adventure but lighter than the ski boots I'd need for a mountain holiday. I tore into the wrapping paper and wedged off the lid. Tears sprang to my eyes. "Oh, Tanner. It's my grandfather's painting!"

"It's the original your grandmother sold after she had the copy made. She helped me track it down. I think she likes me." He grinned.

Blinking back tears, I threw my arms around his neck. "Thank you." My heart swelled at the magnitude of the surprise and the tears spilled down my cheeks. "This is so special." Drinking in the pastoral English countryside, I swiped at my damp cheeks. "Does this mean we're going to England?"

His grin widened. "No."

"Art museums?"

"Hmm, maybe," he said teasingly.

"You said the picture was a clue."

He pulled a smaller gift from the bureau drawer. "And this is the second clue."

"It feels like a photo album." I ripped off the paper and opened it to the first page—a picture of Dad with Jack and a handful of other fraternity brothers. I stifled a frown. "I don't understand."

"When you and your mom were at a dress fitting and I was hanging out with your dad, this album arrived from Ben and Ashley. It'd belonged to Jack and since it had all photos from their university days, Ben figured your dad would like it."

"What does that have to do with our honeymoon?"

"Remember what you said the first time I asked you out?"

"Sure . . . I said yes." I flipped through more pages, confused at what was so special about the album.

Tanner grinned and flipped to the last page of the book. "I'll give you a hint." He tapped on a close-up of five guys, Dad and Jack included, their hands raised, cheering.

My heart dipped. "You're taking me to a football game?"

He pressed a kiss to my hair. "Even better." He produced a magnifying glass. "Check out the wrist of the second guy from the right."

I gasped. "He has a birthmark on his wrist."

Tanner's grin widened. "Does that look like the birthmark you saw the night your grandfather was killed?"

"Yes. I think it is."

"His name is Lester Rhodes, currently residing on a Greek Isle. According to your father, Lester, Jack, your dad, and two other fraternity brothers were in town for a reunion the week your grandfather died."

"Dad's fraternity brother killed Granddad?"

"Can I interest you in a honeymoon to Greece to find out?"

Sandra Orchard is the award-winning author of many inspirational romantic suspense and mysteries, including *Deadly Devotion*, *Blind Trust*, and *Desperate Measures*. Her writing has garnered several Canadian Christian Writing Awards, a *Romantic Times* Reviewers' Choice Award, a National Readers' Choice Award, a HOLT Medallion Award of Merit, and a Daphne du Maurier Award for Excellence in Mystery/Suspense. In addition to her busy writing schedule, Sandra enjoys speaking at events and teaching writing workshops. She lives in Ontario, Canada. Learn more about Sandra's books and check out the special bonus features, such as deleted scenes and location pics, at http://sandraorchard.com.

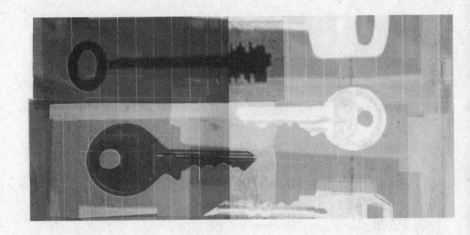

MEET
SANDRA ORCHARD
AT
WWW.SANDRAORCHARD.COM

You can learn more about Sandra's books and access special bonus features, such as deleted scenes and location pictures.

Connect on Facebook **f**
www.facebook.com/sandraorchard

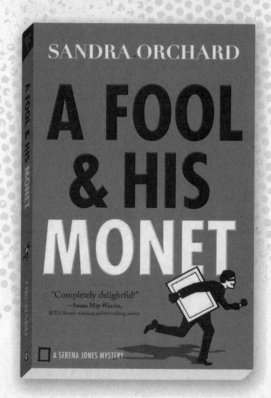

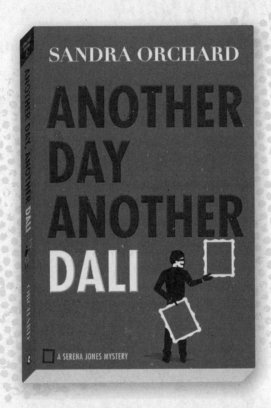